the publican's daughter

A NOVEL

LINDY WARRELL

WATTLETALES
PUBLISHING

WATTLETALES
PUBLISHING

Published by Wattletales Publishing
Adelaide, Australia.
www.wattletales.com.au

First published by Wattletales Publishing in 2022.

Wattletales Publishing and the author pay respect to Elders past, present and future on whose country this story, albeit fictionalised, is set.

Cover Design: Nikki Jane Designs, Canberra
Typesetting: Alycia Tilley, Monique-Mai Designs, Melbourne
Gidgee Tree Image: S.A. Seed Conservation Centre
Printed and bound in Australia

ISBN: 978-0-6453129-0-4 (Paperback)
ISBN: 978-0-6453129-1-1 (e-Book)

Cataloguing-in-Publication entry is available
From the National Library of Australia

Katherine Forster is an ingénue cast into the middle of a wildly unlikely situation, at once violent, loving, primitive, and oddly tender. Lindy Warrell has a gift for compelling narrative that is rare: clear, without being obvious; matter of fact while celebrating the emotional; plausible without sacrificing the surprising.

Howard Firkin

Warrell creates a superb cinematic drama set on Australia's wide purple gibber plains. It is portrayed with raw honesty through a direct line into young Katherine's mind as the city girl's life becomes entwined in the conflicts of people and land. *The Publican's Daughter* is a stark coming of wisdom story of love, loss, heartbreak, and joy.

Shaine Melrose

For my mother, Phyllis May Warrell (1919–1994), and father, Stanley James Warrell (1910–1997), who gave me their world and loved me to bits. I miss them.

Foreword

Far more than a coming-of-age novel, *The Publican's Daughter* is haunting, violent, dream-defiling, and uncompromising. It highlights the dichotomy between the city and outback, between white and black and alarmingly between self-entitled white men and the women who are geographically and culturally unable to escape. The era and the harsh environment make for a prison where there is no place for softness, empathy, or traditional romance.

Protagonist Katherine Forster arrives with a suitcase full of hope which is soon flung open to reveal the dark, not-so-secret underbelly of Wonnalinga. Behind the traditional and halcyon, McCubbin bush scenes that city people have held true for generations is a blight that quickly grows, poisoning the lives and relationships of Katherine and her family.

Akin to the Australian cult movie *Wake in Fright*, a story that the film critics weren't ready for in 1971 yet grew to acclaim at the Cannes Film Festival almost forty years later, *The Publican's Daughter* is shocking and revealing. It exposes a type of Australia that readers are only just beginning to recognise. Warrell's page-turner has a sense of undeniable truth as she recounts the rude awakening of her naïve heroine. A fearless writer, Warrell does not beat around the tainted bush. Instead, she goes in headfirst, bloodied by the thorns.

Despite Katherine's overwhelming sense of hopelessness, she is guided, as most of us are, by the dim light of love on a far horizon. Compelled to seek a better life, she is scantly rewarded by hindsight and hard-won wisdom.

Lindy Warrell is a skilled and natural storyteller whose characters resonate long after reading this novel. The rough ride that is *The Publican's Daughter* is strangely edifying, not the least for its rich portrayal of people, place, and era, but the sense that this story needs to be told. The reader, like Katherine, comes of age in owning a part of history that, although fictional, represents the experiences of our forebears.

Jude Aquilina
Adelaide 2022

the publican's daughter

1

'God, it's hot.' Lillian Forster swiped sticky flies from her face. 'I hope you know what you're doing, Dudley Forster, bringing us to the middle of nowhere like this.'

'That'll be our driver.' Her husband pointed to an approaching billow of red dust. 'You can see the town over there.' He paused. 'Look, it's not far — can you see?'

Lillian turned to watch other passengers being whisked away by waiting vehicles in clouds of dust and laughter as their plane prepared for the next leg of its journey to Alice Springs, then Darwin.

A trickle of sweat tickled Katherine Forster's bare legs. She moved out of earshot of her parents' niggling to get a good look at the absurd posturing of the groundsman guiding their plane for take-off. Muff-eared and dwarfed beneath the nose of the Fokker Friendship, he waved it off with what looked like two oversized table-tennis bats. She could only see the pilot's cap in the cockpit window, as though it alone was reversing the aircraft away from the terminal. The plane turned to taxi then roared into a climb, tucking its wheels into its fat belly. Soon it was a silver speck gliding in a haze of blue.

Katherine sat on her leather case, mooning over the flirtatious steward on The Overland from Melbourne to Adelaide. She blushed. He had grinned at her, handsome and mocking, as she struggled against the lurch of the train to eat chicken soup without either spilling it onto the white linen tablecloth or missing her mouth with the spoon. Once he lifted the cloches from their main course, he retired to the servery; nothing tease-worthy about roast lamb sodden with gravy, baked potatoes and vegetables or a dessert of golden syrup pudding with custard and cream.

On the plane to Wonnalinga, she had been able to relax because the hostesses, being girls not much older than her, didn't bother her at all the way men did. They simply asked, as a matter of course, how she was enjoying her flight. Her flight. She liked that.

Through the glazed oval window, Katherine gazed at changing patterns on the ground; bitumen, red roofs, and tree-covered hills appearing and disappearing in swirling clouds that turned to wisps then returned as dense blobs like cotton wool. Over the desert, the clouds lifted, unveiling a sculpted panorama of fence lines and a rough dirt road alongside a railway line bridging dry riverbeds from time to time. Here and there, scatterings of large and small buildings made up a homestead. Most had dams and clay billabongs nearby, lined with trees like specks in the surrounding ocean of red dirt and purple gibber plains that etched themselves on her heart.

'And this is our daughter, Katherine,' Dudley said, startling Katherine, who hadn't heard him introduce Lillian.

'Katherine, say hello to Mr and Mrs Napper. I think you can call them Pearl and Barney.' Dudley smiled, naming the wife before the husband in an unconscious reversal of custom. 'Barney tells me he is the railway signalman at the station opposite the pub. All the railway workers live next to the station in railway housing, and Barney tells me his cottage is the closest to the big station house itself, where the stationmaster lives.'

Katherine smiled a mute hello, bringing herself into the present and trying not to stare. Barney Napper was a portly chap, bald in beige clothing. Beside him, his wife Pearl stood tall, flamboyant in a floral cotton print frock. Katherine could see in the woman's myopic eyes, magnified by the thick lenses of her black-rimmed spectacles, that she adored her husband. She gave him her complete attention, even as he boasted about the new red Ford Cortina in which he was about to transport the Forsters to their new home, The First & Last Hotel.

'I bought it last Christmas, didn't I, Pearl love? Pity our luck ran out last week when we won the draw — or lost, depending on how you look at it — to see who was going to pick you lot up.' Barney chuckled, pleased with his joke.

Pearl laughed, 'He's quick, our Barney.'

'We won't all fit in that thing, will we? With our baggage.' Lillian looked in the direction of the Cortina. 'You'll have to make two trips,' she told Barney, ignoring Pearl.

Katherine saw a derisive glance pass between the Nappers as if to say, *who does this one think she is?* Katherine felt defensive on Lillian's behalf. She resolved to be wary of this odd pair, especially Pearl. The woman was obsequious and a bit too cocky for Katherine's taste.

'Well,' Pearl stared at Dudley, 'the town's not far, so I suppose we can manage two trips. If that's what Mrs Forster wants.'

Loyal to a fault where his family was concerned, Dudley did not rise to the bait.

'Our bags can come with us in the boot, and Katherine can keep her case here until you come back for her.' Lillian hopped into the front of the car, forcing Pearl into the back with Dudley. He was exhausted after loading their bags after their long trip and sank into the rear seat, relieved to at last be on the way to the pub, bought sight unseen with Lillian's inheritance, without her permission. He looked at the back of his wife's neck. Her short hair lay dank with sweat at the nape, telling him her eyes would also be stinging by now. Lillian had lost her brows to an apprentice hairdresser like herself who, overzealous, had plucked them to extinction when she was just a girl.

Katherine was pleased to be alone for a while. At least the travel arrangement averted a potential scene, so she didn't have to worry about the goings-on in Barney's red Cortina as it sped towards the tiny town. Full of daughterly love for her mum and dad, Katherine looked forward to the adventure of the bush, her understanding of which came from a childhood reading of Mary Grant Bruce novels, she was sure that she'd find a husband in a place where, they said, men outnumbered women ten to one.

Shivering despite the heat in this now profoundly quiet place, Katherine could hear the hot breeze ripple over the folds of the passenger shelter roof. Welcome or omen? She strained to listen to its prophecy as it whistled through straggly trees nearby. It was 1962. She was just nineteen and thrilled to be in the outback.

2

With her blonde hair in a ponytail to keep it out of her eyes, Katherine pushed striped sheets through the wringer in the laundry at the back of the pub, two or more at a time. No matter how wet they were, the first sheet hung would be dry in the desert heat before she pegged out the last. Katherine loved the serene silence of the cool morning on her arms in this place. Her daydreams soared beyond the pub's back fence, over the row of humpies in the lane to the horizon of this vast open land.

'Hello, missy.' Old Paddy's weathered black face peered through the window.

Katherine jumped. Although the old fellow often stopped to say hello when she was doing a big wash, he always materialised barefoot and without a sound.

'Good weather, eh?'

'Yes.' Katherine was shy with Paddy because she could not always understand what he said. Not that he mumbled, but he did seem to talk downwards, as though he let words fall from his body into the atmosphere. His voice was soft. He didn't throw it as Katherine's teachers taught her to in elocution class. She wondered whether people still put their children through the rigours of speech training. It had served some purpose, she supposed. Yet Katherine could not understand why it had been so important to learn how to repeat by rote strings of words written by strangers; dead ones at that. She wandered lonely as a cloud. Or was it 'he'? She couldn't remember. What on earth did that mean? One poem in elocution class about an ancient mariner and an albatross had fascinated her. She had learned it by heart. No, there was another called 'The Love Song of J. Alfred Prufrock' by T.S. Eliot. That made her think of black cats slinking around buildings.

The poem wasn't about a cat at all, but elocution taught her to walk with her back ramrod-straight, balancing three hard-backed books on her head. She used to wonder whether their shape and weight outweighed the value of their contents. Her teacher insisted that good posture was the foundation of proper diction and, by extension, good character.

'You got a smoke?' Paddy waited, a wry but patient look on his face. Katherine took in his faded khaki work pants, gathered lopsidedly at his skinny waist by a long leather belt that was too wide for his emaciated body. It was far too long, dangling as it did past the end of his fly. The trousers must have once belonged to someone with thicker thighs. Paddy's fresh-washed but unironed shirt was also loose but buttoned tight at the wrists. Curly white hair peeked through his stiff open collar.

'Yep.' Katherine extended her packet of cork-tipped Craven "A", apologising for her wet fingers. Paddy tucked one cigarette into his pocket and another behind his ear and murmured something about God looking after her as he went upon his way. Katherine hoped to talk sensibly to Paddy one day about something that mattered, but she couldn't think what.

A knot of sodden sheets prised apart the rollers. The machine squealed and danced across the concrete floor until Katherine turned it off. She wrestled with the coagulated mass of wet stripes, then went back to her dreams and the swish-swash of swirling bed linen.

Katherine liked the laundry, where she felt close to the sky. She loved the caw of crows punctuating the stillness. Their calls reached a darkness in her that made the rough texture of the rust-stained concrete tubs reassuring with her tools of trade lined on the windowsill above them; a bottle of White King bleach, a box of industrial-strength laundry detergent and a scrubbing brush she used on soiled shirt collars and cuffs. The Reckitt's Blue instructions were almost illegible; the print was so small — *Wrap Blue in cloth. Stir while squeezing the Blue in the last rinsing water. Dip articles separately for a short time; keep them moving.*

Replete with its black iron copper in the corner, the pub laundry was a haven from the often-frantic bustle of the house, bar, and kitchen. The acrid stink and oxidisation stains of hot bore water didn't bother Katherine. With detergent, it masked the stink of soiled bed linen, greasy kitchen rags, and bar runners sticky with yesterday's dregs, leaving Katherine to flirt with the purity of the desert air. The only things she hated washing were her mother's period-stained pants.

'Are you there, Katherine? We need you for the lunches.' Lillian's face followed her voice through the laundry door.

'Yes, Mum.'

On Tuesdays and Fridays, the Ghan stopped for 15 minutes at Wonnalinga to fill its tanks with water. Named after pioneer Afghan cameleers who helped open the outback, the train carried passengers from Adelaide to Alice Springs. Some diehards headed straight to the pub, where they got short shrift from Dudley, a stickler for liquor licensing laws. Nobody could get a drink in his pub before 10 am. The locals called tourists locusts because they swarmed in, took whatever they wanted, and then disappeared again as fast as they had come. The foolish among them would run up and down Main Street gawping at everything and snapping anyone with their Box Brownies and expensive Agfa cameras, including — without asking permission — the group of Aboriginal women beneath the old mulga tree in the open allotment next to The First & Last.

Following Friday's Ghan came the Chaser, a supply train with a refrigerated van — the lifeline of the outback. Neither Dudley nor Lillian could drive, so it fell to Katherine in the first few weeks to meet the Chaser for the pub's food and liquor supplies. The previous incumbents of The First & Last had scarpered from town. Nobody knew why and the Forsters inherited their red and cream Commer light truck.

The first time Katherine met the train in the Commer, a good-looking stockman stuck his head through the window of his tray-top utility to wink at her with a leer that matched the teeth-baring bark of his untethered dogs on the tray. She ignored him and turned in time to see a dark green Land Rover pull up on the other side of the Commer in a swagger of dust. Its driver, an older, leaner man, parked next to her, window-to-window, and peered at Katherine, face-to-face.

Soon there was a queue of vehicles behind Katherine. The waiting drivers sauntered around in a flux of light moleskin trousers, blue or khaki shirts, sleeves rolled up, elastic-sided boots and Akubra hats. They greeted each other with whoops and back-slaps. The stockmen made it a point to chat to the pastoralist in the Land Rover, Roger Beaming, and sized her up on the way.

It took Katherine a while to get into stride, loading the pub's goods onto the truck. She could feel the men ogling as she rolled kegs down the wooden ramp the way Dudley had told her to, but before long, the repetitive lifting and stacking of cartons of grog and crates of soft drinks from train to truck revived her natural vivacity. Katherine loaded perishables last so that they could be unloaded first back at the pub. She thanked her stars for not being in shorts and shuddered at the idea of these mocking men gawping at her lily-white city legs. They'd laugh at the way she grappled to re-insert the Commer's gear stick that came right out of its socket on the road.

When Dudley inherited a cheap second-hand grey Jeep from someone who owed him money, the Commer was cast to the elements in a graveyard of discarded vehicles a couple of miles out of town. He then assigned his new offsider, Jimmy Barber, a young man he'd hired from Port Augusta, to meet the Chaser.

One day, with dishes done and frying smells dissipated, Dudley popped his head into the kitchen. 'Two more for lunch, Mum.' He wore a silly man-grin that made him look like an imbecile to Katherine and her mother.

'I'm not your bloody mother,' Lillian growled under her breath.

It had taken no time at all for Mrs Forster, as she preferred to be known, to build a formidable reputation in town. Nobody could expect a meal from Lillian's kitchen outside the designated times. Lunch at The First & Last would be served only between midday and one o'clock. The dining room opened for breakfast between seven and eight o'clock in the morning and dinner between six and seven in the evening.

'Who are they for?' Katherine called after her father's retreating head even though both she and Lillian knew perfectly well. They had seen the Mines Department vehicle arrive in town earlier, around eleven o'clock. It had been parked outside the store ever since.

'Come on. We can do it just this once.' Lillian removed her apron, ran her fingers through her hair and smiled. She was in a good mood, which proved to Katherine that her mother was keen on the senior Mines official, Michael Townsend, who was in town to oversee the development of a petroleum enterprise. Lillian found the man, an engineer, sophisticated and charming. Katherine saw him as a suave flatterer whose attentions she had herself repulsed only last week.

'Hello, Lillian. Katherine.' Michael flashed a bronze smile at the two women as he and an offsider emerged from the darkness of the closed dining room. He stood close to Lillian, his six-foot frame towering over her. 'Thanks for going to this trouble. Thank you.' His eyes glistened with lust as he gazed at Lillian's upturned face.

'It's all right,' Lillian said, lowering her eyes, face flushed. She liked Townsend's deep voice.

Katherine slammed the fridge door and slapped plates on the table for the newcomers. Lillian scowled.

3

'Hey! Katherine! Come in here. The girls want to meet you,' Pearl shouted through the servery from the Ladies Lounge. The Ladies Lounge transformed into a cacophony of women's voices, blouses, and perfume on train days. 'Where's your mum? Bring her too.'

As garrulous as she was florid, Pearl assumed familiarity with the Forsters on the slim basis of having met them at the airport. The bar was packed. Even though Jimmy was learning fast, Katherine was flat out and wasn't about to run around looking for Lillian.

A mixed lot came to town, filling the bar on Friday afternoons. Pastoralists brought their stockmen and, sometimes, their wives, children and governesses. Then there were the opal miners, trench diggers, fencers, graders, dingo catchers and a myriad of other stragglers. All came to meet the Ghan and its supply-carrying Chaser. When the bar got busy, men vied with each other to get Katherine's attention but, as the booze flowed, she became the butt of jokes and critical commentary about her efficiency, mood and appearance. She hated that.

Although men steered clear of the Ladies Lounge, they took an avid interest in which women were there. Katherine and Lillian would have avoided the lounge altogether, but Dudley insisted they socialise with the ladies because it was good for business. Yeah, good for the men, Katherine thought. To her, stepping into the Ladies Lounge felt like climbing into a cage so anyone could look you over from every angle. At least behind the bar, the counter hid half of you.

'Mum will be here shortly, Pearl.' It was a white lie. Lillian would turn up in her own good time. She refused to settle into serious drinking until the pub closed at 6 pm. Lillian didn't like to start earlier because she drank hard and fast to oblivion once she'd had her first drink.

'This is April. April Brown.' Pearl started introducing Katherine when she went back into the lounge to wipe tables and collect glasses. 'She runs the store with her husband, John. He's a bit of a looker.' Pearl's claim jarred. Katherine smiled at April, who seemed tired. April returned the smile with her mouth, but her eyes remained lacklustre, almost lifeless.

Pearl started shouting the names of various women over the chattering din, trying to introduce one woman after another. Katherine kept replacing overflowing ashtrays.

'Leave that.' Pearl grabbed Katherine's arm and pulled her to attention, turning her to face a skinny older woman. 'This is Betty Duke, the Police Sergeant's wife.' Betty Duke, a dark-haired and nervous soul about 40, trembled with compulsive talk. Next,

Pearl turned to Janice, the young schoolteacher from Adelaide. Like Katherine, Janice Cook was new to Wonnalinga. When she finished her teacher training, the government indentured her to an outback post. Janice had a face full of big freckles under a shock of curly red hair. Katherine warmed to her honest eyes and hoped they might become friends.

Pearl plopped down next to Katherine with a heavy sigh. She lit a cigarette then returned to shouting over the hubbub in the room.

'Listen, everyone, let's hear what you think about this one's marriage prospects. Should this blondie here set her cap at William Ringer?' Pearl loved an audience and played up to the other women, turning Katherine's head around by the chin with thumb and forefinger, 'pretty face, too, and, blue eyes.'

Katherine's heart pounded. The woman barely stopped short of opening her mouth to show her teeth, like an animal or a slave. Silent and surly, Katherine willed Lillian to rescue her from this humiliation, and squirmed at being displayed in this manner among these women. These strangers. Katherine determined to hate William Ringer. Yes, she wanted a husband. That was the reason she'd left the city, but that was her business, not bloody Pearl busybody Napper's.

Pearl lost interest in Katherine's marriage prospects the instant Lillian walked into the lounge. While Lillian was short, she had a presence, a certain gravitas unusual in a woman, let alone in such a heavy drinker. Lillian had spunk and did not try to please anyone. Katherine's relief was palpable. She loved her mother and admired Lillian's charm when she was sober, the way she assumed centre stage in any crowd, immaculate as she was today in the white slacks and open-neck shirt that Katherine had laundered for her. Lillian was as fastidious about her appearance as Dudley was about his hair. And his bar.

Lillian walked straight to the servery, asking what everyone would like to drink. Heads followed her. 'My shout,' she said. 'Another gin and tonic for you, Pearl?' Janice asked for a beer, April wanted lemonade, and Lillian ordered a whiskey and dry ginger ale for herself and, without asking, for the Sergeant's wife, Betty Duke.

Jimmy took the order, face taut with concentration. He was still learning the ropes. Rather than confuse him, Katherine went into the bar to make herself sarsaparilla and lemonade. The boy had likely never heard of sarsaparilla. She felt like an outsider to the women's general merriment and was not inclined to join in when she realised that she would have to put her mother to bed later. Dudley always said that it was not a job for him, as a man, to undress his wife when she was like that.

'Time, gentlemen, please.' Dudley's six o'clock call was greeted with howls of feigned objection from the bar and all sorts of lovey-dovey, aren't you handsome words from the lounge when he turned to the servery to say, 'and ladies.' It was his wink that did it. He told Katherine to start cleaning the bar, but Lillian had already called her daughter to the kitchen where William Ringer was making himself at home.

'This is my mate Billy the Kid and his brother Starlight,' William Ringer said, drunk and pleased with his joke. He assumed Katherine and Lillian would recognise him. They did but feigned otherwise. He made them uncomfortable, and they didn't want to encourage him.

'We've had a few too many schooners, ladies.' William spoke through a sly grin, trying to break the uneasy silence. He then fixed his eye on Katherine and announced that he had left a wild gin tied to an old gidgee tree just out of town so that he could bring his boys in for a well-deserved drink after an extended muster. They'd yarded his cattle out by the local dam waiting to be trucked down south to an abattoir. 'My Aboriginal boys are keeping an eye on them.'

Katherine had never heard the word 'gin' before, but Ringer's leer clarified his meaning. She similarly hated hearing Aboriginal stockmen being called boys; they were men. It was the same infantilising thing that irritated Lillian when Dudley called his wife a girl. Ringer's declarations were provocative, intended to show what a big man he was, but her visceral response to William Ringer was to recoil, or, at least, beware.

Here was a man who could tie people up, believing himself to be their owner, my boys indeed. There was entrenched cruelty in William Ringer, yet Katherine was mesmerised by his absolute confidence, the belief that he was born to rule, and she intuitively felt weak.

'Are you girls OK?' Dudley had heard the tromp of boots through the dining room and sensed impending trouble when Katherine didn't return to the bar. It was her job to remove saturated bar runners and wash and stack glasses while he counted the till.

'Come on, fellas, enough is enough.' Dudley stood facing the much taller men. You're all full. It's time to leave the girls alone and go home and sleep it off. The kitchen's off-limits once the pub's closed. You know that. Off you go now; there's good chaps.'

William Ringer turned on Dudley. 'Go home? Who the fuck do you think you are, little dud, dud, dud, Dudley?' He looked around to see if his men were smirking. They were not. He then grinned apologetically and changed his tune. 'Well, maybe you can tell me where to go because you do pull the best beer, doesn't he, fellas?' The others had faded into the darkened dining room and did not reply.

'There's a good fellow,' Dudley said, relieved at William's sudden change of mood. 'The girls are not used to this sort of thing.' Despite the tension, Lillian mumbled that she was not a bloody girl.

'You're right, mate; we're off. No worries. You pull a good beer, Dud, that's for sure,' William Ringer said one last time as he disappeared.

4

The minute Katherine opened the verandah door, her mind and body sagged with the weight of resentment. Lillian was sitting at the kitchen table, smoking a cigarette, waiting for her. She wanted to scream. Tell her mother to stop making excuses for getting up late every day and start doing something by herself. The earliest Lillian emerged from her room was eleven because, she liked to say, 'there's nothing to do in this godforsaken hole.' But it was the town joke that Lillian hid in her room all morning to manage the pain and puffiness of a perpetual hangover.

Lillian used Chanel No. 5 as camouflage. Dudley had given it to his wife for every birthday and anniversary for as long as Katherine could remember. A loyal but expensive token of the love they once shared. Lillian's bedroom stank with a malodorous cloud of stale booze and perfume. It swirled around lipsticks and matching bottles of nail polish, standing like toy soldiers on a Petit Point tray on Lillian's white Queen Anne dressing table.

An altogether delicate and poisonous armoury against marital disappointment and Katherine's glowering disapproval. It also provided refuge from the bush, a place Lillian was determined to hate.

'It's so hot.' Lillian looked up at her daughter as though Katherine might know what to do about it. Lillian had hated the heat since she had waddled into labour with Katherine in the middle of a Melbourne heatwave. 'I had to wear your father's Roman sandals. They were all I could squeeze my swollen feet into.' Lillian never tired of telling Katherine that she had delivered her eleven-pound burden at 3 am on 11 February 1943. While the years obliterated Katherine's unbecoming origins and St Helen's Private Hospital, where she was born, Lillian's resentment persisted with the force of time itself.

'Look at the thermometer. It's 100°F before we even start.' Lillian was undeterred. Katherine walked past her mother in silence to select a record from the small stack of long-playing discs next to her record player, hidden in a corner beside the fridge. Elvis was her favourite. When she was thirteen, Dudley laughed indulgently at her insistence that Elvis really could sing. Dudley was a tenor who sang like Mario Lanza. He could not accept that rock and roll was music in any sense that he understood. She chose Patsy Cline.

Lillian's resentment of Dudley, and by extension, her daughter, was a piece of wartime history. Japanese bombs raining on Darwin for a year almost to the day before Katherine's birth had portent, marking the beginning of the end of marital bliss. A silly story, really, given that she was still with Dudley, yet

Lillian never forgave her husband for not going AWOL from the Bandiana Army Base to be by her side at the birth of their first and only child. To Lillian, a man who truly loved his wife would have gone absent without leave from his army to see the product of his loins which, in Dudley's case, seemed inexplicably to stop functioning after that.

Katherine turned Patsy Cline up to hear the singer's dulcet voice over the drone of her mother's voice. *I fall to pieces each time I see you again.* Katherine's heart swelled with admiration for songwriters who seem to know how people feel, whose words lighten even the burden of being blamed for ending Lillian's brilliant wartime social life. She started to sing along with Patsy to avoid engaging with Lillian's self-pity.

Lillian took the last few drags on her cigarette, and Katherine started on the plates. It crossed her mind that Lillian's fascination with the upward fluctuations of the thermometer might have a subtext. Could it be an indirect and clumsy way of assuming the mantle of a pioneer — *look how hot it is, and I have to work so hard?* Katherine softened towards her mother. The heat did knock Lillian around now. She suffered humiliating hot flushes that caused sweat to drip at the nape of her neck. Her mother was approaching the change. Katherine heard her talk about this with her sisters before they left Melbourne. The change, they said, sent women quite mad — had-to-be-locked-up nuts. Apart from the sweaty flushes, apparent to all, and what Lillian called her cotton-wool heads, Lillian claimed to be handling the change well. At cynical moments, Katherine would remind her mother that her symptoms could be grog induced.

'How many have we got for lunch?' Katherine asked.

'Twelve.'

Mother and daughter worked for a while in silence, preparing for lunch in a companionable division of labour. Lillian turned to the stove to heat yesterday's soup, plugged the electric frypan in ready for the fish, keeping the temperature low until orders came in. Katherine put eight eggs in cold water to boil, testing herself to set out 14 white dinner plates (two extras in case) in even rows on the table in less than the eight minutes it took to perfect boiled eggs for salads. The solid timber kitchen table carried a spread of 24 dinner plates. When the pub was busy, Katherine and Lillian would line another ten on benches. The tabletop bore witness to the pub's history, etched with old finger length cigarette burns that either fell from drunken fingers or spilled off ashtrays and was crisscrossed with knife cuts and carved initials. It was a veritable palimpsest of spilt booze, tears of love declared or lost and the high stakes of after-hours poker games. This silent history under the dinner plates awaited the imprint of the Forster family.

From the coolroom on the verandah, Katherine collected an iceberg lettuce, the bucket of celery sticks she'd sliced to curl in iced water, three large tomatoes, three oranges, and a bowl of sweet beetroot cooked yesterday. From the pantry, she selected a packet of Kraft Cheddar cheese, a tin of pineapple slices and jars of pickled onions and sweet green gherkins that she put on the bench beside her record player. Lillian's private supply of homemade pickled onions — two large jars sealed with wax paper and tied with a Country Women's Association ribbon —

were hidden like guilty secrets behind the cheese. Lillian loved a good, pickled onion when she drank. Guests got mushy slices of factory-produced pickled onions on their salads as a cost-saving measure.

By the time Katherine had garnished the salads with a sprinkle of grated cheddar and a twist of sliced orange, Lillian had mixed her fish batter. Whiting was on today's menu, two large fillets per serve. Katherine checked the refrigerator to make sure the trays of filleted fish, lamb chops, beef sausages and steak — no pork chops this week, they did not arrive on the Chaser — were all OK.

With everything ready, mother and daughter sat down for a smoke, together this time, their separate yearnings mingling silent in curls of white smoke. Patsy Cline crooned on. Like her father, Katherine smoked Craven "A" cork tips. Lillian preferred Rothmans King Size filters. The ashtray that united them sat, precocious among the staid white rows of salad-decorated plates.

'Anything left for me?' An hour later, Dudley poked his head around the corner from the bar. 'Bit of fish would be nice if there's some left.' He always waited until the lunch rush had died down.

Lillian turned the heat of the electric frypan back up from standby and selected four King George whiting fillets, two each for herself and her husband. They loved their whiting. Katherine made up two steak sandwiches, one for her and one for Jimmy, who could eat in the bar to give Dudley a break.

After they'd eaten and cleaned up, Dudley dragged a 75 lb

sack of unwashed potatoes in from the verandah. Once a week, or twice if they were busy, the Forster family sat together to peel, slice and blanch their way through an afternoon to stock up on chips. Dudley brought Jimmy in, too, like the son he never had. Dudley's enthusiasm for a young man he barely knew annoyed Katherine.

As designated peelers, Dudley and Katherine sat on either side of the sack of potatoes to Lillian's right. Lillian sat at the head of the table. Jimmy sat to her left next to any young stockmen in town who volunteered on the day to join the chipping sessions. Katherine's blonde hair, blue eyes and shapely legs were a drawcard which meant no shortage of helpers at The First & Last since the Forsters took over. On busy days, the boys even dried dishes now Katherine was in town. Dudley never asked Jimmy to do scullery duties.

As the cook, Lillian established the protocols. Peeled potatoes were soaked in buckets of water to remove the last trace of dirt. Only Lillian did the slicing. Meticulous about her chips being the same size, Lillian trusted no one to cut them to shape as well as her. She plunged the potatoes into one of two fresh bowls of water on the table in front of her. When the second bowl was full of chipped spuds, she would sluice them, pat them dry in tea towels, then blanch them in smoking hot oil. Katherine's role was to drain the blanched chips onto brown paper, rough side up to absorb fat as they cooled. By the end of the afternoon, four large aluminium trays piled with potato chips blanched to perfection lined the shelves of the Kelvinator refrigerator. Plunged cold from the fridge into smoking hot oil, the pub's chips were Lillian's pride.

'What did you think of the women in the Ladies Lounge yesterday? Dudley asked his wife and daughter as they sat with a cuppa. 'We'd better keep it quiet, so they don't hear us in the bar but, that Sergeant's wife can talk, can't she?'

'Poor woman, can you imagine being married to him?' Lillian responded in sharp defence of Betty Duke, a woman she barely knew but was of similar age. She kept her head down. 'He's a tall bumbling bear of a man whose speech is so slow it's boring. I get impatient the minute he opens his mouth. God knows what it would be like to live with the man. If he were not the Sergeant of Police, I would assume that he was as thick as two bricks. How he found a wife like Betty, I do not know.' Lillian liked the way Betty dressed, as though she were still living in the city. 'She might talk a bit much, but at least she says things worth listening to.'

Dudley didn't persist. He turned to Katherine.

'Did I see you talking to the schoolteacher, love? Do you think you could make friends with her?'

Katherine completed her Intermediate Certificate at school. Teachers streamed her into a commercial course because, they said, she was not up to studying the humanities. Because of a crush on her handsome-but-married teacher, however, Katherine excelled at shorthand. She hoped that her relative lack of education would not affect a growing friendship with Janice Cook in this remote place. Lillian always said that girls more easily find men in pairs, and they were both ripe city girls of marriageable age. They had that in common.

'Yeah, I suppose so', Katherine replied.

Lillian resented motherhood and railed against the expectations put on women with children, and she had grown to believe that husbands — like hers, like Betty Duke's — made women miserable. Yet, with no sense of contradiction, she was keen for Katherine to find a husband sooner rather than later.

'Marriage,' Dudley spoke up, 'spoils women's lives. It changes them into whingeing old nags. Marry a young girl off, and within a couple of years, you will find a frump.'

Lillian flinched at Dudley's heedless remark. Katherine tried to steer the conversation to safer ground. 'Have you seen April Brown's husband, Dad? What do you think of him?'

'He came into the bar the other day, not a bad looking fellow, I suppose. If you like that sort of thing. Bit effeminate if you ask me.' Dudley chuckled. 'That would explain his wife April's miserable countenance.'

Lillian looked as if she would explode any minute. She plunged her knife into the cutting board, slicing chips in silence, head down. Dudley hadn't forgotten the way her sisters had teased her about him. They said he was queer because he wore a flashy camel hair coat and drove a motorbike with a sidecar. Dudley swept Lillian off her feet (as they used to say) by calling on her at the hairdressing salon where she was an apprentice, his sidecar overflowing with carnations and roses. Lillian had never doubted Dudley's devotion, but found it increasingly difficult to conceal her irritation at his gambling and neediness.

'What's wrong with you?' Dudley grew fidgety in Lillian's protracted silence.

'Nothing.' Lillian dried another batch of raw chips, ready for blanching.

Dudley watched her like a trapped mouse waiting for the cat to strike. 'There's always something with you. What the bloody hell am I supposed to have done now?' Dudley had never understood Lillian. There was no point arguing with her. She was better with words than him. He could not bear his wife's silence, which he saw as a deliberate attempt to make him look bad.

'Nothing,' Lillian repeated. 'You always think it is all about you. Well, I'm sorry, Dudley Forster, it is not.'

'Don't worry about her, Dad.' Katherine spoke up, risking her mother's ire. Lillian hated it when she took her father's side, but it was so hard to sit by and not try to stop things from escalating. 'You know Mum. She just goes quiet sometimes.'

Lillian's tongue could be as sharp as her chipping knife, but it was her silence that agitated Dudley. Katherine tried to divert him with a glance at the bar, intended to remind him that Lillian had a worse than usual hangover today, but Dudley was on a roll.

'You think you're too bloody good for me — for this — don't you? You always have bloody well felt like that. You and your whole bloody family. Up yourselves, you were.' Dudley's arms flailed in indignation as he ranted about Lillian never approving of him, how she disapproved of his buying The First & Last Hotel and was just too proud to admit that he had done well. She was bloody well enjoying this place where life was easier for them both than ever before. 'You were not like this when we first met.' He spluttered, looking askance at Jimmy, who, Katherine noted, failed to give Dudley the supportive glance her father obviously sought.

'You think you can run this bloody place by yourself?' Dudley stood, casting his chair across the room. 'You think you know the bloody lot,' he spat at his wife. He stormed out of the kitchen, pausing long enough to dump the chipping pan onto the floor. Boiling oil splashed and burned Katherine and Lillian's rubber-thonged feet.

For most of that afternoon, Dudley sulked in his room, which smelled not of perfume and spent alcohol like Lillian's but smoke and nicotine. Dudley's room was his sanctuary. There, he was surrounded by stacks of paperback Westerns — yippees as he called them — and the racing guide he called his bible. The yippees helped him get to sleep. The racing guide kept him awake with worry. Katherine and Lillian were the only ones who ever knew that Dudley Forster slept all his life with the light on.

'Everything all right in there?' A voice called from the bar. This time it was Roger Beaming, the wealthiest and most respected pastoralist in the district who had been eavesdropping. Beaming commandeered the best seat in the bar facing the short storage corridor between it and the kitchen. He owned a 12,000 square mile property called Myall Creek Station, half the size of England. On a good season, it carried 18,000 head of cattle. Many knew but few dared mention that Myall Creek Station had started out as a sheep property like other stations in the region; the hidden sheep history of cattlemen was never admitted for fear of ridicule. Sheep were for rural areas around cities and towns, not the great outback.

Katherine composed herself and entered the bar with a smile

to reassure the pastoralist that all was well. At the same time, in the kitchen, Lillian threw a thick layer of cooking salt over the oil to soak it up, making it easier to sweep away later. She ran her fingers through her hair to greet Mary Beaming when the woman poked her head in, asking if she could come in as she plonked herself on Lillian's chair at the head of the kitchen table without waiting for an answer.

'I spilt the oil,' Lillian forced a grin and turned to put the kettle on. Mary Beaming, a pioneer pastoralist's daughter, was in the habit of descending unannounced upon various Wonnalinga kitchens when she was in town. As a pastoralist's wife, Mary Beaming avoided the Ladies' Lounge except during race week when it was virtually impossible to avoid mingling with Pearl Napper and her ilk. During the year, Mary Beaming's choice of kitchen accorded with her needs or mood on the day and today, she felt like a drink. That brought her to Lillian. When Lillian offered tea, a flash of annoyance crossed Mary Beaming's face. She was used to getting her way. It would be a long time and many binges later before Lillian learned that Mary Beaming had been a pawn in her father's power game and was married off to Roger Beaming in fulfilment of an unpaid debt. Mary, it seems, had been Roger Beaming's step up in life.

Early in their Wonnalinga lives, Lillian and Katherine were honoured that Mary Beaming dropped in at all. She had come, equipped with recent Myer and David Jones catalogues for the Forster women. Mary carried herself with some of the arrogance of William Ringer and others of that class who had made it their business to welcome people to what they described as their country, their region. They had a proprietary sense of owning not only their vast properties but also the surrounding land, and the town of Wonnalinga. Katherine was thankful that they stopped short of including a welcome to the whole of Australia; such was their sense of entitlement. She did not hold that against Mary, who was pensive today. Doing a favour, the woman told them that they would need to order gowns soon, to be ready for the main social event of the year, the race week ball when women slip off their loose cotton frocks or step out of working clothes and replace them with glamorous gowns. Race week, she advised Katherine and Lillian, was all about mingling and mating. The sons and daughters of the bush met and matched, and she saw no reason on earth why Katherine should not be part of that.

Mary Beaming turned to Lillian, 'She's such a pretty thing. I hear there are bets out on your daughter and William Ringer getting together.' Undaunted, she turned to Katherine, who hung her head in shame. 'Well, who do you like? You must've found someone to throw your cap at by now.'

'Nah.' Katherine was not about to let this woman, let alone her mother, know that she fancied Jimmy Barber. She had no interest in anyone else. Why didn't Lillian pull Mary Beaming up for calling her pretty? Why did Lillian not defend her when this woman described her physical characteristics as though she were a gemstone or a beast up for auction? She was a real person. Not a thing.

Lillian would have gone straight to Dudley if she'd known where Katherine's affections lay. They wanted the best for their

daughter, and that meant finding someone with the right creden-
tials. A boy like Jimmy was far from desirable. Dudley heard
about him through a past customer who put a word in with a
priest in Port Augusta to help him find an offsider. The priest
who recommended Jimmy said he deserved a chance. His parents
were both alcoholics. At nineteen, the same age as Katherine,
the boy needed a break from caring for younger siblings, which
he had done since twelve.

Dudley liked Jimmy from the start, passing on as much as
he could about bar work and the ins and outs of the hotel trade.
Jimmy was soon tapping kegs and cleaning the lines until the
beer sparkled in every glass as Dudley demanded. He pulled
a good beer, too, like his mentor. Katherine took to Jimmy's
animated freckled face the moment she set eyes on him. Jimmy
didn't brag. He carried his lithe physique in a lazy, laid-back
sort of way and was warm, soft-spoken and respectful. Like
Katherine, Jimmy hated alcohol. Jealousy niggled Katherine at
first when Dudley included Jimmy in the family the way he did.
Would Jimmy one day take advantage of her dad's generosity?

Without challenging Katherine's failure of deference, Mary
Beaming proceeded to open her catalogues on the table, offering
the one from John Martins to Katherine and the David Jones
one to Lillian. 'There you go, girls. Feast your eyes on these and
place your orders soon. I've marked the outfits that I've already
ordered to prevent doubling up.'

5

'What brings you here?' Katherine was stripping soiled sheets from vacated beds.

'You should give them a title.' Despite his growing allegiance to Dudley, Jimmy sneaked up on Katherine working in the house.

'What?'

'I'm talking about your parents' fights. I presume the ding-dong the other day wasn't their first. You should give them a title. Then they'd become title fights, see?' He laughed.

'What has it got to do with you?' Katherine was not going to let this boy invade her privacy. The fact that he heard the fight worried her. Did others know?

'The Big Kitchen Oil Spill. How's that for a title?' Jimmy was undeterred, and Katherine turned on him.

'You can't just name a thing like that as though it were no more than a film scene or something. What good would that do?' Even as she spoke, Katherine warmed to Jimmy's quiet persistence. Talking about her parents' fight with another person forced her shame into the open, but as she let the name in, it made the fight separate somehow, like a thing outside of her. It shifted her to a brighter place where she could see it was not her fault that her parents fought.

'It's a good game,' Jimmy said. 'My little brothers and sisters loved thinking up names — no need for stories. Titles do the trick. We had favourite names for different occasions: Who Took the Last Beer, which Dad said when he was pissed and angry and Give us a Fuck, which he said every time he beat Mum.' Katherine winced at the foul language. 'The only fight that we could not recover from was the one we called Crying, after the Roy Orbison song. That's when Dad messed Mum up so bad she left and never came back. That was when I decided to tell the local priest what was happening. Like Mum, I was used to it, but I didn't want to see the little ones cop it too. What if he took to the girls for sex? Or the boys, for that matter. With my father, anything was possible. That's when Father Bob found me this job with Dudley.'

'Where are your brothers and sisters now?'

'They're in foster care, but at least they are being fed and can go to school every day. I get a letter from Father Bob from time to time. He doesn't care if I don't reply. He knows I miss them, and he'll find a way to let me see them when I go home.'

Katherine had never had to worry about little brothers and sisters, and the fighting in her home was not physical. She had never seen Dudley hit Lillian. She'd been shocked to learn that there was such a thing as the sexual molestation of little children.

'OK, The Big Kitchen Oil Spill it is.' Katherine was mulling this over when Jimmy placed a finger under her chin and lifted her face to his. As their lips touched, he pressed himself against her, his penis hard on her thigh.

'Better stop,' Katherine paused for breath. 'Someone might find us.' Implacable, Jimmy unzipped his fly with one hand, covering her protesting mouth with his lips. He tickled her tongue with his, lifted her dress and pulled her panties down. Katherine stepped out of them and lay down on the bed, melting as Jimmy pressed down. The sound of footsteps made them stop, but by the time they'd passed, all he could do was apologise for losing control. Holding Katherine close, Jimmy pulled up her knickers with deft fingers and patted down her dress before standing to pull his trousers up. As he left the room, he brushed his smiling lips on hers.

'Next time,' he said, 'we'll lock the door.'

Scared by the risk they had taken, Katherine went back to stripping and making beds, but her heart sang. She'd had sex before, but it had not been fun like this. Even though Jimmy didn't last, he had aroused her, and that was special. In her last year of school, she and a boy called Steve dared each other to strip naked in the front seat of his dad's truck one full moon night. Their skin glowed a ghostly white. Katherine remembered her astonishment as his penis rose from its dark bed of curls and hardened. They had agreed to look at each other's sex, but in his arousal, Steve pulled her head down, demanding that she suck him 'down there'. She'd started to retch. He pushed her away, banging her head against the passenger side window, then prised her legs apart. As he forced himself deep inside her, she was dry with fear, and the gear stick dug into her thigh. After he groaned his sticky semen into her, he sat up, zipped up, commanded her to dress and started the engine. She struggled to do her bra up and pull panties back on as the truck sped across bumps.

Then, there was Ron, an eighteen-year-old budding musician and guitarist friend of a horrid cousin who threw parties when his parents were away. It started innocently enough with a game of spin the bottle, but all the boys and most of the girls were soon drunk on sweet sherry, which they swigged from the bottle. Katherine didn't drink and was pleased at first when Ron singled her out from among the many girls who seemed unable to resist the allure of a musician. She let him kiss her and returned the petting, but soon, she became fearful as he forced her down onto a sofa, ripped her panties and penetrated her in front of everyone. It hurt. When he finished, he stood up and laughed, winking at his mates as he zipped up. Those who were not attempting a similar play with the drunk girls had crowded around the couch to watch, hands in pockets enjoying their own vicarious erections. The shame of that night was unbearable. Katherine learned the next day that word had spread that she was a slut and had encouraged Ron. That incident decided Katherine to go bush with her parents to wipe the slate clean. She wanted a husband, not ugly sex. Until Jimmy came along, it had not occurred to her that any mechanism would help her forget the stain. She named this incident, Spin the Bottle and took an almost unconscious decision to write about it. One day.

6

Cup Day did not start well for Dudley. Two stockmen pranced into his bar on horseback, hooting and slapping their Akubras against their horses' shivering flanks minutes after he opened the door for business. Katherine watched in horror from the safety of the kitchen corridor. She calculated that there was little more than 12 feet between the front wall and the counter of the L-shaped bar, itself barely 15 feet wide. No horse could squeeze into the small side area. Confined, as they were, the horses snorted through flared nostrils, stress visible in the whites of their eyes. You could smell their sweat and feel their body heat, yet the boys, supposedly excellent horsemen, egged them on. The prancing and half-rearing frightened Katherine. Loud snorts seemed to fill the whole area as the horses repeatedly bumped into each other in distress. What if they went wild and trampled Dudley? The clop of hooves bounced off the walls. There seemed no way for them to turn.

'What the bloody hell do you think you're doing? Get out

now.' Dudley yelled above the din. 'Your horses are ruining the lino tiles.' Even though she was worried about the tiles, her father's words sounded silly to Katherine. It was not as if these yahooing stockmen would be easy to persuade. They were already half-drunk.

'What about a beer, Dud?' One of the stockmen shouted over the thuds and clatter, still on a roll. William Ringer's nickname for Dudley had stuck, adding insult, as they say, to injury.

'Yeah, give us a beer, Dud. What's the matter with ya, Dud?' Attracted by the noise, an accidental audience had gathered outside to encourage the riders with a collective chuckle that incensed Dudley. He stood in high dudgeon, shouting, 'I am not about to let you young idiots tarnish my unblemished liquor licence. I'll call the police.' The threat made the audience laugh louder, but there was more at stake for Dudley. He hated looking foolish to his wife.

'Duh, duh, Dud, don't do that,' the stockmen stuttered in merry unison, not for a moment expecting Dudley to go that far. 'It's only a joke, mate. No harm done.' The horses continued to bump off each other, eyes still rolling, ears now pinned back.

'You are no mates of mine,' Dudley replied. 'And you're harming your horses, you fools. Get out. Get out. I don't know who you think you are, but you're not only making your beautiful animals suffer. You're a bloody public nuisance with no respect for anything. Bugger off! Go on, bugger off!'

Having a spotless bar was Dudley's religion. Trained by her father, Katherine mopped the floor every night with Pine-O-Clean in boiling water and emptied ashtrays into used bulk fruit tins to prevent smouldering butts from flaring up and hide odours. She washed glasses by hand then double-rinsed them in steaming hot water so they would dry to a high sheen and sparkle on the shelves. Every morning, she laid freshly laundered bar runners on the counters, replacing them as necessary during opening hours. No customer of The First & Last would ever encounter the stench of yesterday's smoke and dregs, and yet today, despite all of Dudley's efforts, his bar was being despoiled by horseshit. Katherine would have to clean it up.

'Mum! Mum!' Dudley called out to Lillian, 'Get the police on the phone. These buggers have gone mad.' Lillian was not in the kitchen, so Katherine made the call despite her confidence that any test of wills between her city publican father and a couple of bush-bred miscreants would end in her father's favour. Of course, by the time the police arrived, the horses had gone. The sergeant and his constable had strolled to the pub instead of driving. They were not in a hurry to put paid to anything that might bring Dudley to heel. They did not like his arrogance, as they saw it. The horsemen had forced the horses to rear just enough to allow them to turn on their hindquarters, and they had galloped off down the main street with a new publican story for around the campfire. However, when they later heard what Dudley said to the police, their respect for him grew.

'Who were they?' the sergeant asked Dudley, notebook in hand. Dudley had not yet learned their names, but he had a good idea to which station they belonged. Their Akubras gave them away too. Bushmen mould their Akubras to suit their sense of style and status in the outback hierarchy. It was said that you could read a lot about a man from his hat, more than you might from his walk. The older and more sweat-stained it became, the more a hat was prized, even loved, by its owner. It was an intimate and personal thing.

'I don't know.' Dudley ended the matter. Any fool would know who they were from the vehicles in town, and the only ones belonged to William Ringer and Roger Beaming. Dudley didn't want to piss people off unnecessarily, least of all, the police. He'd made his point by calling them, and that was enough. Dudley might be a stickler in some ways, but he was no keener to get embroiled in police business than the two stockmen. His Sydney slum upbringing had bred in him a profound disrespect for the law in matters such as these, and causing friction would make life more difficult for the family. It might put the pastoralists offside, and they were, after all, good customers. The police closed their notebooks and left.

Katherine shot from the kitchen, wanting to tell Lillian about the horses, only to discover that Lillian had been sitting quietly out of sight in the dining room all along. She'd listened with pride, knowing, as Katherine did, that Dudley Forster would show this town and the people of this region who was boss in his pub. Not that Lillian would ever let her husband know she admired his courage.

Race week had begun, and, with it, the welcome prospect of good takings to keep the pub going for a while. Before long, bodies lay all around, in the dirt or on swags next to vehicles parked at odd angles. Sleeping off the effects of the grog was like a mushroom plague all over town, and mornings woke to jokes about the stench of urine or vomit. Men who soiled themselves in the night slunk around in shame until they were either back home or back on the grog. As a teetotal publican, Dudley was a walking contradiction. He might hate the grog, but he did not like to see his business undermined. It didn't take a genius to figure out that it was not his bottle sales that allowed people to continue drinking when the pub closed. He tried to throw people out before they got paralytic. The store, selling grog on the sly with the full sanction of the law, made it harder for him to keep people in line. Still, people loved the pub for companionship.

The population of Wonnalinga swelled from 60 to nearly 1000 souls of every shape, size and even breed for race week. They came from everywhere; Adelaide, far-west Queensland, Alice Springs and regional South Australian towns like Port Augusta. New cars and heavy-duty vehicles rolled into town alongside bashed-up utes and sedans with sun-faded roofs, carrying every conceivable combination of human, dog and swag. The house filled up, and the bar overflowed with customers determined to drain every last one of the silver kegs lining the Pub's backyard. Despite the store's sly grog, Dudley overcame his distaste for drunkenness when he counted the till at the end of the week. He had ordered well. Katherine and Lillian both knew any fight against sly grog was too big for Dudley to take on. For one thing, he was Ebenezer Scrooge when it came to making money. More importantly, he secretly relied on the police station to disburse his bets.

When the long-awaited ball gowns arrived on the Ghan,

Katherine could not collect them from the Post Office until after lunch because the train was late. The minute she'd put the last dish away, she raced to the post office so fast that, for once, she didn't notice the Aboriginal women sitting in the block next door. By the time she got to her mother's room where Lillian had waited, as impatient to open the parcels as her daughter, the girl was breathless.

'Have you got scissors here, Mum?' Lillian passed Katherine a tiny pair of nail scissors to cut the string. Beneath the brown paper were two shiny-white cardboard boxes, inside of which lay tissue-covered dreams.

In back-to-back modesty, they donned their new finery, then took turns parading, swishing this way and that to catch glimpses of themselves in Lillian's white Cheval mirror. They laughed together, keeping their respective misgivings private. Lillian saw Katherine's black skirt, with its high rear slit, as too old for her daughter. She hated the low-cut, gold-sequinned top Katherine had chosen. It made her look like a tart. Katherine feared that, although the straight, shot-purple taffeta dress flattered Lillian's petite figure, it was so tight that it would roll up to her belly, revealing all if her mother toppled over drunk, as she so often did.

After clearing the kitchen on ball night, Katherine rushed to her room with fingers crossed that Jimmy would be back from the racecourse in time to help Dudley close the bar. Earlier, she had laid her outfit on her bed with the gold sequinned top meeting the waistline of the long black evening skirt so that its back slit fell to the floor to meet her new patent leather stilettos. Sheer, black-seamed stockings and a black lace bra and panties bought in secret completed the paper doll cut-out picture.

Forewarned by Mary Beaming, the Forsters appreciated that the region's women would dress in all manner of organza, tulle, silk or lace evening dresses, elegant shoes and lacy lingerie; the accoutrements of womanhood denied them by heat, dust and hard work. Katherine felt like Cinderella and believed her gown proved that she was more than a publican's daughter, barmaid and cleaning lady. Dressed in fancy clothes, she smiled to herself. Time to go to the ball.

After knocking three times, Katherine opened the door to find Lillian passed out drunk on her bed, taffeta gown still in its box. Holding back tears, Katherine ran to the bar where Dudley counted the till and Jimmy mopped.

'Mum's not fit to go anywhere.'

'Never mind, love. You look nice.'

'I'll walk her there if you like, boss.' Jimmy spoke up.

'Good lad.' Dudley replied. 'Off you go then; I'll finish up here.'

'I'll be right,' Katherine said, turning to the door. She did not want a bloody escort. It made her sick that Jimmy was becoming possessive and sucking up to her father at the same time. He was supposed to be her boyfriend, but this cute boys' club thing he had with Dudley fired Katherine up. Stuff him. Jimmy was not Dudley's son, nor her brother. She was not there for him to curry favour with her father, her father mind you, with her as the mediating object. For the sake of peace, she suppressed her anger.

It had been a long week for Katherine. With the house full, there had been more beds to make, more cleaning, washing and cooking and more time in the bar every day, but she was determined to enjoy the ball. She wished she had Lillian by her side, but at least she would not have to spend the evening looking after her.

Walking down the main street in stilettos for the first time proved a bit more treacherous than Katherine had anticipated; even a tiny pebble could destabilise. The Country Women's Association had festooned the town hall with streamers and balloons and brought a band up from Port Augusta for the occasion. They were tuning guitars and trilling on the piano, try-outs that floated into the chilly night air.

The moon hid behind a cloud, but party lights shone from the entrance like a beacon. Inside the hall, chairs lined the room, delineating a dance floor sprinkled with resin to prevent spills as the night progressed and liquor took hold. Matrons and old men had claimed seats early for good vantage, and small children ran all over the place like puppies on the loose. They would soon fall asleep where they dropped and, except for the littlies, would be packed under a pile of warm blankets in cars with windows ajar. Hardly recognisable in fine apparel, the district's women greeted each other with bright lipstick smiles and flushed cheeks. Men stood outside in drinking clusters until the music started and, after that, between sets. They'd traded their work garb for starched white collars, dinner jackets and brand-new cream moleskins, high-heeled boots shining like the occasional hatless Brylcreemed head. Katherine revelled in being alone without someone hovering protectively over her as Jimmy would have done. She breathed in the excitement.

As the night wore on, the music slowed from upbeat to gentler rhythms. Liaisons formed among the singles while parents and employers arranged marriage alliances. Lights dimmed as everybody settled, dancing cheek to cheek with a preferred partner. Katherine left before the last dance. She was too tired and sober to keep fending off old men and fumbling, yahooing drunks. William Ringer kept his distance, but she could feel him watching her, and that, too, pissed her off. Bloody men, they all assumed they had rights over her in the way they appraised — no, consumed — her body with lustful eyes.

As Katherine stepped out into the crisp night to walk home, she decided that Jimmy deserved to be left at home sulking. Thought dissipated and, as the raucous music grew quiet, Katherine surrendered to the gentle light of the luminescent moon.

When she got home, Dudley was nowhere to be found. She wanted to tell her father how much she'd missed Lillian at the ball and that she'd been too tired to enjoy it. More than that, she'd felt like the odd person out among town and station women alike. Men always showed a keen interest, at least in her body, but the local women, especially married ones, kept their distance. Ready for bed, disappointed and lonelier than she'd been for some time, Katherine slipped into her nightdress, folded her evening clothes back into their white city box, which she shoved into the bottom of her wardrobe.

The moment her head hit the pillow, she fell into a deep slumber until a fondling hand crept between her thighs and roused her. Thinking it was Jimmy, she arched her body to receive him until her hands found rough stubble instead of Jimmy's soft curls. She recoiled.

'Who are you?' Katherine shoved her assailant to the floor with the abnormal strength of surprise and anger. The man grunted, yanked his trousers up and struggled into his boots, hopping on one leg then the other as he made for the door. She could hear him move across the gravel towards the road. Katherine recognised Zygmunt Symanski. He was the fellow who, only yesterday, had menaced Dudley with a broken bottle, demanding money. Dudley had stood his ground till Symanski calmed down, and only then did he lend the man enough to get him out of his difficulties. Her dad was good with drunks.

The reassuring crunch of gravel stopped, bringing Katherine back to the moment. She peered into the chill night, where she could see Symanski's silhouette against the moon. There was no mistaking the rhythmic jerk of the man's shoulder. He was masturbating in the middle of the backyard, facing her door. Katherine brought herself to climax as she watched.

When she was sure that Symanski had gone, Katherine got up, yanked her nightie off and stripped the bed. Covering her nakedness with her dressing gown, she glided barefoot across the lawn to the incinerator. The grass was damp and cold underfoot. She camouflaged her bed linen and nightie with handfuls of dead leaves, planning to burn the items with pub waste in the morning. Flames against the night sky would attract anyone for miles around, and questions could be asked. Feeling unclean, Katherine tiptoed up the corridor to the ladies' bathroom, where she began to relax under a hot cascade of pungent bore water.

Next morning, Police Constable Barry Johnstone came to the pub looking for Zygmunt Symanski — who he called Ziggy for short — a Polish opal miner from Mintabie.

'What's out there?' Katherine asked, hoping her question would divert attention from her discomfort after last night's episode.

'Nothing much. Mintabie's a small opal mining site about 150 miles out of Wonnalinga where men with dubious pasts go to grovel in the gravel for a fortune.' The constable smirked. 'Not many believe there's opal out there, but local Aboriginal people reckon it is. They say that a German fellow made big money years ago from a rare vein of milk opal. It's hard work digging through the tough layers of rock and earth and takes a special kind of desperation to want to do it.'

'Well, I haven't seen any Polish-looking man, not that I'd know what one might look like if I did. I'll call you if I hear a foreign accent. I'll tell Dad, too, if you like.'

'Yes, please. How're you finding it here? You've got rings under your eyes. What did you get up to last night?'

Katherine sensed the constable's cock quivering and turned away. The man's blue-eyed stare was cold and hard. For a moment, she felt almost sorry for Polish Ziggy, as she had last night when he left her room with nothing but unsatisfied longing in his hand. She had no interest in what he'd done to attract police attention; this policeman was using him as an excuse to get to her.

When the constable left, Katherine headed off to the laundry only to be confronted by Jimmy saying he wanted a private word.

'What is it?' Katherine tried to be patient despite her tiredness and the disturbing encounter with the constable. The inclination to tell Jimmy to go to buggery was strong, but something about his frown stopped her. He was serious for once.

'Your dad had a rough night last night. You need to know he was hiding from you when you got home. When we closed the bar, he told me how well we'd done on the day and how pleased he was that race week had been a great success. The kegs had held, and the till was bursting. He was tickled pink. After the bar was done, I was about to head off to my room when Dudley asked me to stay and have a cuppa. We sat together congratulating ourselves that cup day had gone without a hitch, except for the horses, of course. We were relieved that we could get back to normal tomorrow when the town emptied again.

While we chatted, what, at first seemed to be unremarkable whispers and giggles outside, gave way to hoots of laughter and the sound of boots stomping on the roof above the bar. Dudley guessed it would be Roger Beaming who had won the Wonnalinga Cup. The hooting started at the racecourse when Akubras went flying into the air to the cry, *yippee, onya Roger, we're beaming for ya*.

We listened for a while. Then Roger Beaming started yelling over the others, *come on, Lilly Pilly, up you come, there's a good little filly*. Your mum must have woken up and got it into her head to go to the ball by herself, in her nightie mind you, only to be waylaid by Roger Beaming and company heading the other way. She would still have been full despite a couple of hours sleep, yet here he was dragging your mum to ultimate degradation and encouraging her to stomp with the rest of them on the roof over your father's head.

'It broke my heart to see him, such a proud man, sink to the floor, heart crushed. I asked if he wanted me to call the police, but David Duke's voice was the second loudest up there. Dudley rocked himself, repeating over and over that the whole world had gone mad. He asked God how much a man had to take. Thinking of others as always, though, he was frightened that someone might get hurt if they fell. They were all drunk as buggery. And there would be insurance to worry about. Most of all, he said, he wasn't about to lose Lillian like that. He straightened his back and marched outside and, from the middle of the main street, shouted with as much authority as he could muster, telling everyone to get down from the roof immediately. As you would expect, raucous laughter was the reply. After that, he sent me packing, saying I'd need my beauty sleep. He would wait, he said, keep guard, till Lillian was safely on the ground. He didn't want to bother you.'

7

Katherine could see humpies in the back lane through a small opening in the corrugated tin fence at the rear of the block where Aboriginal women whiled away their days talking, laughing, and surrounded in the heat by babies, little ones and lean yellow dogs. Women entered through the opening, and while men occasionally called from there, they rarely came in. Facing the main street at the front, the block was prime real estate when it came to watching the town's comings and goings, especially as nobody heeded the women. It was almost as though they didn't exist. For Katherine, though, walking past, feeling their eyes upon her, was a challenge. She averted her eyes, too shy to say hello. Her embarrassment was so acute — as it was when she first encountered Paddy — that she walked poker-straight past the women with her stomach clenched and staring straight ahead. No matter how many times she visited the store or Janice Cook, who lived in the tiny shack next to it, she had not yet been able to tame her discomfort.

Even though Janice was a qualified schoolteacher, she was not eligible for government housing as a single woman. Katherine was shocked. According to the Australian standard of domesticity, the government teacher's cottage was allowed to stand empty, waiting for proper occupants, a man supporting a wife and offspring. The girls agreed that it was outrageous, but what could they do?

Despite the discomfort of being on show on the way, Katherine liked going to the store. Dudley had become a bit iffy about her doing so since he discovered that the Browns sold sly grog, but there was little else to do on a quiet day. This morning, she'd plucked up the courage to ask Paddy if he could introduce her to the Aboriginal women, then it would be easier to say hello as she passed. It didn't feel right not to. She'd already stopped calling the block 'vacant' the way everyone else did. Sure, there was no building on it, but the large slice of earth under the big mulga tree was undoubtedly occupied.

The storekeeper's liquor licence permitted him to deliver booze to stations. It did not allow him to dispense alcohol in town as he did. Openly. Bush people often turned up at the pub, drunk at opening time. Aboriginal people could be seen drunk at any time, although it still was against the law for anyone to sell grog to them. Dudley refused to sell one illegal drop. Katherine couldn't help being a bit sorry for the storekeeper's wife, April, who clearly had problems. She seemed always to be an unshed tear away from a well of sadness. Her golden-haired little ones, a little boy, aged three and a girl aged two, drained her. She was often alone with them, working in the store while her husband seized any opportunity to get out of town to visit railway sidings, cattle stations and Aboriginal camps where he sold booze. Gossip had it that he also had an Aboriginal woman on the side. With that much to hide, no wonder he sold sly grog to the station people when the pub was closed. Katherine was getting the hang of how things worked in Wonnalinga.

The store displayed its wares in a hierarchy of social value. Starting right next to the front door were shelves stacked with cigarettes, tinned and dried food and soft drinks. Also close to the entrance, sometimes on a rack outside, there hung a Tropicana of loose, floral, cotton dresses called *muumuus* after their Hawaiian origin and known locally as gin's dresses. No white woman would be seen dead in one, despite their appeal in extreme heat where the slightest breath of air on legs could cool you down. Baby products nestled further in, on one side of the store: fly-net hoods to protect little ones from the sticky desert flies that could blind a child, Nestlé's Lactogen, a powdered substitute for mother's milk, dummies, bottles, teats, cloth nappies and lots of cheap toys. The wall opposite stocked men's items: moleskin trousers, jeans, fitted stockmen's shirts with studs, elastic-sided boots and Akubra hats that gave status to styles. Browsing items like books and records were at the back of the shop, away from light fingers. Thought to be black.

Today, Katherine was after music. She loved reading, but her taste was eclectic. She sometimes bought books from the store but ordered directly from suppliers like the Mary Martin Book Shop in Adelaide.

'I'll have this,' Katherine passed an LP called *GI Blues* to

April.

'You like Elvis then?' April asked.

'Yeah. I saw the film in Melbourne a couple of years ago.'

'I miss that, going to the proper pictures,' April continued. 'Little children,' she said with a shrug. 'Still, I wouldn't be without them. They are a blessing.'

'Must be hard up here,' Katherine had no knowledge of babies and children but wanted to appear kind.

'We get by,' the older woman replied. 'You going to have babies?'

'Pardon?' April's question caught Katherine off guard. She had grown up listening to Lillian talk about how she had spent the war years when Dudley was in the army lugging her pudgy baby and trudging the streets of Melbourne to find accommodation when landlords would not rent to husbandless women with infants. Her mother's stories told Katherine she was a burden, which caused her to sublimate the idea of having babies, with a contradictory vow to be a better mother than Lillian. It'd be easy. She only had to forego the grog.

'Yes, probably. When I'm married.' Katherine bridled at having to answer such a question on the spot like that. She wanted to say that, of course, she would have children. That's why people get married. The idea that there would be any choice in the matter had never occurred to her. She pondered this on the way home and, again, forgot to worry about the Aboriginal women watching as she passed by.

When the pub was quiet, the days were long. Since Jimmy took over meeting the Chaser, Katherine and Janice met on the pub's front verandah on Ghan days to watch the goings-on, a bit like the women parallel to them in the block next door.

'It's late,' Janice said. 'The train.'

'Yeah. If it doesn't come soon, even Mum might get to see it arrive.' The girls giggled, enjoying the way their friendship had blossomed in recent months. They stared at the heat waves rising along empty tracks and strained to hear the train over the omnipresent caw of crows to little avail. Station people in town to meet the train were far more attuned to the subtle sounds and silences of the plains, which meant that, for these two city girls, the first sign of the approaching train came from vehicles pulling up at the station across the road. Men in the bar could hear the damn train sooner than they, announcing *here she comes* inside before the girls could discern the slightest atmospheric change out on the verandah.

'Have you met Wendy Milton yet?' Janice broke the spell. 'She's a fettler's daughter, but rumour had it that her father sent her to a good school, so she's a bit educated. She's going to fill in at the Post Office and help in the store. April needs a break from her kids and keeping house for that husband of hers more than in the Post Office, but it's something, I guess.'

'Was that her arriving yesterday in the blue ute I saw? She's tall with dark hair.'

'That's her. Her father pulled her out of the railway siding where she'd been camping. Unless he stayed awake all night, I don't know how he kept the other fettlers out of her bed. Perhaps he didn't. Anyway, they put her up in the shack with me. Come and meet her tonight.'

'You girls got nothing to do but line up like wall-flowers along the front verandah?' Lillian joined them, and, in that interruption, all three women missed the train's arrival. When tourists hit the verandah wanting to take photos, Lillian whispered, 'Mary Beaming told me they call them grasshoppers around here. They come in droves, eat everything in sight and leave.' She laughed, turning to Katherine, 'Come on lazy bones, lunchtime.'

'See you, Janice.' Katherine followed her mother into the kitchen. Katherine loved her mother's company on days like today, so she didn't correct her; tourists were called locusts, not grasshoppers. It was an easy mistake to make because a locust is a type of grasshopper but only locusts swarm. Paddy told her that.

By the time Katherine showed up at the shack after dinner, Billy Snowden and Ian Taylor, the two stockmen who worked for William Ringer, were already there. From the state of them, drinking had started early. It was odd to see men at the shack because, for as long as Janice had lived there by herself, it had been a man-free zone.

'You want a beer?' Billy passed a bottle. Katherine felt like an idiot for bringing three small bottles of Coca-Cola, expecting only to find Janice and Wendy Milton. Lillian always chided her for taking free drinks for friends. She said it was trying to buy friendship. If that were true, what did it mean that men in the bar bought each other drinks all the time, which was called shouting, something that mates did. Maybe shouting was reciprocal, but then you might ask why the two stockmen tonight had brought two full cartons of beer with them. What sort of reciprocity did they expect from that?

'Nah. I'll stick to Coke. Thanks anyway.' Katherine wanted a clear head, not that she cared what Jimmy would think of her being in mixed company, but she did not like the effect of alcohol. Dudley would disapprove. For a man who no longer made love to his wife, her father was adamant that all men were after one thing and one thing only. Katherine sighed. At least he had no idea of some of the things she had endured from men, and she wanted to keep it that way.

'Come on, don't be such a party pooper.' Ian Taylor glanced sideways at Katherine and wrapped his strong arms around Wendy's pliant body as she straddled his knees, nuzzling his neck. She was drunk and didn't bother to acknowledge Katherine, who squirmed at the undisguisedly erotic play that made her wonder how anyone could ever find a husband if all men wanted was sex.

'I'm not.'

'This is Wendy,' Janice piped up a bit too late, 'Wendy, this is Katherine.' Janice was at it too, drunk and snuggling into Billy Snowden on the couch. The introduction was as peremptory as Billy Snowden's hand was proprietorial. It climbed along her friend's thigh till his fingers disappeared up her skirt.

'Wendy, nice to meet you.' Katherine's greeting fell on deaf ears. The surface of the lime-coloured Laminex table she sat at was tacky with spilt beer. Sober and out of place, she lit a cigarette, inhaled deeply and blew smoke rings into the fetid air.

'How was dinner?' Janice was torn between Billy's amorous persistence and the demands of friendship.

'Yeah, good. Not too busy.' Katherine stood up to leave. 'Can't stay though,' she lied, 'I've got early breakfasts in the morning.'

'I'll come over tomorrow then.' Janice's voice was thick, now, with a mixture of guilt and desire.

Katherine heard 'bye' and 'see you around' from Ian and Billy, followed by a collective sigh of relief accompanied by smirks she caught a glimpse of in a backward glance.

Not usually afraid of the dark, Katherine felt strangely vulnerable walking home, as though night itself was the harbinger of evil. She thanked the stars for being bright, but the front door was locked when she reached The First & Last. All the lights were off, which meant that Dudley, Lillian and Jimmy had gone to bed early. She lit a match to see her watch. It was midnight. Overcome by an urge to talk to Jimmy, she headed towards his room. She tapped on his door, not wanting to disturb her parents, whose rooms were close. She waited, ear against the door in the dark corridor for what seemed like an eternity. Not a sound. No reply. With a sigh, Katherine headed to her room, her sanctuary. She crossed the gravel yard, humming a comforting Paul Robeson lullaby, 'Lula, Lula, Bye Bye' that Dudley used to sing to her when she was tiny and scared.

Not bothering to turn the light on, Katherine went to lie down to watch the stars through her wire screen door. In summer, it let the slightest waft of air caress and cool her skin.

'Christ, Jimmy, you gave me a fright. What are you doing here? On my bed? I stood outside your room for at least ten minutes, wondering why you didn't answer my knock.'

'I've been waiting for you,' he said, waving her down onto him. 'Look. Look what I've got for you,' he waggled his erect penis at her. 'I've been looking after it for you.'

'Is sex the only thing you men can think of?' Yes, she had gone to Jimmy's room, but she would not have dreamt of making herself at home on his bed in his absence. Had she been wrong about him? Was he the same as all the others? Was the difference between the sexes simply that men assumed they would get away with things? Those boys at the shack would lie around hardening their dicks, too; if they had the slightest inkling that they could get away with it. Katherine had no doubt they'd got them out the minute she'd walked out the door.

'How would you feel if I lay in wait for you with my fanny open for the whole world to peer into?' Katherine was crude in her anger. Her room was a private place, somewhere she could be herself and not have to please anyone. And here was Jimmy, acting as though he owned it. Owned her. Katherine questioned whether she should trust Jimmy as much as she did. After all, he was a man.

'Come on, Katherine. Don't be like that,' Jimmy pleaded, opening his arms, still unselfconscious about the tumescence lying in wait across his trouser zip. Katherine hesitated. Jimmy started fondling himself again, grinning. 'Please, pretty please.' He moved to make space for her to lie down beside him. 'Come on,' he implored with increasing confidence until Katherine told him to pull his head in and his trousers up and go to bed in his room.

8

When Gregory Sharmer walked into The First & Last Hotel, he didn't notice the gilt sign over the main entrance proclaiming Dudley and Lillian Forster as its licensees. Nor did he see the large white lettering 'Ladies Only' when he entered the Ladies Lounge. With no apparent interest in his surroundings, he thumped for attention on the servery between the lounge and the bar. Katherine pretended not to hear. She had been keeping an eye on the stranger from the moment he came in and intuited, before his American accent confirmed it, that this man in sunglasses and fawn desert boots was a foreigner.

'Move your suitcases away from the entrance,' she called to the man over her shoulder as she served her bar customers. It wouldn't hurt to make him wait. 'Someone will trip if you leave them there.' Not until she heard him drag his cases to a more sensible spot, did she deign to look at him.

'I'd like a room, please. With a bath.' Katherine figured he was about 27, maybe younger, but he had a bearing about him. He wore tailored slacks and a beige cotton shirt with cuffs. Firm, tanned, and hairless forearms caught her eye. He flushed as she looked him up and down, attempting to mask his embarrassment by tossing his head back and running his fingers through his thick, brown curls.

'No rooms with baths here, but we can give you a room with a verandah that opens onto the back lawn.' The size of those suitcases, covered as they were with an intriguing collage of coloured stickers from around the world, told Katherine this man was used to extra space.

'OK. That'll be fine.' Gregory Sharmer recovered composure enough to return Katherine's gaze with speckled blue-green eyes — like a cat's, Katherine thought — mocking.

'How long do you reckon you'll stay?' Katherine searched for the accommodation book under the counter, hoping to hide her reddening cheeks because his eyes now seemed to be undressing her.

'Well, that's not sure right now. I guess I'll take three months to start with and let you know from then, if that's OK with you. I'll be going bush some, but I'll need a room each time I return to town, so it would help if I could keep it on. Can we come to an arrangement?'

'You'll have to ask Dad about that.' What would this man do if Dudley refused to bring accommodation rates down? Of course, he would. Dudley was a soft touch when someone was nice to him. There was a lot to find out about this man, what he did for a living, what brought him to these parts. Katherine was intrigued. All she knew about America came from Dudley, who believed the Americans, not the British, saved Australia from the Japanese in World War II. On principle, Katherine would not let an American accent sway her. She did not intend to be like the Australian women of her mother's generation who, Lillian taught her, let the United States military buy them for the price of chocolate and nylon stockings.

'Room 7,' she said, it's the last on your right as you go down the corridor.' Gregory Sharmer did not move. Katherine pointed over his head to the corridor.

'You go left over there, past the sign that says *guests only beyond this point*.' The man still didn't move. 'The bathrooms are at the end of the corridor, and you'll find the men's toilet opposite the ladies' right before you get to the back door. Meal hours are seven to eight for breakfast, twelve till one for lunch and dinner is six o'clock sharp until seven. Tell us if you are not going to be in for a meal.' Hoping she did not sound too much like her mother whose rules she had just recited, Katherine gave the man the key he had been waiting for.

She forgot to ask his name and address.

Next morning, after Katherine put the first lot of sheets in the washing machine, Paddy poked his head into the laundry. 'Morning,' he said, 'you got a cigarette?'

'Here.' Katherine passed her packet of Craven "A" to Paddy, knowing that the old man would take two and tuck one behind his ear. It had become a ritual.

'An American booked in yesterday, Paddy.'

'Yeah.'

'You knew? 'Katherine was still unused to the speed of the bush telegraph even though it stood to reason in such a tiny town that no stranger could put a toe to the ground from train, plane or car without someone seeing or hearing about them. Flat, open plains offered no place to hide.

'Those old girls told me,' Paddy said, thrusting his chin in the direction of the mulga tree next door. 'They watched that man walk to the store, white socks and all. Those flash boots he wears leave ripples in the sand.' Paddy allowed himself a little giggle.

'Desert boots,' Katherine told him. 'They're called desert boots.'

'He's here to look at my people.' Paddy said. 'Research.' He took a deep puff of his freshly lit cigarette.

'Well, how's he going to do that?' Katherine had heard of research once through a school friend whose Canadian father worked in a laboratory, a word the girl's family pronounced as 'labratory' the same way Australians say 'lavatory.'

'He got it wrong already,' Paddy continued. 'He arksed them old girls straight up if he could go out bush with them. Told 'em he wants to follow 'em round like he wasn't there. They told him quick smart he had better arks me first. That fella doesn't know much yet about our people, that's for sure, up and talking to our old women like that.' The humour had left Paddy's voice.

'I'd like to meet those women one day, if I could?' Katherine's curiosity might have offended Paddy after he'd just complained about the American, but the words came unbidden. She'd been holding them in, waiting in fear of rebuff or, worse still, she worried that her meeting the women might get tongues wagging. People around here are quick to say a man has 'gone native' when he consorts with Aboriginal women. Would it be the same for her?

Paddy took the last deep drag on his cigarette, dropped the butt, stamped it out with his bare, calloused foot, smiled at Katherine and headed on his way.

9

Ever since that horrid day in the Ladies' Lounge when Pearl had just about traded her, Katherine had deliberately shown no interest in William Ringer, a man with more money than education, tact or good sense. Nevertheless, she accepted his invitation to his claypan party because she was curious. It felt safe enough, knowing that Janice and Wendy would both be there. She'd just have to put up with Billy Snowden and Ian Taylor, who had invited them. William would behave anyway. Rumour had it that he was smitten with the new Myall Creek Station governess, Helen Drysdale. She looked after Mary Beaming's sister's children after that unfortunate woman's husband ran away with a young tourist to Queensland. Helen was a city-bred, convent-educated snob as far as Katherine was concerned. Ringer and the governess deserved each other, but Katherine couldn't resist the offer of a ride in his new Toyota Land Cruiser, one of the first in the country. She didn't hint at an invite for Jimmy because he would have made her go with him in the pub Jeep.

They headed off to the claypan just outside town where Ringer and his men had set up camp after yarding his Old Bore Station cattle to be shipped for auction on the next train south. William Ringer inherited the property named after the Great Artesian Basin by his grandfather from his father. Without its bore water and ancient artesian springs, livestock could not survive in the desert.

William pulled up at the claypan in a well-practised, flashy tyre-spin at the precise distance required to cause a threatening cloud of red dust to fly up before floating to the ground without smothering everyone. Playing grand host, he pulled his hat off in a flourish of welcome as she stepped down to earth.

'This is Samuel Kingston — just call him Sam,' he said, introducing Katherine to a young Aboriginal man, adding in a whispered aside, 'Sam's a half-caste. Mixed blood. And this is Reggie Kahn, Sam's half-Afghan half-brother' — he laughed at his cleverness — 'not a real brother as we think of it. They're really all brothers or fathers or uncles to each other. Reggie hails from the Alice or somewhere north of there. Can't always be sure as those fellas move around a lot, go walkabout.'

Sam kept his eyes modestly downturned as he greeted Katherine, but Reggie Kahn held his head high, his black eyes searing right through her unabashed. She flushed and turned to ask if William intended to introduce the other Aboriginal men who sat at a distance from the campfire in the shadows.

'Nope. The black mob's job is to oversee the cattle all the time, taking turns to sleep,' Ringer said. 'No need for you to meet them. Sam can join us, but those old fellas up there,' he pointed as he spoke, 'can't. Sam's got a ticket to say he is to be trusted like a white man, and they haven't, and Reggie's an Afghan, so he doesn't need one, so he can sit here with us too. The blacks call those tickets dog tags. It gives 'em the right to drink booze. It means they are exempt from the Natives Administration Act. In short, they have citizenship rights.' He did not explain how hard the certificates were to get or how restrictive they were in practice. They had to be carried at all times and produced on demand. The government could revoke them on a whim. William chuckled, his interest in Aborigines waning as he ripped open a carton of beer. He passed long brown bottles of West End draught to each of the men. Katherine said she liked Southwark Bitter best because it was sweeter.

The men looked at her as one and laughed, 'It all makes ya drunk quick enough.'

Even though she could not easily discern their faces in the dark, Katherine did recognise Paddy among the Aboriginal men beyond the fire. His sandy coloured Akubra stood out in the night with its tall crown and pointy rim. As everyone settled in, Sam produced his guitar. He and Reggie began to croon mournful country songs that Katherine had never heard. William shared his bottle with her, and, not wanting to be called a wowser as she usually was, she relented and took a swig or two.

The hard ground grew softer to Katherine the longer she lay there, resting back on her elbows, listening to the guitar and the lonely wail of country love songs. Extending her newly shaved legs, crossed naked at the ankle, Katherine tilted her head back to look up at the sky. The moon shone softly on her long, blonde hair. She had never seen so many stars, trillions of silver speckles, sparkling like diamonds in the moonless black sky. She imagined that if she traced between them, she would be able to read their stories.

'You gonna lie right down?' William Ringer stood over Katherine. He had spread his swag on the ground right next to where she lay. 'You must be uncomfortable there, with stones biting your bum. Put it here.' He patted his swag.

Katherine looked over at Janice and Wendy. They'd started petting on swags with Billy and Ian earlier and were now under the flaps, knotted together in front of everyone. No shame. Some things should be kept private.

'No, I'm fine,' Katherine replied, sitting upright in a vain attempt to clear her head and appear respectable. Her body tingled and flushed as she recalled how Reggie had looked at her, then nausea swept through her from drinking too much. Still, her mind was clear enough to not want Aboriginal men to see her lying beneath canvas with William Ringer, especially not Paddy. She glanced towards those who were still awake, looking towards the campfire. Sam and Reggie were still wide awake, too, swigging beer from the same bottle, passing it back and forth so that their two voices became one in their songs, punctuated by maudlin howls.

Katherine stumbled and almost fell into the embers as she rose, needing to vomit. Ringer caught her around the waist as she lurched blindly, manoeuvring her to the periphery of the camp. When she stopped heaving, he led her back and lowered her into his swag without asking a second time.

Her head swam 'till she passed out with a receding shudder of nausea.

Katherine woke to birdsong when the first sliver of silver light peeped over the horizon. She watched the sky diffuse to a pre-dawn grey before she noticed her undies on the pillow, scrunched beside her face as though someone had placed them there deliberately for her to find when she woke. Her hand reached out from under the swag and snatched them beneath the blanket. Still lying flat on her back, she bent sideways to slip them over the left foot then the right without moving too much. She lifted her bottom slightly to pull them up, and as she did, her hand touched a damp spot on the sheet below.

It felt as though she might have wet herself, but, no, the dampness was tacky. The night had not been innocent. She lay still, trying to work out how best to get out of the swag without disturbing the man beside her. She did not want to see William Ringer's face and was glad he'd covered it with his Akubra. Let him suffocate on the greasy stink of his sweat. His stentorian snore reassured her that he would not wake in a hurry. As she wriggled out of his swag, using her elbows, a whiff of his stinking boots parked at his head made her hold her breath until she was standing up.

The morning was bright and bitterly cold. Janice was already awake, sitting pensive and alone by the campfire embers on which there was a new log, just starting to take.

'I didn't think you liked William.' Janice spoke softly, not wanting to wake anybody.

'I don't know how I ended up in his swag. How did you go with Billy? You really do like him, don't you?'

'Yes,' Janice turned away, tears welling up. The two girls sat in silence, each lost in their own worlds for a few minutes.

'Billy's got a child with an Aboriginal woman from over Coober Pedy way,' Janice blurted out, 'He told me out of guilt last night after we made love.' Janice choked back a sob. 'He told me he was falling for me.'

'Let's get out of here.' Katherine said, jumping up. She wanted to divert her friend, but she also wanted to escape before Reggie appeared. She remembered the intense desire he awoke in her and knew he had seen that with his darkling eyes. Even the recollection aroused her. 'Let's go for a ride.'

'Can you ride?' Janice asked. 'I've only done it once before.'

'Doesn't matter. You game?'

'If we can get one of the boys to saddle up for us.' Janice looked around. 'They're all still sleeping.'

'Sam's not.' Katherine said, smiling at Sam, who was now waiting for the billy to boil. 'Please, Sam,' Katherine said, 'we'd love to go for an early-morning ride. Can you saddle up a couple of horses for us? No good asking the others, look at them sleep, lined up like corpses on a battlefield.' She made herself sound more cheerful than she felt with a hangover and soiled crotch. She hoped fervently that nobody, not Reggie, not Sam and certainly not Paddy, had witnessed what William Ringer had done to her in the night.

Not one to waste words, Sam smiled his assent, taking the billy off the fire after making sure the lid was tight to prevent flies from falling in. 'It's hot enough for anyone who wakes up,' he said as he placed the billy in dusty embers before signalling Reggie to come and help. Reggie ignored Katherine, and the two boys strode ahead of the girls, leading them towards the cattle yards where stockmen had tethered the camp horses to scraggly trees.

'Those are gidgee trees or stinky wattle,' Sam told the girls with a giggle when they wrinkled their noses. 'They smell real bad when there's rain.' The lowing of cattle grew louder. It was as though someone had changed stations on the wireless, the sound of livestock tuning out the grunts and snores of the sleeping stockmen and Wendy's giggling and groaning as she again tussled under canvas with Ian. By the time Katherine was astride her horse, she had decided it would be best if she never saw Reggie again.

Whatever Katherine and Janice lacked in riding experience, they made up for in naive trust in their ability to find their way back to the camp. They walked the horses in silence for a time, but as soon as Katherine spurred hers into a canter, Janice followed suit. Hearts pounding, they rode across the plains high in the saddle, hair flowing, laughing with youthful exuberance. They had no plan, no real idea of how to stop, but they gave the horses free rein. Katherine recalled Jimmy's game. What could she call what had happened last night, Cuddles at the Claypan? That would work unless she missed her period. Then nothing would expunge the consequences. She would be trapped.

'We'd better head back,' Janice said, breaking through Katherine's growing fear. 'Better not get lost, or all hell will break loose.' As a schoolteacher, Janice was trained to put a stop to willful behaviour, even in herself.

The girls turned their horses around and were soon relieved to see the clump of trees that marked the campsite on otherwise open plains. They spurred their horses to a gallop till they reached the camp where the click of hooves on gibber gave way to a quiet whoosh on the sand. They dismounted to a camp now empty except for William Ringer, Billy and Ian. They had lined up in wait for them at the yards — one two three — like the troopers in Waltzing Matilda, their scowls as uniform as the legendary soldiers' colonial red coats.

'Where the hell do you think you've been?' Ringer's face was ashen. 'We've been worried about you,' he said in a controlled voice burning with six hot feet of rage. He looked only at Katherine. 'Haven't we?' Ringer turned to his men, commanding their assent.

Billy and Ian nodded, but they kept their heads down, hiding their faces beneath the brims of their hats so the girls could not see cowardice in their eyes. That was the way of William Ringer's men. Ringer was the boss.

'We just went for a ride.' The words sprang from Katherine's mouth despite knowing she did not have to justify herself to this man who had used her the night before to satisfy his lust while she slept.

'Yeah! And who went with you?' William's mouth curled into a sneer. 'Blackfellas.' Katherine had seen him switch mood in an instant before but never with such hatred in his voice as he declaimed.

'No. Sam and Reggie just saddled horses for us, didn't they, Janice?' Katherine looked around for Reggie and Sam, hoping her friend's reassurance might help dissipate Ringer's anger.

'That's right.' Janice agreed, looking vainly for support from Billy, who remained passive and silent, eyes glued to Ringer.

'Sam, and Reggie? Sam's fucking Afghan mate?' Ringer's body had become as rigid as his stare. 'That sly black bastard.'

Ringers' mention of Reggie Khan caused Katherine to catch her breath. Had William seen what passed between them? Desire was hard to conceal from watchful eyes around a campfire. If so, perhaps that contributed to his rage. Was Ringer trying to give her a lesson by treating her like a slut? She stood her ground.

'You can't go accusing us of anything.' She came back at him in a loud, firm voice.' I am sorry that we took your horses without asking, but we could hardly get permission when you were snoring your head off. How was I to know you'd carry on like this?'

William Ringer threw Katherine a sharp look, turned on his high-heeled boots and strode away without another word. He gave cursory instructions to a stockman Katherine had never met to chauffeur the three girls back to town in his Toyota.

The pub was quiet when Katherine got home. There was a morning chill that the sun, peeping over the horizon, had not yet dispelled. As soon as she was safely inside her room, Katherine tore her clothes off with shaky hands. They were caked with red dust and reeked of vomit, fatty barbecued beef, stale beer and William Ringer. For a frozen moment, she stood naked in front of the mirror before popping her dressing gown on. With matches in the pocket and a bath towel over her shoulders, she headed once again to the incinerator. Only when the evidence of her shame was in cinders did she drive to the public bore-water showers on the flat halfway down the airport road to meet Janice and Wendy as they'd arranged.

'Where have you been?' Dudley materialised at the back door as she passed it, on his way to the toilet half asleep, the fly of his striped flannelette pyjamas agape and his genitals visible behind dangling white ties.

'I've been horse riding with Janice,' Katherine said.

'All night?'

'Of course not. Wendy, Janice and I went to a party at the claypan with William Ringer and the boys early on.'

'Where did you sleep?'

'In swags. They had extra swags.' Katherine was amazed at the ease with which she came up with half-truths for Dudley. It was not as though she had done anything wrong, yet she could see her father did not believe her.

'What were you doing at the incinerator?'

'I just burned some rubbish. We're off now to have a shower down the road.' Katherine wanted to divert her father's attention.

'Who's we?' Dudley asked, his voice now predatory with anger.

'Janice, Wendy and me. Like always.' Katherine wanted to make her father feel guilty. She refused welling tears. 'Who did you think was going?'

'Make sure you're back on time for work. The house needs cleaning, you know.'

Dudley turned his back on his daughter.

Katherine was overcome by a yearning to speak to her mother, but Lillian would not wake for hours yet.

Katherine was the first to reach the shower block on the flat halfway down the airport road. She revelled in the heavy splish-splash of steaming hot bore water with its malodorous flow of mineral salts as it cleansed every part of her body. The high-pressure syphon relaxed her tired muscles, and her hangover dissipated in the steam, drowning out the sound of her friends' arrival and their chatter.

Katherine and Janice had often gone to the public showers for fun. They made a pact to meet outside of town after a party to gossip out of earshot. Including Wendy made no difference. The block had no doors, inside or out, and, while the girls could see for miles across the plains, nobody could approach by foot or by car without being seen. There were four roses mounted side by side on concrete walls over concrete floors, stained to the salts' dark red ochre colour. For the girls, after-party bathing ranked higher than the parties themselves as they stood naked, side-by-side, wrapped in friendship and hot water against the early morning chill.

By the time Katherine got back to the hotel, it was past 7.30 am. She had a quick cup of tea before heading into the house to knock on the American's door; he was the only house guest. Even though Gregory Sharmer was a permanent guest, Katherine still made his bed and cleaned his room daily when he was in town. Gregory Sharmer did not take breakfast, neither in the dining room, as he was entitled to, nor in the kitchen where he had started to take his other meals with the Forsters when it was quiet. In the mornings, the American made his special coffee with sugar, no milk, boiling water in the kettle Dudley lent him. She was a bit early, but he was usually up by this time. He took a while to answer, so she knocked again.

'Come in.'

'Am I too early to make your bed?'

'Not at all. Come on in.'

Sharmer unlocked the door. After quickly cornering the sheets like they do in hospitals, Katherine threw the chenille spread over the bed and stood up. The American's gaze had stroked her from the moment she came in the door.

'Do you need a clean towel?' Katherine knew Sharmer would say no because towels in this heat dried quickly and, in her experience, men equated dry with clean. In any case, Gregory Sharmer was an easy customer in this way, content for his linen, including the towel, to be changed only once a week. And his feet didn't stink like William Ringer's, and other stockmen's feet did. Worse than rotten eggs, the stench permeated bed linen until it was almost impossible to wash out. Sometimes, Katherine had to boil vile, stinking sheets in the copper for hours before the odour faded. When a man with stinking feet stayed a week or more, the stink penetrated the mattress ticking, which occasionally meant a replacement if a good airing didn't help.

'No. Just sit by me for a minute.' Sharmer patted the freshly made bed. 'I'd like to get to know you a little better.'

'I'm not supposed to fraternise with the customers in their rooms.' Katherine made the rule up on the spot.

'Please.' Sharmer smiled.

Prim with feigned obedience, Katherine sat briefly at the edge of his bed, letting her eyes wander over to the stack of books and papers sprawled on the other single bed; evidence of scholarly life. She stood up. 'Dad would hit the roof if he saw me sitting here like this.'

'Sorry.' There was something practised in the way he had simply let her sit. He had not tried to touch her. Then he said, 'I'll wait.' Katherine stood up and almost tripped in her haste to get out of the room. She could cope with rough groping, but, not this, this waiting.

'OK, I'll meet you in the kitchen one day soon. After lunch.' Katherine was curious about Sharmer but in no hurry to encourage him. She could not help wondering — echoing what she believed would be her father's view of the matter — what a man like Sharmer would want with a girl like her.

Nobody noticed that Gregory Sharmer slid through the darkened dining room into the kitchen every day for a week, looking for Katherine. He didn't know the laundry was her hiding place.

It had been several days since Paddy had last dropped in on Katherine in the laundry, and, as always, he took her by surprise.

'Hello, Missy.'

She offered Paddy a cigarette, but he declined. 'Big problem, that camp day', he said, looking Katherine straight in the eyes, as he had never done before. His tone was different too. She cringed to think that he might have lost respect for her. It would be no surprise if he'd seen her under the canvas with William Ringer. Everyone else would think she was a slut by now.

'Sam. He's in hospital. Gone to Alice Springs all bashed up. Reggie too.'

'Is Reggie bashed too?' Katherine could have bitten her tongue for questioning her old friend. His eyes were so full of pain.

'Nah. Just Sam in hospital, Reggie's bruised but had to be with him. They always together, them two.'

'William Ringer and his boys, they took to Sammy at that claypan. Beat him up real bad. Broke coupla ribs, smashed 'is nose and cheekbone. Missed 'is eyes, but they must've used a heavy stick too, not just fists. His shin's busted, and he said they lay him out on the ground spread-eagled like and whipped his feet. Flying Doctor took 'im to the Alice, and soon as that plane left the ground, Reggie jumped in 'is car and headed north too. Those young fellas are gone now. Not coming back.'

Paddy had never before said so much to Katherine at one time. She stood rigid, hoping he would not sense the guilt in her heart. Did he know that it was she who had asked Sam and Reggie to saddle the horses? Did either of the boys say anything to him? Could Paddy have noticed the sexual energy between her and Reggie? Katherine thrilled again to the possibility of the young Afghan boy. Her emotions were so powerful they'd begun to draw her towards something she could not yet name.

Had she known a bit about bushmen, Katherine might have been alert to William Ringer's intentions from the dismissive way he spoke about the dog tags. How could she not have guessed from the cruel look in his eyes after the horse ride that it would not be enough for him just to shout at her?

'I am so sorry,' she said, 'how could that have happened? Why?' Tears came, unbidden, self-pitying.

Paddy patted Katherine on the shoulder, saying softly, 'That's finished now.'

10

'What do anthropologists actually do? How on earth do you study people?' Dudley chuckled at his own rhetorical question. 'Come to think of it, people spill their guts to me when they're drunk, but I guess that's different.'

'That's a tough one, Dudley. How long have you got?' Sharmer smiled, intending to disarm, but Katherine did not miss the patronising glint in his American eyes. She looked down at her plate and cut into her roast beef, allowing a flush of shame to subside.

Jimmy and Lillian perked up at Dudley's questioning. They were also curious to hear what the American had to say. Lillian was trying to get the measure of this man whose eyes had danced all over her and Katherine since he arrived. Could she accept him as a good catch for her daughter? As though reading her mother's mind, Katherine's anger rose. Would Lillian never let her take charge of her own fate?

'We don't need all the details,' Dudley spoke up. 'The layman's overview is good enough. You know, I've always said, if you educate a fool, you get a bigger fool. Every academic I've known argued up and down and around a topic without ever getting to the point.'

'Anthropology is really just the study of human diversity. We look at material culture — you know, the stuff of museums and galleries — as well as study the economic, political, religious and aesthetic aspects of the lives of groups of people. The sort of anthropology I do has a somewhat philosophical bent, but we live among our people, so it is grounded in fieldwork. That's why I'm here. To record the Aborigines' daily lives, see how they interact with each other and document their kinship system, beliefs and practices. We call that ethnography. The higher aim is to contribute to the sum of human knowledge about natives before their primitive ways of life die out.'

Katherine almost laughed at the man's pomposity. She wasn't sure whether Sharmer ignored Dudley's bait or didn't understand it. 'Do you just follow people around with a notepad all day or what?'

'Nope. I use a tape recorder as well. And a camera of course.' Gregory failed to hear the scorn in Katherine's voice. He seemed oblivious to others' sensibilities.

Still, as Sharmer continued talking, Katherine felt her own perspective shift. If only for a moment, she could see her parents through his eyes before returning to scepticism. She told him his work sounded like prying and asked why he didn't look at how Aborigines and whites interact rather than treat Aborigines like a species apart. He didn't reply.

'What do you say to entice them to put up with you?' Katherine would hate it if someone presumed to sneak around, looking at her at every moment of the day. For all she knew, he might be doing that already. She remembered how scared she was as a child at school in religious instruction. The minister insisted that God was omnipresent. He could see her, even in the darkest recesses of her home, room, or mind. She had been terrified to think that nothing she did, thought, or felt was safe from scrutiny. As for a foreigner like Sharmer writing things about Australian Aboriginal people to publish for the world to see, to know their way of life, that had to be mortifying for them. Did anthropologists rely on the fact that Aborigines in the desert had a slim chance to read about themselves and complain if the man got things wrong? Would Sharmer use real names? No matter how Sharmer wrote his up findings, Katherine decided, it must take the hide of a rhinoceros to be an anthropologist.

'That's fascinating.' Lillian created a diversion to give Katherine time to cool her heels. 'It's not something everyone would want to do, travelling to remote places like this to head into the desert alone for days or weeks at a time without the comforts.'

'Going bush is the best thing of all,' Gregory was relieved, thinking he had Lillian on-side. 'Sleeping under the stars is God's blessing, although I have to admit goanna meat smoked on coals is not easy to stomach.' He turned to include Dudley in the exchange with a chuckle. 'The Aboriginal people love it, but, to me, it's an acquired taste. In the end, it'll all be worth it because I'll get a PhD from this stint of fieldwork. I'll publish, of course. A decent publication about the Aborigines of Central Australia will put me on the road to a professorship, as I plan.'

'Thanks for letting us grill you, young fella,' Dudley ended the conversation. 'Pity we're not in the city, I could have introduced you to a different Australian tradition. Australian Rules Football.' Dudley grinned at the preposterous idea that his own culture could be an anthropological subject. After all, nobody could call Australians natives.

'I'd sure like that. Another time?' Gregory was serious. Again, he missed the Australian humour, whether mocking or self-deprecating.

'Right. Jimmy, it's your turn to clear the table. Katherine, you wash the dishes. Nice talking to you, Gregory.' Lillian instructed everyone what to do, leaving Sharmer no option but to retire. Lillian needed a drink, but she would not start until the American left the kitchen.

'I'm off to my yippees.' Dudley loved his paperback westerns; they put him to sleep. He turned and called out over his shoulder, 'Make sure you turn all the lights off when you've finished, kids.' He winked conspiratorially at Gregory and guided him to the door.

Lillian glared at her husband's retreating back. Silly bugger left his light on all night. How dare he call her 'mum' one minute and 'kid' the next? She had long given up hope that Dudley would see her as a grown woman, a separate person, distinct from himself and his bloody moods.

11

'You were very quiet at dinner with Gregory the other night,' Katherine wanted to stir Jimmy up.

'Well, there was nothing much I could say with that Yank showing off.'

'You're jealous.'

'No, I'm not.'

'Yes, you are.'

'Who's jealous of whom?' Lillian interrupted the young ones in the posh telephone voice that took over when she was drunk. She slumped at the kitchen table, sighing into a half-empty butcher glass.

'Nobody and nobody.' Katherine was not fooled by the small beer glass. She could smell the sticky-sweet aroma of top-shelf liqueurs on her mother's breath, far more pungent than the bitterness of hops.

'It's nothing, nothing at all.' Jimmy left the room.

'Coward.' Katherine called after him, cross to be left alone with her mother, who was not yet drunk enough to pass out but sufficiently pickled to pick a fight. Lillian was renowned for being hurtful in this state. Jimmy was piss weak. Katherine hated how her mother became emotionally absent and overbearing when she was drunk, insisting that she work harder. In her deepest self-pity, Katherine's imagination cast Lillian as Cinderella's wicked stepmother. Lillian's drunken trump card for keeping Katherine in line was to say at every opportunity that Katherine was just like her father, moralistic, self-righteous, and hard as the hobs of hell.

'Oh. I get it. You're seeing Jimmy.' Lillian exclaimed with alcoholic insight.

'So what?' What are you going to do about it?'

'I'm going to tell your father in the morning, that's what. He won't like it at all. Not one bit my girl.' Lillian was not intentionally mean. One uneducated man like Dudley in the family was enough for her, and, as the oldest son in a family of orphans, Jimmy had no prospects. How could he have, when he was responsible for ne'er-do-well siblings who would cause nothing but trouble in his life?

'Why all the secrecy?' Lillian's mouth became ugly with disgust. 'You're having sex?'

'Please don't tell Dad.' Dudley was capable of making Jimmy's life unbearable if he knew. Although he treated the boy like a son, he could sack him.

Life in The First & Last settled down for a week or so, at least on the surface. Kitchen and bar routines were easy to maintain in a quiet pub. The laundry was up to date, the bar and kitchen sparkled in readiness for the next onslaught of guests. The anticipatory quiet unnerved Katherine, who grew more vigilant each day, expecting an outburst from Dudley.

Lillian was a little chilly towards her, but she clearly hadn't reported the situation with Jimmy to Dudley. Nor, it seemed, had Jimmy told her parents about the night at the claypan. Yet, with so much at stake, Katherine felt like an outsider in her own home. She couldn't relax and missed the soft tread of Gregory Sharmer's desert boots on the linoleum.

The American had acquired an Akubra, which he liked to place on the servery in the Ladies Lounge, copying what the local bushmen did in the bar. He didn't get it that a ladies' lounge was a place for women and that a man's hat on the servery was a thing out of place. Like him. Nor had he personalised the Akubra's shape, although it sported a few fresh smears of red dirt and the band had the beginnings of a greasy sweat ring.

When he showed up, Gregory's smile told Katherine that he was pleased to see her, too.

'How 'bout a schooner,' he asked with a slightly awkward, settled-into-the-outback swagger. Katherine grinned. At least he was no longer drinking butchers like a woman.

'How did it go?' Katherine asked, dying to learn more about this fieldwork thing he called participant observation.

'Good, good. I'll tell you more about it later after I've had a shower and a nap.' Gregory swigged his beer in a single gulp and, with a wink, headed to his room carrying his red-dust-coated swag on his shoulder with pride.

'Is that your new boyfriend?' Jimmy saw the spark of attraction pass between Gregory and Katherine as he came into the bar.

'What do you mean?' Katherine was defensive.

'I'm beginning to think you made all that up, that stuff about the claypan,' Jimmy said. 'I reckon you asked for it.'

'Asked for what?' Dudley heard the last remark as he, too, came into the bar.

Katherine froze, looking on in horror as Jimmy turned to her father.

'Your daughter slept with William Ringer at the claypan.' Jimmy's words rushed from his mouth loud and hard with hurt and hate.

Dudley turned to his daughter in disbelief.

Lillian joined them from the kitchen, drawn to the bar by Jimmy's outburst. 'Have you been sleeping with William Ringer as well?'

'As well as who?' Dudley's mouth was agape.

'Well, since you ask, our daughter has been sleeping with your precious Jimmy here, in case you'd like to know.' Lillian turned to Katherine. 'But, what's this about William Ringer?'

Katherine burst into tears, wanting to confide in her mother, to tell her the truth that she'd been too scared to disclose at the time. 'Yes', Katherine answered her mother's implicit question. 'Yes, I had a few drinks, but so what. He did it while I was asleep. Mum. Dad. He did it while I was asleep.'

Dudley and Lillian united in horror, too overwhelmed to hear Katherine's plea. People did silly things when they were drunk that they'd try to wriggle out of later. Drunks and gamblers had taught them that much over the years. And they lie. Why would their daughter be any different? It made no sense that Katherine was drunk enough to sleep through an ordeal like that, oblivious to it, yet know she was raped.

'How on earth do you think you'll ever find a husband if you carry on like that?' A new fear grew in Dudley that his beautiful daughter might yet follow in her mother's tracks with the grog.

'You don't love me. You've never loved me. You always think of your precious customers first. William Ringer raped me. The man is a drunk and a bully, and yet, here you are standing up for him against your own daughter.' Katherine trembled in a confusion of hurt and disbelief.

'Calm your bloody daughter down!' Dudley yelled at Lillian, who, at that moment, had nothing whatsoever to give her daughter by way of comfort. Dudley turned to Jimmy, who stood aside in silence to watch once he threw the bomb. He'd learned early on that life with the Forsters was like tiptoeing on eggshells.

'And, don't think you're off the bloody hook either, sonny Jim.' Dudley stared at the young man.

'I love Katherine.' Jimmy found a smidgen of gumption. 'I wanted to marry her, but she's been funny ever since that night at the claypan.'

'Well, if you don't believe her, what do you expect?' For a second, Dudley appeared to be siding with his daughter, but Katherine understood her father's way of drawing people out until it was too late for them to act. He then shooed Jimmy away as though he were an insect. 'Just get out of my sight. I'll deal with you later.'

Katherine emerged from her room at three o'clock that afternoon, tears spent, anguish echoing in puffy eyes. She bumped into Gregory in the corridor.

'What happened to you?' Gregory asked.

'Nothing. It's all right.' Tears threatened to return at the unaccustomed gentleness in Gregory's voice.

'Looks like something to me, but you don't have to talk about it if you don't want to.'

'Ta.'

'Do you want to go for a little drive to the dam? We could take our bathing suits.'

The promise of cold water lapping over her appealed to Katherine. 'I'd like that.'

'Meet me outside; I'll bring the Jeep around. And bring an extra towel for me if you can.'

Katherine was vulnerable, and Gregory snatched the moment. He stood ready to open the passenger door as she approached his dark green Jeep. Katherine hung her head, slightly unnerved at the sight of the American's swag on the roof rack. In the pub, he stowed it under his bed rather than risk it being stolen, which meant he'd loaded it for her. Gregory liked to show off that his American swag was better quality than the married man's swags used by locals. She sat forward in the passenger seat as he started the motor, but when he turned in the direction of the dam, Katherine stopped him. 'Go that way,' she said, pointing south. 'Bridge Hole is in that direction.' She pointed. 'It's a bit further, but there are lots of trees, and it's better. I love it. You've got to wade through silky mud that slimes between your toes until the water's deep enough to float. The water is murky, that's for sure, and there's a risk that you might put your foot on a sharp tree stump or an animal carcass, so you can't dive, but it's like a secluded oasis.' Gregory had already turned the car around and was heading south. Katherine started to enjoy herself being away from the pub, her parents and Jimmy for a while. Out here, surrounded by the vast expanse of red earth and purple gibber stretching flat out to the horizon, she could breathe. It was a desolate landscape scarred only by occasional fence lines and fading vehicle tracks like those she'd seen from the plane. Here and there were carpet mounds of saltbush on which cattle and native animals grazed. A twisted knot of acacias lined dry creek beds with an occasional free-standing gidgee tree on the plain. Whether red dust or purple stones, the desert made Katherine feel as though she was the only person alive, the only one who counted. She had come to believe that it had the power to purify and cleanse, and she needed that. It opened her heart.

Gregory parked under a large eucalypt with clusters of drooping, grey-green leaves. She felt safe in its shade. Galahs screeched as they fluttered up from its branches in a noisy cloud of pink and grey when the Jeep drew to a standstill. Katherine and Gregory sat in the silence that followed the birds' departure, the air between them charged by arousal.

'Do you want a swim first or a drink?' Gregory had brought lemonade. 'Best drink this before it gets hot.' He passed a bottle of lemonade to Katherine. The bubbles tickled her nose.

'Thanks.' Katherine could no longer ignore Gregory's intent. He said, 'first'. It wasn't hard to guess what came next. She held her breath. Her heart pounded like a paralysed native animal in the bright beam of headlights for interminable minutes.

'I want to make love to you.'

After the shock, Katherine thrilled to Gregory's desire. Nobody had ever asked her before, not like that. It was as though he'd given her permission to say no. Other men in Katherine's life had just taken her, even Jimmy, although he was gentle, and she wanted him too. When she danced, if her partner had an erection, he'd take it for granted that she wanted sex. No discussion. Sometimes, like her friends, she would succumb to someone's importuning just to get rid of them. But this. Being asked. Being asked to decide and agree to have sex sent thrills of fear through her body. She trembled. Did he want her naked? No matter how many self-deprecating thoughts crossed her mind, Katherine was ready.

'Did you hear me, Katherine?'

The way Gregory rolled her name off his American tongue heightened Katherine's arousal.

'Yes, I heard you.' Her voice was deep but faint.

'Shall I roll out the swag?'

'Yes.'

There was nothing more to say. Pensive now, Katherine watched as the American retrieved his swag from the roof rack and threw it on the ground. He undid the wide leather straps, graceful, for a man. 'Down you get,' he commanded as he helped Katherine down from the car, too late for that swim.

Gregory stood facing Katherine, his gaze penetrating. Katherine lowered her eyes, but he took her face in his hands and kissed her softly, pressing his body to hers. Gregory was hard but not in a hurry. Still, he made her wait. Katherine swooned.

'I want to watch you undress.' Katherine had never stood naked before a man and clutched her shirt to her breast. When he was naked, Gregory tore the shirt from Katherine's hand, standing proud before her. Mesmerised, she let him gently lower her onto his swag. His slow rhythmic lovemaking transported her. He waited so they'd climax together. Gregory's ability to hold back scared her. She'd never reached orgasm with a man before.

They laughed, rising in unison to tiptoe down the bank to skinny dip in muddy water. The surface was warm, but it was freezing below, tickling their satiated bodies. Afterwards, they lay side by side, two white bodies in the dappled shade of the eucalypt, oblivious to everything except each other until swarms of flies brought them back to reality.

12

Pearl burst into the bar moments after Dudley opened the doors. Her eyes and hair were wilder than Katherine had ever seen.

'Shoosh, everyone. Have you heard the news?' Pearl waved her arms to gather people around her.

'Come on, woman, spit it out.' An impatient jeer started.

'Well.' Pearl paused. 'President John F Kennedy was assassinated at 3:30 this morning.' The bar talk stopped. 'Barney heard it on his new shortwave radio.'

Barney fancied himself a radio aficionado, but the news was Pearl's domain. A veritable repeater station, the woman regularly updated Wonnalinga on significant social, cultural, and sporting events from around Australia. And snippets of town gossip as though she were a Walkley's Award-winning journalist. Admittedly, today's announcement was momentous, and Pearl was keen to cement herself and Barney as vital links between this town and the world at large.

Katherine burst into tears.

'You're a duffer,' There was surprise in Dudley's voice.

'Don't think I'm stupid. I know who that is. I know Robert Menzies is the Australian Prime Minister, too. Men in the bar talk politics all the time, arguing about this and that, left and right.' Menzies repelled Katherine, in whose mind he was pompous old bugger whose bushy brows hid sinister eyes. But President Kennedy was charismatic. Katherine couldn't be sure whether she felt that because he was good-looking or because she had grown up with Dudley declaiming that we wouldn't be here today if the Americans had not become our allies in the war. Her father's words instilled in Katherine a nebulous view that America stood for something honest, enduring, powerful and protective. And now, the man whose office protected Australia during the war was dead. Assassinated. With her emotional world already in turmoil, Katherine felt unsafe. She did not know about Martin Luther King's inspirational speech three months earlier, calling for equality for African Americans, a call for change that would echo down the generations. Yet, she intuited that Kennedy's death marked a turning point and, with that thought, left political wrangling to the men.

Katherine was late to Pearl and Barney's party that night because Dudley insisted that she count the till before she left. The first person she bumped into was Gregory Sharmer. Strictly speaking, the door opened as he was passing, knocking a beer from his hand. His trousers were wet. Katherine offered a flustered apology. Being with Sharmer at the waterhole hadn't changed

Katherine's uncertainty about the man. She had no clue how to behave with an educated American. Her nerves jangled. Would he make another move tonight?

Pearl's compulsion to introduce Katherine to everyone in sight offered a distraction. 'Have you met Bruno yet, Katherine? This is Bruno Moretti, our new stationmaster.'

'Bruno, nice to meet you.' Katherine extended her hand to the short, stocky man in front of her. Bruno was not unattractive with his tight black curls and eyes so dark they shone black. His skin was a bit swarthy for her taste, but he had a certain animal charm. However, any sense of attraction vanished the moment he took her hand in his. It was repulsively limp, damp and fat, with fingers sprouting black hairs. Katherine had never met an Italian, so she decided to give him the benefit of the doubt. For now. Dudley would have said that the limp handshake could be an Italian custom, not a sign of weakness. Yet her stomach squirmed at his touch. Bruno flashed Katherine a quick grin, withdrew his hand and turned to survey the room.

The party was to welcome Bruno. People were pleased to have a stationmaster. Three months before the Forsters arrived, the previous incumbent had beaten his wife around the head and face. She died two days after the Flying Doctor Service airlifted her to the Royal Adelaide Hospital. The man also shot both of his dogs and his wife's chickens. Police did not lay charges until his wife died. The court exonerated the stationmaster. The judge decreed that the stationmaster's wife's death was an adverse effect of the isolation that drove men crazy in the bush. He placed the stationmaster on a good behaviour bond. Within a month, the only thing people remembered about the unfortunate woman was her fresh hen's eggs. They missed those too.

Leaving Bruno and Sharmer to their own devices, Katherine went in search of her mother. Lillian was in the kitchen, already half full, which made Katherine resent her father. Why did she have to be the one to look after her mother when she was legless? Katherine, not Dudley, undressed her mum — his wife — to put her to bed. For a moment, she yearned to get away, which made her want a husband even more.

Back in the lounge, Katherine sat next to Gregory on Pearl's low-slung, mustard-velvet couch, pressing herself into the opposite corner to him. She wanted to have fun. Taking the beer he offered, Katherine tried to stop worrying about Lillian, just for a while.

'What do you reckon?' Katherine turned to Gregory. 'Only Pearl would choose mock regency-stripe wallpaper to go with a mustard couch.' Gregory grinned at her in a way that turned the half-light of the standard lamp, with its maroon lampshade, into what Katherine imagined an opium den might look like. Dudley described seedy dives where bad things happen as opium dens. Her heart thumped with guilt when she saw a thoroughly domestic plastic floral display on the mantelpiece in front of framed family photographs.

'Now, is it safe to sit closer to you with a fresh beer in my hand?' Gregory smirked. Katherine grinned but felt hemmed in. The smirk was indecent and quite contrary to the publicly serious demeanour she had grown accustomed to from the American. Gregory lounged back, legs stuck straight out in front, ankles crossed like a woman, making his trousers pucker at the fly. He sprawled his arm along the back of the couch behind her, cornering her. Gregory had become proprietary.

Just then, William Ringer showed up, stockmen in tow. Katherine hadn't seen him since the claypan incident and was angry and fearful all at once. She sat still as though stuck to the couch. Pearl frowned at Ringer's noisy posse of drunk followers. She was aware of his cruelty towards Reggie and Sam and had not invited him or his coterie of hangers-on.

'The whole town is here.' Sharmer said. 'And half the station people.' He waved his hand in front of Katherine's face. 'Well, I suppose there's not much social life in these parts. I wonder where all the Aborigines are.'

'Why do you ask that?' Was Gregory Sharmer's laid back assumption of closeness to do with their visit to the water hole or, had he heard about the claypan incident? Maybe it was both or, was he being sarcastic? Katherine wished the man to buggery, willing someone to come to her rescue. She wriggled forward, wanting to stand up. 'Everyone's in the kitchen or on the verandah.' Gregory held her back, caressing her shoulder, holding her. He tried to kiss her, but Katherine pushed him away, saying, 'I need air.' She took off to the back of the house, past the bedroom doors lining Pearl's long corridor. Gregory followed. He was toying with her, and she felt like prey in his benign resignation to whatever she said or did. He bided his time, waiting to pounce. It was creepy.

'Oh! There you are.' Katherine's tension abated when she found Janice and Wendy in the kitchen. Ringer's men, Ian Taylor and Billy Snowden, hadn't yet joined the girls. (Katherine could hear her mother correct her — *they are women, not girls.*) Ringer's men were out the back drinking, getting primed, they called it. They had offered to help Barney with the barbecue. Still, Katherine, Janice and Wendy agreed that the boys (there it goes again, Lillian's voice talking about infantilising people) were more likely to hassle the poor man. William Ringer had arrived uninvited with an appeasement gift of half a bullock over his shoulder, a killer, the other half of which he sold to Dudley that afternoon. Katherine was not impressed.

Someone changed the music and turned it up loud. Katherine jumped but didn't recognise the song. She watched the stockmen snap tops off bottles with their teeth, swigging beer, only pausing long enough to take a drag on their cigarettes. The kitchen was stuffy, with so many people standing around. Smoke and raucous laughter filled the room, making Katherine light-headed. She moved towards the verandah to get some air.

Outside, when her eyes adjusted to the semi-darkness, she could see Bruno Moretti sprawling over someone on an old settee. Katherine recognised the bare white legs glowing around Moretti's bulk. She recognised the panties at the ankles. It was her mother, drool dribbling from the corner of her mouth, her lips swollen with desire, and eyes wild with grog. Moretti lifted his head, blank eyes staring in Katherine's direction as he came into Lillian. When his body lost its tension, he made as if to rise, but Katherine stopped him with a powerful slap to his face. He looked stunned but tried again to stand. Lillian moaned and grasped his hand, trying in vain to guide him to her own urgency, but the man jerked himself away. Katherine started beating Moretti around the head, again and again, and again, screaming. 'You, filthy pig. I hate you. I hate you. I hate you.' She could not stop. 'That's my mother, you animal.' Her face turned white, as though she had lost blood, but her body turned rigid and violent with pain as she relentlessly pummelled the man.

'Come on. That's enough.' Gregory and William Ringer both came running at the sound of a fight. Each took one of Katherine's arms to drag her off the frightened stationmaster. Katherine looked from one to the other, vacuous, and crazed. Those who'd been egging Moretti on and gazing at his antics with lascivious eyes got even more excited until they became aware of the humiliation and shame in Katherine. When Moretti ran away, not a soul followed.

As the energy of madness drained from Katherine body, tears of sadness sprang forth for her mother. Lillian was unconscious, so fragile, so frail, and so very alone. Katherine leaned down, pulled Lillian's panties back into place and sat with her mother's head in her lap, stroking the brow of this precious, unconscious woman whose foolish secret yearnings had been exploited by a horrid, horrid man.

Katherine trembled and was still unsteady, dazed. Gregory sidled up to her, pretending support but caressing her instead just as Lillian woke, asking for a drink. The only people left on the verandah were Constable Barry Johnstone and his Sergeant, David Duke. They had witnessed everything but were as drunk as Lillian, unable to enforce any law. Ringer disappeared. Katherine asked Barney to drive her home with her mother.

She turned to Gregory, who was hovering expectantly. 'There's no room for you.'

The last thing Katherine saw as she left Pearl and Barney's was Paddy sitting in the back yard with a group of his people just beyond the flyscreen-filtered light from the kitchen. They had been there all along, missing nothing.

Katherine half-carried, half-walked Lillian to her room, undressed her and put her to bed. It wouldn't be long before Dudley would learn what had happened. People tended to joke about others' infidelities in public, and her mother would be neither exempt nor pitied. As for Bruno Moretti, he would be forgiven soon enough; the town needed its stationmaster. For Katherine and Lillian, the story would be much harder to live down. It was not until she lay on her own pillow that Katherine succumbed to her own unhappiness. She wished that she could talk to Jimmy, but she did not have the energy to go to him. Not tonight. He had stopped going to parties where Gregory Sharmer would be. Jealousy was eating him up. She fell asleep, aching for lost friendship. He would have been able to think of a fitting title for tonight's events. She could not.

Katherine dreamed that it was she, not Lillian, who was paralytic. Her father was poking her in the ribs shouting, *Wake up. Get up — you're just like your bloody mother.* Then Lillian's voice intervened, telling Katherine, as she often did when drunk, that she was uncaring and selfish, *just like your bloody father.* Katherine started running barefoot over sharp gibber stones that blistered her feet in the desert heat. She could not escape the hurt stalking Dudley and the beating heart of her mother's disappointment. Waking in fright, Katherine dragged herself out of bed, grabbed a pair of scissors then stood staring at her face, wild in the mirror. She slashed and chopped at her long blonde hair, cutting it shorter and shorter. A jagged new reflection grinned back. Gleeful at the wreckage she'd wrought, she gathered her hair in a towel to take to the incinerator. As she lit the fire, a wind blew up, and it magically took the nose-wrinkling stench of scorched hair with it.

13

On the morning after Pearl's party, Katherine couldn't get to the laundry fast enough to breathe the fresh air and find relief for her pounding head in the quiet. Last night she'd tossed and turned, dreaming grotesque scenes of her mother and Moretti and re-living the shame and terror of her violent response. Katherine wished for time, to comprehend, to recover, but with questions tumbling non-stop in her mind, it was as though madness was imminent. How could she show her face in public, now that she had beaten a man? What would people think of her mother? Could Lillian ever live this down? Could she? A fleeting image of Lillian helpless, so lost inside herself, brought tears. After all the drama of race week, Katherine feared that Dudley may not cope when he found out about the situation, as he surely would. Even though he didn't get out much, he'd hear about it somehow. Tongues wagged wildly in the desert where there was nowhere to hide. How could they, as a family, face the town's derision? How could they?

'Good morning, missy.'

'Oh! Paddy.'

'What's the matter?'

'Nothing.' It took effort, but Katherine refrained from blurting out the whole Bruno Moretti thing. She did not want this old man to think the worst of her even though she was sure as if she had seen him with her own eyes that he'd witnessed it all in the dark beyond the party-lit perimeter of Pearl and Barney's house.

Before Paddy asked, Katherine proffered her open cigarette packet. The two stood toe to toe (as Paddy put it) in amicable silence while he lit her cigarette, then his. How fast Paddy's cigarettes burned down. Like a lot of bushmen, the old man drew smoke deep into his lungs with the drawback, holding it almost to the point of no return before returning it to the world in a rush of white spirals through his nostrils.

'You wanna meet those old girls? 'You can go with my daughter, Grace. Come here after lunch today.' Paddy threw his cigarette butt on the ground and extinguished it barefoot.

'Oh, thank you.' Katherine's heart leapt at the invitation. It was as though Paddy had promised escape from the vortex of pain, sex and booze that was consuming her. She'd long wanted to meet the women, and now she was going to. She looked into Paddy's kind brown eyes. He knew.

Lunch had not been busy, but the air in the kitchen was electric that afternoon. Dudley would not look his daughter in the eye. After learning about William Ringer and calling her a slut, Jimmy had been distant too. His job was safe, though. Dudley might have reacted to the idea that Jimmy was her lover, but so strong was his unacknowledged desire for a son, he treated him as though nothing had changed. Lillian was subdued, although there was no mention of Pearl's party.

Katherine sat in the kitchen with Lillian and almost jumped with surprise when, for the first time ever, Lillian admitted that she had a shocking hangover. It came as no surprise that Pearl's party was not mentioned beyond that because Lillian often blacked out when she was drunk. Still, how could her mother not remember something like that? Did she not recognise the tell-tale physical leavings of sex, of Moretti? Katherine wanted to scream, to tell her mother everything, to prepare her for when the story got around or just throw it in her face. Words refused to come.

Katherine stood to go. With dishes done, the kitchen was spotless and ready for dinner.

'Where are you off to?'

'The store.' Katherine looked at her mother, whose energy wilted beneath her gaze.

'I think I'll have a little lie-down.' Lillian did not comment on Katherine's short, rough-cut hair. She didn't seem to notice.

'OK. See you later.' Katherine was tempted to stay with Lillian, not out of guilt but because of a powerful desire to protect. Still, Paddy would already be waiting in the lane behind the pub, ready to take her to meet the women as promised. Katherine wondered if they'd sit under the mulga tree next door where everybody would see her. She hoped not. One scandal at a time for her family was enough.

'You got good feet for walking?'

'How far are we going?'

'Little bit far, that's all.' Paddy pointed towards the middle distance across the flat.

His gait was slow and steady, so Katherine had no trouble keeping up even in rubber thongs, although sharp stones threatened to destabilise her at times. Paddy walked barefoot on gibbers without faltering. He may have a soft heart, but her friend had tough callouses on his feet.

Soon, a cluster of eucalypts appeared, about half a mile away. Katherine had never seen them from the laundry because of a slight rise in the land that hid them from her vantage point. Although trees promised water, many of the waterholes and billabongs around Wonnalinga were dry. As they drew closer, Katherine saw the women sitting in the shade of a scraggly tree that somehow managed to survive in desert conditions. Katherine rued her ignorance about this land, its vegetation and the creatures that inhabited it. She recognised only the goats that the Aboriginal women tended, camp dogs and an occasional goanna or sleepy lizard sunning itself in the open. She feared snakes. Cattle didn't count.

She looked down at her feet in shyness, several yards from where the women sat. Paddy's daughter Grace came towards them. Paddy introduced the two girls. Grace was tall and beautiful, with a high forehead. A smile lit her face, her dark eyes wide open and aglow with friendliness. Grace spoke excellent English. The main reason Paddy had stayed in town as much as he had over the years had been to ensure his daughter's education. His own generation had not been allowed to go to school. While Paddy could communicate in English well enough, he was illiterate and took pride in his daughter's ability to read and write.

'Come. Meet the aunties.' As soon as Grace offered the invitation, Paddy said goodbye, turning back to town. He told Grace to walk Katherine home later. 'Can't let the girl be by herself in this country,' he said with a giggle, 'Not yet.'

Six women sat in the sand at the edge of a dry billabong, where water would once have been. Katherine did not take in all their names at first, but one old woman commanded her attention, Paddy's sister. Aunty Evelyn did not talk much at first. She observed as others asked Katherine how she and her family liked living out bush. They giggled when they asked her about her boyfriend, but their question made her cry.

The women soothed her in soft voices with unintelligible words. Katherine's shyness melted away. She had never experienced such gentleness and was soon talking about all the things that had hurt or worried her, especially the stuff about Pearl's party. What happened there dwelled within her soul like an evil spirit. They did not judge, not for a moment. A couple of women slid close to Katherine to sing in their language and stroke her, letting Katherine sob until she was empty. She didn't understand, but their words brought healing.

A week later, Paddy brought Katherine a message from Grace, asking her to come to Bridge Hole. Katherine was drawn to Grace and welcomed the chance to become friends. Straight after lunch, she climbed into the pub Jeep and headed to the waterhole.

As Katherine pulled up in the shade, Grace emerged from the water, tall, slender and as beautiful as Katherine remembered, even with her curly black hair wet and flattened on her forehead. She admired the way Grace's skin glistened over lithe muscles.

'Do you want to go for a swim?' Grace called out as she towelled herself.

'Nah, I'll go in when you're ready to go again. I brought some Coke.'

'Thanks.' The two girls sat down on a canvas groundsheet, side by side in the dappled shade, facing the waterhole. Katherine imagined they'd look a right pair from the outside, she with pale skin and recently shortened blonde hair in a sky-blue bathing suit and black-haired Grace with dark skin and red togs.

'Can you get sunburned?'

'Not like you, pinkies.' The girls giggled. 'Too much sun is not good for anyone.' Grace paused. 'Are you all right now? You know. Your mum, well, she's just unhappy, poor bugger. Don't be cross with her.'

'I know. It makes me sad, but I'm scared that Dad will find out. It's like waiting for a volcano to erupt, one that could destroy my whole world.'

After a lengthy pause, Grace spoke again.

'You know, I had an aunty who fell in love with a white fella. He was a World War II soldier. Did you know our people fought in that war?' Grace answered herself. 'Well, they did, lots of them. Nobody knows much about that. Back then, white men were not allowed by law to go with black women. It was hated by your mob as much as a black man going with a white woman is now. Anyway, that aunty loved her white man so much, and he loved her back and treated her well. When he came back from the war, he bought land and built her a house. They had one kid, a little boy who died from measles. When that white uncle died years later, the government took the land and house away from my aunty, leaving her with nothing. Nothing. After all those years together — half a lifetime — it was as though she was just rubbish, a rubbish person who didn't even have the right to exist.'

'How could they do that?'

'Well, they did. Not only that. Aunty had to get special permission from the Protector of Aborigines to get married in the first place. Black people were never free like other people. The Protector had to fill in a form saying she was capable of living with a white man. Capable, mind you. She was deemed incapable of owning and running her own land even after years of managing it with her man. Nobody cared that this country is all Aboriginal land and was her people's land in the first place. The poor old girl never recovered.'

Katherine could think of nothing to comfort Grace, who had shown in such a gentle way, that her family's beloved country, this country, was rent in two; one world where the rules worked for the whites and another, cruel world that caught the Aborigines in a racial net.

'Tell me about your family.' Grace asked with tact that relieved Katherine from having to respond. Grace's quiet wisdom impressed Katherine, who decided to ask Gregory if she could read some of his books. She wanted to learn, not be so ignorant.

'My dad was a soldier in the Second World War. His father

fought in World War I. Dad only went as far as New Guinea, but my granddad died of war injuries — I never met him. Chlorine gas. He suffered for a long time before he died, but at least as Dad used to say, he died on home soil up in the Atherton Tablelands in Queensland. He'd worked there before the war as a horse strapper. That's where my father got his love of the gee-gees.' Katherine chortled. 'Well, he loves gambling. Dad doesn't train horses; they've got him trained to lose money. Mum hates it.'

Grace mentioned another uncle, her mother's brother, who had gone to New Guinea. 'Could be they met each other up there, your dad and my uncle but, he's gone now too. Died in Adelaide from too much grog. Finished.'

The conversation lapsed for a while. Katherine was uncomfortable; it was as though Grace's first story carried a deeper meaning, a message that she hadn't quite grasped. She found her disquiet hard to throw off.

'What about that American, then?' Grace asked, giggling as she did so.

'What about him?' Katherine was getting used to the fact that talk about sex and men brought forth giggles from Aboriginal women.

'You interested in him, or what? You'd better go for him before that Helen Drysdale snaps him up, or maybe Wendy Milton. She aims high that one.' Grace was teasing, of course, but what caught Katherine unawares was the way she spoke with such authority about Helen and Wendy's possible intentions. A flash of jealousy stabbed her, but Katherine cast it aside because she'd never had such an exciting talk before and didn't want to break the magic.

'No. Well, I dunno.' She decided to be honest. 'When he first came, the American, I thought he was a bit of a — you know — a weakling. Bit soft or something. But he was so nice to me.' Tears scalded Katherine's eyes and throat as they did every time someone was kind, but it was getting worse. Katherine had not lost the sense that her mind was loose these days.

'You had a hard time the other night.' Although matter-of-fact, Grace's voice was gentle again. 'You know, your hair will grow back.'

'Were you there?'

'No, but I heard. You know, those old women did too, that's why they helped you. They told Paddy it was time for you to meet them.' Katherine was side-tracked by the way Grace said, 'I heard' instead of saying, as she would herself, 'so and so told me.' Things like that make a difference in how one fits into the scheme of things. The women under the mulga tree had invited Katherine to meet them. Her mood lightened on hearing that.

'You know, I came here to this very spot with Gregory the other day, before Pearl's party.'

'You came here? Together?' Grace was intrigued, and, as Katherine confided the details, the two girls laughed out loud. They kept talking about men till giggles grew into great guffaws that lifted them off the rug and into the murky water to cool down, shared secrets sealed in a knowing and maturing friendship.

14

When a formal invitation arrived for Mr Dudley Forster and Family to attend a New Year's Eve function at Myall Creek Station on 31 December 1963, Dudley declared it was about time. It would do his girls good, he said, for them to have some fun. For once, Lillian was too excited at the invitation to complain about Dudley calling her a girl. She took it as a sign that her friendship with Mary Beaming would blossom, that Wonnalinga society accepted her. Katherine was sure Lillian's enthusiasm was as much about the fact that Michael Townsend had offered to fly them to the station in his light plane. Although Katherine's mistrust of Townsend would not budge, going to a station felt like a fairytale come true. In her excitement, she almost forgot that Paddy had called the place wild, a *myall* place. Now she understood from its name, it wasn't the creek that was wild but the station itself.

On Dudley's instruction, Jimmy drove Townsend, Lillian and Katherine to the airport early in the morning. Lillian and

Katherine had never been in a light plane before. Katherine tried to conceal her delight from Jimmy. He'd been such a sourpuss lately that she would have preferred to drive to the airport herself, but the pub needed the Jeep.

'Watch your speed, Jimmy.' Lillian took umbrage at Jimmy's surly face.

'Sorry, Mrs Forster.' Jimmy took his foot off the accelerator. He was not contrite. Katherine could see through his act — and Lillian's — as her mother attempted to assert authority for Michael Townsend's benefit. Lillian had plans for him that required a safe trip to the airport without Jimmy's tornado of speed, gravel and jealous anger.

Katherine stared ahead. She no longer cared that Jimmy still believed she betrayed him with William Ringer. He had relinquished his right to say anything to or about her after creating a rift in her family. She'd never forgive his duplicity. Katherine caught a glimpse of Lillian, snuggling next to Townsend in the back seat. It was the first time ever that her mother had not claimed the front passenger seat for herself. When they got out, Jimmy took off in a fury of dust, speeding home without a backward glance.

'You girls wait there,' Townsend said, pointing to an area off the tarmac, behind a gate. 'You'll be out of harm's way while I check the plane.' Notably, Lillian did not react to his calling her a girl.

Townsend flew a little white and blue Cessna 175 Skylark, a far more comfortable mode of transport than a Jeep bumping over rough corrugations for hours. The Cessna might cruise at

100 miles per hour or more, but Townsend's display of concern for their comfort didn't impress Katherine any more than Jimmy's huff and puff. The plane looked a bit like a biplane with the bottom wings missing. She had no respect for him right now. The man drank into the wee hours of the morning, and, as he would know, the law prohibits pilots from drinking for a full 12 hours before take-off. A lot of people in these parts ignored the rule, but he was a professional pilot. Lillian's longing for such a crass person was almost too painful for Katherine to bear.

The trip took just under an hour. Townsend flew the plane closer to the earth than the big Fokker Friendships go, so Katherine could see kangaroos thumping their mighty tails across the flat (she was now comfortable saying 'the flat' like the locals instead of 'plains'). Hundreds of galahs suddenly soared and swooped in unison, delighting Katherine as they momentarily stained the ground or peppered the trees in pink and grey before screeching back into flight. A wedge-tailed eagle caught her eye as it glided towards the sun. A flurry of tiny wings drew her back to earth as a mob of budgerigars alighted on a dead tree, their greens and yellows making it look like an abstract floral arrangement. Small groups of cattle dotted the landscape, the ubiquitous shorthorns favoured by local stations for their high-quality beef.

Paddy had taught Katherine to recognise different cattle breeds and look for birds. Over 150 bird species lived in these parts, including some not found anywhere else. The more she talked to Paddy the greater her respect for him grew. His knowledge spanned many landscapes, the natural one he called his country and the pastoral industry he had worked in for most of his life like his father before him. He was knowledgeable about the lay of the land in white society, and he was more politically astute than most. Katherine learned not to question Paddy. She learned instead to listen, heed his every word and understand when he dropped unsolicited treasures of information. Always, with Paddy, in his own time or when he decided she was ready.

On the day he took her to visit the aunties, he nattered about how outback roads were built along Aboriginal trade routes and storylines, close to the sites and tracks of their ancestors. Storylines, he told her, took people to meet different mobs, and to places where they could sit down for ceremonies, arrange marriages and do business. Early whitefellas were ignorant of what country meant in the Aboriginal way. But now, some station people — Paddy qualified it — know a little bit here and there.

While smooth enough, the landing forced Katherine back into the present moment. As they alighted, Mary Beaming greeted them with glossy smiles and the false flattery Katherine had grown to expect from the woman who believed she was queen of the outback. Roger Beaming strode up to Townsend to shake the pilot's hand before he had a chance to place chocks under the Cessna's wheels. Back at the homestead, first beers came out at 9 am.

After lunch — the Beamings prided themselves on being excellent hosts and had put on a mouth-watering barbecue — Michael Townsend found Katherine sitting on a divan on the verandah and plonked himself down next to her.

'Where's Mum?' Katherine asked, 'I haven't seen her for hours.'

'She's drunk,' he said, waving others to join them while placing a proprietary hand high on her thigh.

'I asked you to tell me where Mum is, not what state she was in.' Katherine stood up as she spoke, forcing his hand to drop away.

'Round the back, on the homestead lawn.' Townsend replied with a coarse laugh. He was very drunk but held his grog well, a sign of a real man in these parts.

Katherine found her mother sprawled on the ground at the back of the homestead, clasping the Hills Hoist with one hand and holding a bottle of beer in the other. Lillian lay in the dirt, legs askew, skirt crinkled high around the waist, exposing her cottontail-covered fanny. Bare legs. Painted toenails. No shoes. Katherine rushed to her mother in time to cover a breast that was threatening to spill from her bra.

A group of men encircled the clothesline. One broke rank, interrupting an ugly gale of laughter to tell Katherine that Lillian had been dancing around the clothesline, holding it as though it were a Maypole or, he continued with a leer, a maybe-dick. Katherine watched in horror as Roger Beaming, bloated with grog and self-satisfaction, kept egging Lillian up and at 'em even though she was prostrate and barely conscious.

Beaming glanced at Katherine but barely lowered his voice, so fascinated was he with his capacity for rhyme — 'Lilly Pilly the little filly, badly wants a big fat willy.' He winked at her and smirked at the men. 'Here's trouble,' he said as though Katherine was a joke. She turned on him with wild eyes, trembling in pain and anger, but her familiar madness lacked heat. This time, she channelled her disgust into icy words.

'Leave my mother alone.' Her tone stopped the insane laughter. One by one, the men slunk away, passing Michael Townsend with lowered eyes as he came to proffer a fresh bottle of Johnny Walker to Roger Beaming. Katherine was appalled. The pilot placed a protective arm over Roger Beaming's shoulders and escorted him to the homestead where the dutiful Mary would be making a show of cleaning up, not letting on that the Aboriginal women on the station would do it properly later. Katherine sat alone in the dirt with her mother, who, mercifully, had passed out.

Townsend's voice trailed behind him as the two men walked away. 'We have cause to celebrate, old mate. It was announced on the wireless this morning that drilling in the region has produced South Australia's first commercial gas flow. Mining will seal our future.' With a wide grin, Townsend gave Roger Beaming a congratulatory backslap.

15

'What about them mines? They gonna bugger up this country or what?'

'Where have you been? I've missed you?' Katherine had not seen Paddy for a few weeks.

'Out on that station.'

'All this time?'

'Yep. Not working, just sitting down with them other fellas 'bout this mining business.'

At first, Katherine was deaf to the distress in Paddy's voice. She was still wound up about Lillian's latest fall from grace out there. Paddy would have seen it all, but the way he kicked the soil with his big toe told her he was worried about something bigger than her petty concerns.

'What do the others say?

'We dunno what to expect. Could be OK, but not sure. Those mining people got plenty of money. They are friendly with that pastoral mob. But people in the Territory, they're speaking up about bad treatment from the pastoralists who took their country. There's going to be trouble for the Canberra government soon. That Northern Territory mob are not going to take it anymore. You watch. Soon, something will happen. I'm thinkin' we can do something about mining too.'

Katherine still had not figured out how, in the middle of nowhere, as Lillian loved to describe where they lived, someone like Paddy could know what was happening as far away as the Territory. Although Paddy had no formal schooling, his English was easy to understand and comprehensive. Aboriginal boys like Paddy often learned in boys' homes. Others picked up Aussie English up on the two-way radio used by the Flying Doctor Service or from working on a station. Even at the police station, they listened. As Paddy would say, they had ears. Gregory Sharmer may have told him things too. The American spoke interminably on the phone to people overseas and interstate. He read every newspaper he could lay his hands on as part of his research: *The Daily Telegraph* from Sydney, *The Advertiser* from Adelaide and Melbourne's *The Age*. He communicated on a routine basis with other academics at the University of Sydney, where he was a doctoral candidate. Gregory was always the first in line to pick up the papers that came by plane, and he poured over them, even though they were already out of date.

No matter how he got his knowledge, Paddy was worried that spiritual places connecting his people to the land were being destroyed in other parts of the country and could happen on his land. Katherine was in awe as Paddy confided his fears, that her friend trusted her enough to talk about such vital matters when she could not think of a single thing she might do or say to help.

The next person to confide in Katherine at the beginning of 1964 was Janice, who plopped herself on the end of Katherine's bed one night after the bar closed to announce that she was pregnant. 'They're sending me away,' she said, bursting into tears, 'I've been sacked. The government has bloody well sacked me.'

'Why, because you're pregnant? Did you tell them?'

'No, you're the first person I've told. It's because of Billy.'

'That doesn't make sense.'

'It does to the Aboriginal welfare people who must have told the Education Department. You haven't forgotten, have you? He fathered a child with that Aboriginal woman from Coober Pedy, and everybody knows about it. He tried to keep it a secret, but I can tell from the way people look at me lately that they think I've disgraced myself just by going out with him after he has done *that* with her. Somebody who doesn't like me must've reported it.'

'It is not as though half the men in the district haven't done the same thing, though.'

'True, but somehow, it's the idea of half-caste kids that upsets them most. Miscegenation is a dirty word.'

'What's that?'

'Oh! I learned about it at university. It's about mixing breeds. You know, kids with black mothers and white fathers, like that. The idea of sexual mingling disgusts a lot of people, not that they would admit it, mind you.'

Katherine brought to mind all the Aboriginal kids she'd seen, who, as Paddy had pointed out to her, were branded by physiognomy as the offspring of well-known pastoralists. Pioneer pastoralist families let their young sons go with Aboriginal girls. If a girl got pregnant, they'd marry her off to a poor white stockman who'd pass the child off as his own. He'd be rewarded with a lifetime guarantee of work. She dared not mention this to her friend. Janice's career as a teacher was already over, at least in South Australia. Things were always tougher for women. If a woman has a child out of wedlock, her prospects of marriage and her whole life would be ruined. A woman in that circumstance could well find herself homeless. She knew of parents who had turned their backs on unmarried, pregnant daughters. Again, impotent to help a friend, Katherine watched in sadness as tears scalded Janice's precious, freckled face.

'What are you going to do with your baby?'

'I don't know. I'm booked to catch the Milk Run on Saturday night. I know it's silly, but the idea of leaving by plane in the pitch dark at midnight makes me feel so ashamed.'

'I'll be there to see you off, don't you worry, I'll drive you there. Will your parents meet you in Adelaide?'

'I don't know. I don't know what to say about losing my job, let alone announcing the pregnancy. I am not sure which would be worse.'

Katherine told Janice about a school friend in Melbourne who got pregnant at 16. The parents sent her friend to a Catholic home for wayward and pregnant girls in New Zealand, where the baby was born. The home forced the girls to work hard during pregnancy, but at least they were away from the prying eyes of the world. Nuns arranged adoptions, and the girls, many from

Australia, would tell everyone when they returned that they had been on a working holiday.

Katherine looked at Janice. 'If you want to go to a place like that, you could visit a priest outside your local parish and ask what is available. There must be somewhere in Australia, maybe in Melbourne or Sydney.'

Neither girl mentioned abortion.

Katherine was bereft at the prospect of losing Janice.

When Katherine and Gregory went back to Bridge Hole, he laid back with hands beneath his head, a portrait of post-coital ease, unaware that the mottled shadow-play of eucalyptus leaves made him look ugly. Katherine was ill at ease. She missed the easy camaraderie she had shared with Jimmy, who she could confide in. He at least had an interest in her. Gregory was different. Lately, he was difficult to talk to, which she found annoying at times. He showed not one shred of interest in her, so absorbed was he in his work and allegiances with men, mines and stations, in Wonnalinga and university in Sydney and even America. Katherine began to believe Lillian was right, that men were not genuinely interested in a woman except for the way a woman made them feel. You can only hold a man's interest, Lillian would say, by asking him about himself. Yet, here he was today, questioning her. She watched Gregory sit up. He stretched like a lion and began to pry, smooth talker that he was, but she was on guard the minute he mentioned Paddy and Grace. He didn't know about Aunt Evelyn, but he was grilling her about her friends.

'Tell me about your work.' Katherine was testing Lillian's theory. He seemed taken aback for a moment, but it worked. The minute Katherine gave him her full attention, he backed off.

'I've been gathering kinship data. You know, who is related to who and how. Aboriginal people have such a complicated kinship system, not at all like ours, which is pretty much the same in Australia and the United States. A person's mother's sister for them is like a mother, and a person's father's brother is a very particular type of father. It's fascinating.'

Gregory wanted to compare Aboriginal society with that of the American Indians, but the idea proved untenable because, he said, 'Aboriginal society was organised in terms of kinship, not chieftainship. What about you, though?' He was nothing if not persistent when he wanted something. 'You seem pretty close to that old man, Paddy. 'Sharmer's gaze was so acute it forced Katherine to lower her eyes.

'Sort of, but he's an old man, you know?'

'What about that pretty daughter of his, Grace, isn't it? Do you see a lot of her?'

The questions felt like a succession of poisoned darts, sharp, lethal and difficult to sidestep.

'Oh, we just talk girls' stuff, you know,' Katherine remained nonchalant. How could this man think she'd just tell him about things she had learned from her friend? Good job he had no idea of the aunties who had healed her. Those things were not his to know. The longer she remained silent, the more intense Gregory became. Could he think so little of her integrity or so highly of his charm and persuasive powers that he believed she would succumb to his enquiries? If the Aboriginal women did not share their practices and knowledge with their men, then she had no intention of telling this white man a single thing. After all, she was Lillian's daughter, so talking about private things was not in her nature. And, by now, she agreed with Lillian that no man could be trusted to apprehend the suffering of women with any degree of empathy.

As soon as Katherine got home, Lillian besieged her with questions about where she'd been all afternoon. Katherine lied, saying that she'd been at the shack until the girls cadged a ride to the dam for a swim. It seemed out of character that Lillian had even missed her while she had Michael Townsend in the kitchen drinking tea and flirting. They were both suspiciously flushed.

'Ah, Townsend, I figured I'd find you here.' Gregory walked into the kitchen moments after Katherine, his tone of voice commanding the older man's attention. 'I need a word if you don't mind.' Sharmer nodded to Lillian and Katherine as though they should vacate the kitchen so that he and Townsend could have some privacy.

'No,' Katherine said. 'Not here. You can meet elsewhere. The kitchen is our home, not your place of business.' Katherine was sharp, and Lillian's face contorted in disbelief at Sharmer's temerity, believing he could evict her from her own kitchen. Townsend followed the anthropologist, leaving the kitchen without so much as a glance at Lillian, who moments ago he'd been trying to seduce.

Katherine wanted to scream at these arrogant men, tell them that they should talk to the Aboriginal people and let them know what lay ahead, not be cooking up plans in secret that will change lives forever. Let alone in her mother's kitchen.

'Your hair's looking better now that it has started to grow again,' Lillian smiled at her daughter.

16

From the other end of the house where she was stripping beds, Katherine heard her father singing. For the first time since they moved to Wonnalinga, his lovely tenor voice filled the morning air. When Katherine was little, Dudley sang light opera favourites in Italian and danced her around the room, her tiny feet on his. Sometimes he'd twirl on tippy-toe and sing, holding up his pyjama legs, turning flannelette pyjama pants into a magical tutu. Katherine laughed until her tummy hurt.

'You sound happy, Dad.' Katherine called out, following his voice to the bar, her eyes bright with tears. He added flourish as though singing to a lover, like Mario Lanza in The Great Caruso — *when you are in love, it's the loveliest night of the year.* Dudley was a film fan, and Katherine loved going to the pictures with him. He treated her to a vanilla Dixie ice cream that she wrapped her palms around till it melted a bit, then twirled with a tiny wooden spoon till it was soft and creamy in its cardboard cup.

Lillian never went. She said she did not like sitting next to strangers in the dark. Years later, Katherine found out that the real reason was that Lillian found Dudley's innocent enjoyment of make-believe embarrassing. He lost himself in characters and their on-screen stories and unselfconsciously laughed out loud at the silliest of jokes. Yet, his voice bewitched her then and still did. Lillian listened to her husband singing with a heart full of memories, her eyes glistening with sadness.

Once, when Lillian was drunk, she'd confided in Katherine that she'd held Dudley back, that he would have been happier with a life on the stage like his dancing sisters. Her sisters had him pegged as a homosexual. Men did not have to be homosexual to like the stage they said, but a lot were, and Dudley loved performing. Lillian had reason to question Dudley's sexuality herself as they never slept in the same room, let alone the same bed after Katherine was conceived. Loyalty held her back from asking for fear of the answer.

'You silly pair of duffers.' Dudley smiled. 'I'm OK because I reckon we'll soon be on top of it for our second race week. The kegs have arrived, the fridges are full of food and….'

'Hello, you.' Jimmy poked his head through the Ladies' Lounge servery as though something had spirited him there. Nobody heard a car pull up.

'Oh! Look at you, all covered in dust,' Lillian smiled.

Jimmy had driven his first car, a second-hand and somewhat beaten-up Chrysler Valiant, non-stop from Port Augusta.

'What are you doing back?' Katherine was confused. Why

would Jimmy turn up like that? Since he dumped her and her mother at the airport on New Year's Eve, she hadn't heard a word, not a single word, no letter, no call. Nothing.

'Dudley asked me to come to help for race week, and here I am.' Jimmy smiled as though nothing had changed.

'I'm off to the laundry.' Katherine tripped in furious jealousy as she left the kitchen. Dudley was singing because Jimmy was coming back. He'd organised it without even talking to Lillian. Or her. Shaken to her core, she sat on the laundry stoop, head between her legs, waiting for the clamour of her heart to ease.

'You OK?' Grace tapped Katherine's shoulder, her face a study in concern.

Before Katherine could reply, Dudley yelled from the kitchen. 'Katherine, Katherine, come here quickly. Your mother's hurt herself.' She stood up so fast she might have fallen had Grace not caught her by the arm. Grace followed Katherine to the kitchen in case she swooned again.

'What happened? Where's Mum?' Katherine looked at Dudley with fear in her eyes.

'Settle down, Jimmy took her to the AIM, and the nurses have already called the Flying Doctor. The plane's on its way. She was wearing thongs and accidentally trod on hot coals that spilled from the fuel range. When she went to steady herself, your mum put her hand flat on the stovetop. Her whole palm and all her fingers are badly burnt. The nurses will look after her. You need to take over the lunches. Right now.'

In the lead-up to race week, the bar was already frantic and, by 11.30 in the morning, orders had started coming in. Katherine wanted to go to her mum but did not have the energy to argue. Shaken and unsure of herself, she took over but asked Grace to come and help. Bugger Dudley. After the surprise he'd sprung, she wasn't going to ask his bloody permission for anything ever again.

By midday, the two girls were ready for the fray. They moved fast. Frypans were on the bench ready for grill and fish orders, salads plates sat in readiness under a twist of orange, and bowls of additional ingredients waited safely in the fridge. Two pans of oil sat smoking on the fuel range, ready for chips. The kitchen was hot, but Katherine thanked her stars it was May, not February, the hottest month of the year.

Grace was a quick learner, and Dudley was happy to put her on the payroll. The longer Lillian was away, the easier Katherine found the cooking, with Grace to help. It had been easy to show her the ropes, and they were becoming close friends. They even whiled away their afternoons under the mulga tree next door. Katherine had lost her shyness and no longer cared what people said about her. She had not set out to learn about Aboriginal people she'd never even heard of until she came to Wonnalinga. Nobody taught her anything about them at school. She didn't know they existed. But they'd been so kind to her, and she was dying to learn more about their lives. A new world had begun to embrace her.

One afternoon, the group was abuzz when Grace and Katherine showed up. It took ages for the women to stop giggling long enough to let them in on the fun. Different mobs of people were coming to the races this year, from as far away as Queensland and the Top End of the Northern Territory and Alice Springs. And a few would come from down south. As they took turns naming men they'd known years ago, everyone burst into lascivious laughter saying, 'Big men now, that mob. What will he look like now, that one? Old and fat, maybe, and white hair?' They danced up a cloud of dust, stamping exuberant feet. They turned to Grace and Katherine, saying, 'Young ones coming too, better look out now.'

Amid the merriment, Aunty Evelyn beckoned Katherine to sit down beside her. 'You know,' she said in the soft voice she used to heal Katherine, 'When the white fellas here have their races, we do ceremony. People come from all over, stockmen mostly, but their families too. They get a lift with their bosses, and we get to see our relations from far away. Some come into town for the races. Others like the pictures, but most camp a bit far outside town. At night, we all go there, tell stories and fix marriages. Like that. When the races are in Queensland, we go there. Same thing. When everybody sits down in Alice Springs, Tennant Creek — same. Nobody talks about these things. But our people got pushed off their lands, and sometimes, those other mobs have our people living with them, and they live with us. Sounds a bit mixed up, but we still know who we are and make right marriages for our young people. This year, Paddy wants to find someone for Grace. She's the right age for that now.

'At the ceremonies, old people are there. The proper ones to tell the stories and the ones that must look after things for their country, our country. Stories follow the old people's trade routes and trace our history across this land like spider webs strung together with songs. People now call them Songlines because we sing to remember our ancestors who walked this land, created this land. Our songs tell us where to find shelter, water. Like that. That's all now.'

Evelyn ended this short disquisition in that familiar way. Elders like Evelyn and Paddy talked about important things with deliberate intent. Grace too. Words were never wasted. Katherine felt privileged.

One day, under the mulga tree, the women reminisced with raucous giggles about exchanging sexual favours for goods or services. There were stories about this or that taxi driver, who, they'd heard, would drive a woman from Port Augusta to Adelaide and back if she asked — nearly a four hour drive each way — for sex. It'd be good to know which ones to ask, they announced, with deep belly laughter.

A young woman began to cry, breaking hilarity's thrall. Respectful silence enfolded her. 'What you cryin' for, bub?' Aunt Evelyn asked. The girl hid her face and whispered of her pain at not having her little boy with her. Then she told her story. A pastoralist where she lived gave her to his pubescent son so he could learn about sex. The laughter died down. Aboriginal women's giggles only belonged when they conferred sexual favours or fancied someone. This was different. This young girl had a child to a station owner's son. One day, they announced that her child had been sent down south to a decent school. That was a lie. Her child was stolen. The station owner adopted him out to someone she did not know without her consent. The station owner was not interested in his son's paternity rights. He wanted to hide the child because his lineage was stamped on the child's face and would ruin his son's reputation. No decent white woman would marry him if it got out that he'd had a kid with an Aboriginal girl.

It took several days for the weight of the girl's sadness to lift from the afternoon gatherings because it had brought back memories of other unbearable losses.

As Katherine spent more time with Grace and the women, Wendy Milton stopped visiting. At first, Katherine attributed her friend's absence to her love affair with Ian. Or, possibly, Wendy might be jealous of her friendship with Grace. It was not until Roger Beaming told Dudley to get rid of Grace because it was bad for business that Katherine realised what was happening. She was being ostracised. Even April at the store had grown diffident towards her, and townsfolk were less friendly than they had been. Subtle it might be, but lines had been drawn that made Katherine miss Janice even more. She was glad her friend had escaped.

17

The town was talking. People had seen Katherine Forster out and about with Gregory Sharmer. Pearl broadcast her view that Sharmer was a real catch for a publican's daughter. In this estimation, being American elevated him above William Ringer. Tonight, Katherine and Gregory were at the pictures together for the first time. They did not have to hold hands. Blind Freddy, as they say, could see that they were close.

The Wonnalinga Community Association ordered films from down south to screen on Fridays, Ghan nights. Barney was the projectionist, Pearl collected entrance money, and between them, they organised everything. By the time people arrived, they'd set up a dress circle of picnic chairs in rows on the dirt under the stars, with an aisle down the centre. Front seats filled early. Aboriginal people drifted in when it became dark, never approaching the chairs. They sat on the ground in the shadows on the offside of the seating away from the main street. From there, Paddy told Katherine with a chuckle, they could see two shows for the price of one, one in the dress circle and another on the screen. Not much escaped their keen eyes.

Lawrence of Arabia featured last week the story of a white man going mad in the desert that proved, according to Paddy, how hard it was for any man to live on another man's country.

Katherine sat through *To Kill a Mockingbird* with Gregory without much comprehension. When he asked if she enjoyed the film, she said she preferred musical comedy. *To Kill a Mockingbird* disturbed her. 'I don't even understand the title', she said.

Gregory told her she was a silly little thing. How could she not be moved or impressed by the hero, the white hero lawyer who stood up against his own community for a black man wrongly accused? 'Where I come from,' he said, 'everyone appreciates the bravery of that.' Katherine felt stupid.

After the show, Katherine helped Barney and Pearl stack the chairs and put them back into the hall where they lived. Barney packed the film back into its tin, safe and sound for the return trip, and, as soon as he and Pearl had cleaned up, they headed home. Katherine turned to Gregory. He was about to kiss her when the sergeant called his name. He strode off, leaving Katherine alone in the dark.

Sergeant David Duke and Constable Barry Johnstone were standing near the front of the hall with an Aboriginal man. Katherine could not hear what was being said, but as her eyes adjusted to the pale moonlight, she could make out a tableau. After they spoke for a minute, Gregory stood languidly by, watching the sergeant pin the man's arms behind his back and then start beating him. For the next few incredible minutes,

Katherine witnessed the two policemen pummelling the Aboriginal man in the face, head, and abdomen and, when the man stopped struggling and fell to the ground, two pairs of police boots took over to kick him in the back.

Katherine backed herself away from the scene to hide in the shadows. She found a secluded place in the back lane where she crouched, shaking and close to tears, waiting till she felt safe enough to make a run for it. She jumped when a gentle hand reached out to pull her up with a whispered shoosh. It was Paddy.

'Did you see what they done?' The old man whispered, 'That's my cousin-brother. They mighta killed 'im and no witness 'cept that American.'

Katherine hung her head.

Paddy whispered. 'You seen it, don't worry. You say nothing, OK. This is not your fight.' Katherine's tears stung with guilt, knowing that to accept Paddy's offer was the coward's way out. And, yet, deep down, she understood that he was protecting her from something more than being a witness to the violence she had just seen.

'What is it?' she asked, not expecting an answer from a man who did not waste words.

'Nuthin' to bother you. You go home now and sleep sound.'

As Paddy walked beside her, silent in the dark, Katherine's mind churned. She longed for the earlier certainty that she'd had with Jimmy. He would know how to find the right title for the incident at the pictures. Police Brutality is all she could come up with. It sounded as dull as a newspaper headline if there was such a thing as a newspaper willing to print a story about two white policemen bashing a solitary black man half to death on a dark, outback film night. Who would report it; tell the story? Nobody. That's who. Despite Paddy's assurances, she wanted to report the incident but was flummoxed; where could she go to report a crime committed by the police?

Katherine decided to tell Jimmy in the morning when he came to stock the bar before either Dudley or Lillian greeted the day.

'What do you want?' Jimmy was playing a distant game

'Something happened after the pictures. Something awful,' Katherine confided, keeping her voice low. 'Come here, I can't shout out.' She beckoned Jimmy to follow her to the back verandah where their conversation would not be overheard, and they could see anyone coming. He listened, intent as she told him the story, which told Katherine he was as aghast as she was at the enormity of what she had seen. His apparent jealousy of Gregory suddenly seemed to dissipate.

'Paddy told me not to worry, that it is not my fight, but I can't ignore it. Can you write to your priest? Tell him? Ask him if he can help? What do you think?'

'Did you see who the Aboriginal man was?'

'I didn't recognise him, but Paddy knew him all right. Said it was his cousin-brother but didn't say his name. You'd have to ask him.'

'Leave it with me. I can find out from the Port Augusta end.' He returned to the bar, leaving Katherine at the kitchen table to wait for her mother. Her heart was fit to break. Jimmy had been kind, but she was certain from the way he spoke that they would never again be more than friends, even if she ever saw him again, which she doubted.

Later that afternoon, Jimmy asked Katherine to mind the bar for him while he went to the Post Office Agency to call Port Augusta. He returned with the news that the Aboriginal man had come close to death but was expected to recover in the Port Augusta Hospital. They had whisked him away by Flying Doctor first thing. Jimmy did not tell Katherine that the man had accused Gregory Sharmer of fathering a child with his daughter, aged 13. When the police questioned Gregory Sharmer, he said the man was lying, and they had taken his word without question.

Next day, Father Bob telephoned Dudley to tell Jimmy he should get back to Port Augusta as soon as possible to look after his youngest brother. His foster parents had kicked the boy out for beating up their biological child. For Jimmy, the news that he had to go home came as a relief. The Forsters had always been demanding. He was well on his way back to Port Augusta by the time Katherine discovered he'd gone. When she checked, his room was empty. He had packed everything, including his swag, and there was no sign of his car. Katherine sat on the bare bed where they had first made love and cried.

Katherine soon learned that the Port August court system whitewashed the evil she'd witnessed at the pictures. After he had recovered from his beating, the Aboriginal man was put on trial. The Wonnalinga police charged him with aggravated violence in a mad transposition of events whereby the victim became the guilty party. Sharmer didn't appear, but the law in its pomposity found the Aboriginal man had lied.

The local press lacked the courage to publish a piece about a miscarriage of justice despite written remonstrations by Jimmy's priestly mentor. No legal saviour for the Aboriginal man. Katherine shuddered at the memory of Gregory Sharmer lecturing her from his moral high ground as though he were Alabama's Atticus Finch in *To Kill a Mockingbird*. The American's lofty pronouncement, like the man himself, was a joke.

A few short months later, a 13-year-old Aboriginal girl delivered a half-white baby just outside Wonnalinga. Like so many other little ones fathered and disowned by whites, the child would be called a half-caste.

18

Gregory left on the Milk Run the night after the beating, like a thief in the night. From the perimeter of the airport floodlight, a few Aboriginal men watched him go. Katherine had no idea about his departure until she went to clean his room on Sunday morning. It was empty. Gone from the second bed was his brown leather case. Gone, too, the cornucopia of texts that had lain all over the place. There was no knapsack. No desert boots under the bed. Nothing remained of Gregory Sharmer except his Akubra. He'd left it sitting on top of the hotel Bible on the bedside table in a final salute to Wonnalinga. Sharmer was not coming back.

Katherine stripped the American's bed. In a matter of days, both Jimmy and Sharmer had slipped out of town and from her life. Both scarpered, without so much as a thank you or farewell. She had no tears. Instead, Katherine congratulated herself in the mirror for having kept a part of herself from Sharmer. As she cleaned the mirror, she admired the way her hair shone again as it grew back. So absorbed was she by her own image, she knocked the tin of Ajax she had been using to clean the mirror off the dresser. It tumbled to the floor, spilling white powder everywhere, coming to rest in an awkward spot in the corner beside the single wardrobe. Katherine moved the robe to get at it and heard a thud. A leather-bound diary with a gold clasp fell to the floor. It must have been wedged between the robe and the wall. She slipped it into her apron pocket with little immediate curiosity, finished the room and headed off to the laundry. As she loaded the washing machine, her spirits rose. As she pegged out the washing, the sun warmed her skin. When she had finished, Katherine sat on the laundry stoop, turning the diary over and over in her hands.

'My people are happy he's gone.' Paddy did not hold back when Katherine told him what she was playing with. He'd turned up silently as usual. 'He'll get his degree using my people's stories all right. His career will be good, his life. He's not the first and won't be the last to build himself up at our expense, with his stories about who we are. That man was rubbish, a rubbish man. Your life is better now.' There was an unusual hardness in Paddy's voice.

When Paddy left, Katherine took herself to a quiet spot in the shade on the lawn beside the house. Sensing that Paddy had indirectly given her permission to read it, Katherine expected the notebook would contain information about Aboriginal people in the area. She sat down to read.

Wonnalinga, Australia — On the Personal Side of Things.
This is a diary of my personal experience of the wilds of

the Australian outback. When there is nobody to talk to, a man must reflect on his reactions and responses to his environment, his wishes, yearnings and desires.

May 1962

I finally reached 'the field' for my research after several gruelling months under the tutelage of Professor X in Sydney. I shan't name him as I did not like him at all. I am staying in a small outback town called Wonnal-inga in desert area of northern South Australia. The hotel is dreadful. The rooms have neither air condition-ing nor bathrooms. I have to queue with other guests for the privilege not only of bathing but also of going to the toilet. There is only one male and one female toilet at the end of the accommodation corridor in a place that can accommodate up to 20 guests; most are men. I, therefore, use the women's toilet if I get stuck.

The daughter is a rude young thing. Blonde and rather pretty, petulant and somewhat intense. She came here with her family from Melbourne for what purpose one cannot imagine. She could be tainted in some way and cannot find a husband whence they came. Nobody knows why the father — Dudley is his name — brought his family all the way out here anyway. Must be something wrong for city folk to come to this godforsaken place.

Katherine rubbed her forehead as though in pain. She and her family had done so much to help this American man. They welcomed him to family meals in the kitchen and looked after his things when he went bush. Dudley even lowered the tariff for him while he travelled around. Who could have guessed he was harbouring such horrid thoughts? Katherine despised duplicity. Letting herself be seduced by this man was a dreadful mistake. She was tempted not to read on, but curiosity overtook good sense.

July 1962

Late yesterday, I returned from the bush, as they say hereabouts when one goes out of town and into the desert country. It took some time before a group — a family really — of Aboriginal people who camp about 30 miles out on a station called Ingeburra agreed to let me work with them. Nobody knows where this name originated, but it doesn't matter, as I have nothing to do with station people when I am in the field. I stay alone with my subjects in situ for longish periods to learn by necessity, observation and participation in their way of life. I detail all that in my official notes which I keep separate. Here, I record my personal, visceral response to the people.

The group I am studying is composed of women whose men work on the station, their children and the old people of the tribe. The legs on these people are skinny, and the kiddies' tummies protrude. I doubt it is malnutrition — more like nature's deformity. The people are healthy, but I've never seen such stick-like legs before. Of course, they walk a lot, not having ready access to vehicles.

The young women are tall, bare-breasted, nubile and proud. Their hair is tangled and unkempt, yet they have luminous brown eyes and the longest black eyelashes. Are they beautiful? Not if you value fine features. Their thick noses are flat and lips thick, but there is a bearing about them that draws you to them. I find myself semi-aroused by these creatures most of the time, even though they giggle each time they see me. Do they sense my physical attraction? Does it show on my face, or do my eyes betray me? When lust begins to overpower me, I return to Wonnalinga to play with the publican's daughter.

NB. No matter how desirable I find the Aboriginal women, I am unsure whether I could go with one. As a race, they smell different; it's a musky, smoky perfume that seems stronger after they have eaten Goanna meat, a food they all prize. I can't work out if it is the animal's flesh or the smoke of the campfire mixed with sweat — there are no showers and few watering places out here. (I wonder if the people for whom the Goanna is a totem, which proscribes eating their meat, smell too? How does one find out such things?) I may stink the way they do after I eat Goanna with them — hard to tell by yourself. My natural, nay, cultural body odour could well revolt them. I might ask one day. I must stop writing now to burrow further under the canvas as my cock is hardening.

November 1962
Dudley, the publican — Katherine's father — gave me

a hard time one night. The man thinks he is much more intelligent than he is. Dudley is guileless, not a fool, but without much education, if I guess right. He has his eye on me as a catch for his daughter. So does the mother, Lillian, but she's a whole different story. If I didn't already have the daughter, I could bed the mother. Need to think on that. Back to Dudley. He asked me what an anthropologist does. How am I supposed to answer that? Should I say an anthropologist lives with strange people, mostly natives, and writes about them? In truth, these Australian people are all natives to me, natives of a country not my own. Australians are just as challenging to comprehend in many ways as the Aborigine; maybe more difficult. I can't let the man know I want his daughter to distract me from the Aboriginal women now, can I? I know many anthropologists go with native women. My mother would be appalled if I was to do so, but the temptation is strong...I hope I can continue to withstand my own urges.

December 1962

Lillian, Katherine's mother, is a lush, a drunk who is sexually frustrated and in her menopausal years when women's desires can lead them astray. She has taken a fancy to a senior Mines Department official who has her wrapped around his little finger. Katherine disapproves, but Lillian is no fool. She is watching me with her daughter. She'd accept me as a formal suitor for

Katherine, but I doubt she'd approve of my rooting her to defray my sexual frustrations from the camps. To have a root is the Australian term for a screw. Fuck is used but less often than I expected.

Forget Lillian. I have decided to make a serious play for Katherine. She is coy, but that won't last, and she is a tempting morsel. Is she, or is she not a virgin? Maybe not with a publican for a father — who knows what types she has been around or with. I don't care.

Christmas Week 1962
Good fortune, Katherine succumbed to my advances at the waterhole today. Yes, she was on the rebound. Something that Jimmy the barman did to upset her — I don't know the whole story. I took her at Bridge Hole, on the ground — well, on my swag, to be precise. She was lovely. An innocent but not a virgin. Am I starting to have feelings?

Katherine held the diary close to her chest, holding the idea that Gregory might have felt something for her for a moment. Was Gregory honest back then? Hoping to find out, she turned the page only to find the next few had been roughly torn from the diary. There was pretty much a blank year, but Katherine was mesmerised. It was as though she could see inside someone else's head.

November 1963
The most horrific scene at a recent party. Katherine lost

it when she saw her mother rooting around at a party drunk with the new stationmaster. She became insane with rage. Quite a sight. I didn't know she had it in her. I forget how the silly girl got home. I was too pissed to do anything sensible after helping others pull her off the man before she killed him. I think I helped, but my memory's pretty vague. Anyway, the incident hinted that there could be things about the girl I don't know, so I'd better be careful. I don't want to get too embroiled if there is something amiss in her mind.

Something wrong with her mind? The fucking idiot. Katherine slammed the diary shut, going over in her mind the way the American had worn her down, pressed himself on her. The diary drew her in again. This time, she read with trepidation.

December 1963

I haven't written anything for a while because there is one black girl in camp who excites me to the point that I don't think I can hold myself back much longer. Even with Katherine in town to take the edge off my urges, I cannot keep my eyes off this girl and am at risk of disgracing myself with a public erection. She is so dark her skin glistens, her legs are skinny beyond belief, but her breasts are ripe and full, with dark nipples that thrill to the faintest touch of air. She carries herself with pride, and her forehead is so high she looks like a princess. I long to bury myself in her, and I wake every morning in camp with my hand still on my cock, striving to think of ways to separate this girl from the watchful eyes of the older women.

I was in luck today, though. The adult women went walkabout to find bush medicine for a couple of the smaller children who had a fever. The girl offered to stay behind with her younger sister to look after them. I know she is interested in me by the way she looks up at me through her eyelashes without lifting her head. It is a knowing look. I am aroused now, just remembering. I must be careful and, yet she came to me, looking that way, and I saw her incline her head, just the faintest movement urging me in the direction she was heading. I took it as an invitation to follow her as she walked towards a mound at the foot of a nearby pile of giant rocks. She had left her younger sister sleeping in the camp with the two sick little ones. She was partially hidden behind the most prominent boulder. When I stepped around, she was urinating. She looked up quickly but did not seem alarmed at being disturbed. I watched as she cleaned herself and covered the urine with sand.

As she began to move, I took her in my arms. She stood still. Alert but not responding. When I touched her, the girl's pubic hair was still slightly damp. I unbuckled my belt and took down my trousers. In a moment, I had come. When I released her, she turned and walked back to camp without a word.

I left the camp before the older women returned from

their gathering expedition.

The entries ended there. Gregory must have lost this volume, having to pack in a panic, ready to flee. Katherine flicked through the pages again, and two slips of paper fell out, undated entries that he'd tucked between the last page and the back cover. She unfolded the first.

One

I made love to Katherine this afternoon, but I know now the white girl is not enough to stay my lust for the Aboriginal girl I want to possess, who I want to keep pressed to me so I can force myself into her. There is even part of me that wants to hurt her, to leave my mark.

This convinced Katherine that Gregory had misread the girl. She wouldn't signal him to follow her when she was going for a pee. Was it rape? What he did? She read on.

Last time I went to the camp, the women welcomed me back, saying with joy that little ones were no longer sick. I replied, saying I was pleased for the children, but what they would have seen in my face was relief. The girl had said nothing. We sat around the campfire from dusk. I listened to the women talking about family, identifying who belonged to who. They worked out which side people came from, the mother's or father's side, as they were to meet another group soon for ceremony. Marriages and alliances are formed at such gatherings. Kinship infor-mation must be up to date.

That night, I lay on my back, wide-awake under the stars. All the women were asleep, some of the older ones snored. The camp dogs were quiet, warm near the fire and the bodies of women. I noticed that the girl was lying apart from the others. I rose and circled the camp, far enough outside the perimeter. Even a crunch of stone would be enough to wake someone. The girl was awake, so I beckoned. She rose and came to me. We walked silently in the night towards the rocks, and there, I took her again and again. Her black skin was smooth to the touch. No wonder they call it Black Velvet.

The next night we rose again from our beds to unite in silent passion under the stars. I lived for this sex, night after night. During the day, I took notes and pretended everything was the same, but it was not. I could not get enough of the girl who spoke not a word to me. The way she opened to me in her vulnerability brought out a violent carnality I did not recognise. I began to be rough with her. I could not resist the urge to harm. A form of self-loathing grew out of my sense that I was debasing myself with these people, this girl. A new level of violent arousal began to permeate my trysts with Katherine too. She did not complain.

Katherine read this passage repeatedly, trying to figure out why the girl would go with Sharmer in the night. Was she too scared to tell her mother what was happening, too afraid to say no to this man of authority? That was it. Katherine felt sorry for the girl.

Two

When I pulled up on the next visit, the men of the camp were waiting for me. I first assumed they were back from the station, but they were all standing tall, looking at me. Had I not been overcome with foreboding, I would have taken a photograph of their nobility. The Noble Savage, I knew that I should not harbour such views as it dehumanises. I jumped to the ground, kicking up the red dust. When the senior Elder walked towards me with purpose, I shook in fear.

I can't say what happened next, not even on these pages. All I will admit to is being humiliated in front of the entire camp: men, women, girls and children. Afterwards, even the dogs shied away from me. How had they found out about the girl? I wondered. Had she, who had never spoken to me, told them? I could not see her. I suspected the old girls had hidden her.

Back in my vehicle, on the way home, I figured that I'd had a lucky escape. They could have killed me there and then, but they didn't. Nobody ever needs to know what happened. I had more than enough data in my field notes to write my PhD. This could have been God's way of ending a torrid situation that may have sent me mad or caused me to do something stupid. A lot of men who go with Aboriginal women cannot leave. In these parts, it is common knowledge that men who 'go native' can never return to their rightful place in the white world.

At least I did not sacrifice my foreskin in a male rite of passage designed to move young men from their mother's house into the world of men to 'buy' more stories and secret information as a few of my academic compatriots have done. That, to me, would be an absolute abuse of power and privilege as not one of them goes on to live like a Man in Aboriginal terms. No. They go back to their own worlds, gain fame and fortune writing about things that should remain unspoken.

It is time for me to leave Wonnalinga before I lose myself.

While Gregory may have feared the loss of himself, Katherine had started to wonder if she had a self to lose. As the diary's contents swirled around and around in her mind, Katherine realised that she'd been waiting to find herself by finding a husband.

She wanted to scream at Pearl, who thought William Ringer, the rapist who tied Aboriginal women up to trees and beat their sons for talking to a white girl, might be a good husband for the likes of her! As for Lillian, would she still see Sharmer as a good catch if she knew the depth of his depravity? It seemed to Katherine that nobody had any idea about what makes a good marriage.

Nobody asked her what she wanted. All she'd had from any

man was sex with vested interests. Sex from schoolboys determined to impress their mates. Sex to save Gregory from his self-destructive weakness. As for Jimmy, jealous Jimmy, manipulative Jimmy who lied to ingratiate himself with her father, who probably aspired to follow in Dudley's footsteps like a son, how could she trust any of them? Did she have no value at all?

19

Lillian's hand had healed well by the time she returned to Wonnalinga. Dudley did not ask his wife why she had stayed away so long. He was thrilled to see her back.

Katherine and Grace had a good routine for doing the lunches without Lillian, but Katherine worried when her mother started emerging from her room later each day. Lillian fell into the habit of slipping into the kitchen mid-afternoon after the girls left to make a cuppa. Without turning the lights on, she sat smoking and staring into the gloom for long periods. Over time Lillian ate less and less, and only went into the bar or Ladies Lounge if someone convivial was there. After dinner, Lillian retired early to her room, where she drank alone.

While still immaculate, wearing white a lot of the time, Lillian lacked vitality. It was as though nothing mattered to her now. Dudley berated himself for his wife's condition, making it all about himself. But, for Katherine, it was as though the sun had gone down.

The laughter died at The First & Last until the day Paddy showed up outside the laundry, carrying a little crossbreed puppy, the runt of a Blue Heeler-Bull Terrier cross litter born on Myall Creek Station. He gave it to Katherine, saying it was not for her, but Lillian, who'd secretly asked him months ago to find her a pup. He'd waited, he said, to find the perfect one.

'Tell your mum, this is no camp dog,' he said. 'People say camp dogs are savage, but not this little fella.' He tickled the squirming puppy around the ears.

'Yes, and full of mange, ticks, worms and fleas,' Katherine replied. 'Oh! And rabies most likely.'

She and Paddy chuckled together.

'Did you know that some of those white doggers looking out for dingo-scalp money, they shoot our camp dogs to claim the two quid bounty for ears like this fella's? They don't fool us, but we trick the buyers too. We make false ears by sewing together pieces of dingo hide to make 'em look like they are from a dead dingo.' Paddy spoke with a big grin. 'This one's no camp dog, no dingo in 'im for sure. He's a fair dinkum cattle dog.'

Katherine smiled her thanks as Paddy headed back down the lane. She held the puppy's plump little body tight. He was wriggling hard trying to lick her face, and she didn't want to drop him on the way to Lillian's room. Katherine burst in on her mother without knocking, put the puppy on Lillian's sleeping body then opened the blind and window. The room reeked of cigarette smoke, Chanel No. 5 and alcohol.

'What, what, what are you...' Lillian peeked out from beneath the sheet. She sat up to take a sip of water from her bedside table. After a sweaty, boozy night's sleep, her short hair stood up like a cockie's comb. She tried to maintain a grumpy charade because she'd been woken so early, but Lillian could not ignore the joyful tail-wagging ball of fur that Katherine had plopped on her tummy. The pup panted with mischief, his long pink tongue anxious to please. Lillian pulled the little fellow to her chest, cradling his soft belly next to her heart, his pumping legs splayed. 'You came a bit late, little one, but you're here.'

'You'll have to give him a name.' Katherine said.

'In my own time. Give me a minute to wake up properly.' Lillian kept fondling and patting the puppy's inquisitive little head. 'All right then, let me look at you.' She hooked her thumbs under his forelegs and took a peek. 'You're a boy, aren't you? How about we call him Paws? Look at the size of these.' She pressed on the puppy's toes which spread wide. 'He has to grow into these big feet.'

'Paws it is then.' Katherine loved the name if only because Lillian laughed her warm rumble of a laugh that Katherine had not heard for so long. 'OK, Paws.' Lillian nuzzled his soft underbelly. 'Off you go to Katherine; I need a shower.'

Katherine took the puppy outside for a pee, giggling to herself when he squatted like a female dog. He seemed delighted with the steaming yellow trail he had left behind. She gathered Paws into her arms and ran to the kitchen to show him to Grace before starting the lunches. She then banished him to the back verandah for hygiene reasons. When she shut the door, his yowls got so loud before lunch, they brought Dudley from the bar at the exact moment that Lillian walked in, on time for a change.

'What on earth is making that racket?' They shouted simultaneously, loud enough to end the yowls for a moment and, looking into each other's eyes, smiled fondly in their shared love of puppies.

David Duke, Barry Johnstone and Barney Napper arrived in the kitchen for poker that night at 7.30 pm. Paws had been fed and put to bed with a ticking clock and a hot-water bottle buried under blankets. As long as he heard voices from the kitchen, he was quiet. Dudley and Lillian had hosted a card game at the pub for a while. They learned to play during the war years and taught Katherine to make up a six. The only downside was the whingeing of the town's two policemen, vigilant in case they were caught gambling in the pub after-hours. It didn't stop them drinking.

Katherine had no sympathy for them. They hadn't worried about who might have seen them bash that defenceless Aboriginal man. She would have preferred neither of them at the table, but at least during play, the constable couldn't leer at her the way he did when nobody else was around. Barney was a good poker player who liked a bit of light relief away from Pearly, as he often called his wife (the town followed suit). He told Katherine that he preferred all-male games, but this was the only decent game in Wonnalinga. 'Beggars,' he said, 'can't be choosers.' Sporting new spectacles, almost identical to his wife's but with thinner lens — Pearl bought them, of course — Barney announced that now he could see, there was no point in trying to bluff because he would miss nothing. Nothing! His little joke brightened the mood.

Dudley placed two new packs of cards on the table, pulled a deck from one, peeled off the cellophane and extracted the jokers. He didn't like wild cards in his game. As host, he shuffled then placed the deck at the centre of the table. The sergeant cut first, but Barney won the first deal with an ace. He shuffled the cards anew and, with deft fingers, flicked one at a time to all the players. The Forsters picked up their five cards in one swoop, as did the two policemen, but Barney picked his up one at a time, teasing both himself and others. Impatience was thinly veiled. With no betting limit, they played in silence for high stakes.

On poker nights, Dudley sat at the stove-end or head of the kitchen table where Lillian did the chips. Lillian preferred to face him from the other end, closer to the bar. Visiting players lined the sides of the table, Barney sitting next to Katherine, opposite the two policemen.

There was no mystery as to why Lillian got drunk faster than everyone else because, each time she went to the bar to fetch drinks for people, she tippled from the top shelf. Katherine had long since measured the levels in spirit and liqueur bottles before the game to check just how much her mother managed to consume. Lillian liked the heady, sweet stuff: Crème de Menthe, Cointreau or Crème de Cacao. At the table, she drank beer one for one with everyone except teetotal Dudley. It amazed everyone how, no matter that Lillian was pissed to the point of oblivion, she still won hand after hand after hand. Dudley's wife was a much luckier and cannier player than anyone else. Not even Barney in his new spectacles could read her. Nobody took Lillian for granted as a poker player.

'What? Come on, you said something,' Lillian lifted her head from where it had been resting on her folded arms. Her out-of-focus eyes tried to find their mark on Dudley's face. Words failed, her mouth sagged, and her head fell forward. Seconds later, she jolted upright again, lifting her head so high she was at risk of toppling backwards. When her words came, they were unintelligible. Katherine watched in anguish. Lillian's head wobbled like a blancmange.

'Wipe that drool from your mouth, woman.' Dudley turned to his guests with a forced smile. 'She's not herself tonight, fellas. Time to call it quits if you don't mind.'

'Who do you think you are, Dudley Forster,' Lillian's pride kicked in. 'You're nothing to me. Nothing at all, do you hear?'

Dudley blanched as his guests filed out. They'd seen it all before and did not want to get embroiled in the family's business.

When Lillian tried to stand, she swooned. Katherine jumped up fast enough to catch her under the arms, then wrapped her own firmly around Lillian's waist to steer her out of trouble.

'Come on, Mum, how about I take you to your room?'

Lillian pushed Katherine aside and plopped back down onto her chair, muttering. Dudley stalked out of the room, leaving his daughter to look after his wife. Katherine pulled a chair close to her mother and put her arms around her. Their heads touched. She could smell stale cigarette smoke in Lillian's thin hair, alcohol on her breath and Chanel No. 5 at her throat and wrists; the familiar blend of love, beauty and decadence that was her mother.

'What is it, Mum?'

'He was there, waiting for me in the dark.' Lillian pointed towards the house.

'Who was, Mum? Who?'

'I've wet myself.' Lillian cried, not maudlin tears, but a wail as though she was in pain.

'Never mind, Mum, I'll take you to the toily then get you into fresh panties and your nightie.'

Walking down the corridor giving ballast to her mother was arduous and halting. Katherine backed Lillian into the toilet cubicle and sat her square on the pan. 'Don't stand up, or you'll trip.' Katherine whisked her mother's wet trousers and panties away from around her ankles, so she wouldn't trip if she tried to get up without help. Experience told Katherine it was time for a smoke when Lillian's body folded in two, where she would sleep, head on knees. It was best to wait because, after a snooze, Lillian was more amenable to being sponged, dressed in a clean nightie and knickers, and put to bed.

Half an hour later, Katherine had finally settled Lillian with a glass of water on the bedside table in case she woke in the night with a dry mouth. As she turned to leave, Lillian stopped her.

'There's more.'

'More what?' Katherine was expecting to hear more about the man who had waited in Lillian's room.

'Your father. He keeps secrets, but I know he's been gambling much more lately with bigger stakes. If he doesn't stop, we could lose the pub.' Lillian passed out, lying on her bed almost inanimate, mouth open, still dribbling. When she ate chocolate in bed as she often did in the night, Lillian's drool would stain the pillow brown. Chocolate was hard to wash out.

For the first time since coming to Wonnalinga, Katherine was overcome by fear. Her mother's words set her body prickling with ugly anticipation as she walked to her own room. She was on edge, expecting someone or something to leap out of the dark to attack.

Katherine slept fitfully that night.

20

Unlike the quiet suburban streets of Melbourne where Katherine grew up, there was always something happening in the bush. The pub often hosted politicians, mining executives, foreign travellers, priests, actors, writers, musicians and academics like Gregory Sharmer. The latest crowd to invade town was a bunch of rogue rally car drivers. A journalist covering the rally dropped by in a helicopter to refuel, giving Dudley advance notice that he could expect a group of drivers who had gone AWOL from the Ampol Around Australia Trial. The journalist had lunch and took off within the hour. The rogue rally drivers were not as newsworthy as the teenage runaways from rural Victoria that he'd covered for *The Advertiser* a while back. That story won him an award, and he had hoped his coverage of the rally itself might bring another, but he didn't like his chances with rally dropouts.

A couple of days later, five battered cars carrying 14 drivers and their offsiders turned up at The First & Last at seven in the morning. They introduced themselves as rogue drivers, had a hearty breakfast and retreated to their rooms to rest after asking Dudley to organise a bush barbecue for them one night, with fresh-killed meat. They'd pay well for what they described as the full bush experience.

The drivers wore an unofficial uniform of white t-shirts under checked flannelette shirts, with white overalls and leather jackets branded like their cars by sponsors. They had set out from Sydney ten days ago, travelled the back blocks of New South Wales up to Queensland and across to Port Augusta before splitting from the trial. The remaining contestants continued east from Port Augusta to Victoria then back to Sydney.

With thousands of points lost after mechanical problems, it was no use trying to get back into the race. They had to stay put in Wonnalinga until they could get spare parts up from Adelaide. They planned to head north once the cars were back on the road or until they ran out of cash. The local mechanic agreed to let them use his workshop for a fee when their spare parts arrived. With that organised after their rest and lunch, they spent a lazy afternoon before showing up in the bar an hour before closing, showered, shaved and in clean clothes, preceded by wafts of expensive cologne.

Dudley bumped into them dressed in shorts and a raw-fat and blood-spattered apron carrying a tray of freshly cut steaks. He ran embarrassed fingers through his tousled hair, greasy from butchering the side of fresh-killed beef William Ringer's boys brought in for the drivers' barbecue. Dudley had worked flat out to organise a second 44-gallon drum and large grille to act as a brazier to keep people warm outside at night in the middle of winter. It was rare to see him dishevelled, let alone smelly and grubby as he was. Katherine felt sorry for her dad and offered to butter bread and slice onions and potatoes for the barbecue while Dudley beetled off to shower and change.

After her own shower, Katherine could not decide what to wear. As Dudley asked, she wanted to look her best if she was to be hostess, yet comfortable enough to cook, pull beers, and clean up after the party. The self-pitying notion that she worked as hard as Cinderella did not stop Katherine from wanting to be attractive to these city men who she found worldly even though they wore the same sort of desert boots that Sharmer did. That man. She wished he'd not come to mind. Would they be like Sharmer? Do all men harbour dark and disrespectful ideas about women while smiling to one's face? Or was just the American who thought of Australians, if not as natives, as wild colonials, living on the outskirts of civilisation, as he knew it?

Bugger him. Katherine applied light makeup, not wanting to look like a tart. She took her brown suede jacket from the back of the wardrobe and rubbed her hands over its softness to see its colour change. She hadn't worn the jacket for ages, but it was as good as new, even after enduring extreme outback summers.

The back lawn looked good. Barney had dotted it with trestle tables and chairs under spotlights that threw an unnatural circle of white light around the space. The lighting was so bright under the gum trees that you had to move out of the ring to appreciate the speckling stars in the night sky, flickering like a million trillion fireflies.

The barbecue was open to all comers who had to pay for food and drink, which didn't stop inquisitive locals from pressing around the visitors. Katherine took a moment to check everything before looking for Lillian. Already unsteady on her feet, her mother wore black slacks for a change, with a red jacket matching her long, enamelled fingernails. She was playing kitten with a man she had cornered. The scene brought back bitter memories. Katherine sighed, anticipating a long night.

'Hello, Katherine. What can I get you? You are Katherine, aren't you, the publican's daughter? My name's Eddy. This is Brian. We're both from Sydney and live close to each other on the beach at Bondi.'

Katherine smiled. 'On the actual beach?'

'You know what I mean.' Eddy wasn't at all defensive.

'Well, Bondi's fine, but I'm from Melbourne, so I'm pretty fond of St Kilda beach.' She smiled. 'I'll have a butcher, thanks.' They laughed together at the interstate stupidity of having different names for beer glasses.

'So, what brings you to a place like this?' Eddy asked.

'I could ask you the same thing,' Katherine retorted.

'Be serious. This is the first time we've been so far into the outback of this country, and to find a pretty girl like you, a Melbourne girl at that, living here, comes as a surprise.'

'I came with Mum and Dad. For a better life.'

'And?'

'And what?' Katherine was uncomfortable, unused to what seemed like genuine interest. Unwilling to discuss the disturbing things weighing on her mind, Katherine asked herself why she was still here, and not for the first time. There hadn't been a moment till now to think about it. With Lillian heading towards alcoholic oblivion and Dudley, well, taking them all to the poor house, her family was disintegrating, and she was often scared. Katherine bent down to pat Paws to hide her discomfort. He rarely left her side unless he was with her mother, who spoilt him rotten.

'I'm sorry, we're sorry, we didn't mean to pry.' Eddy sounded sincere. 'Let me get you that beer. Back in a moment.'

Brian smiled. 'Eddy didn't mean to be impudent. He's a good fellow. We're both interested in the people we meet along the way.' He chattered on, telling her they were sponsored by Holden. Brian was the driver, and Eddy, the navigator. They met at university, where they both studied medicine. The rally had been a hard slog for them as rank amateurs. Their adventure would end when they ran out of money because sponsorship didn't cover extracurricular travel. But they'd made a pact to do something exciting together when they qualified, and, well, here they were.

'How long did it take you to become doctors?'

'Four years of study and two years interning in a hospital. Eddy is interested in research and is planning to do a PhD. Ah! Here he is now. Cheers, everyone.'

Katherine relaxed with Brian and Eddy as far as she could while keeping her eye on Lillian. Dudley tried to keep an eye on Lillian too but soon had to attend to guests when it was time to serve the barbecue. He had decided to do it the easy way, no plates, no salads; just meat, potatoes and onions on bread with Rosella Tomato or Worcestershire sauce to taste. Fresh fruit and vegetables wouldn't be replenished till Friday morning's Ghan arrived. Tomorrow, Dudley announced by way of an apology, he would make sure the boys would have the pub's most excellent roast beef with baked root vegetables then. 'Mum's baked potatoes are the crispest you'll ever taste,' he promised.

'It won't be Mum cooking.' Katherine had seen her mother fall. After refusing food, Lillian was legless.

'Mum, you're making a fool of yourself.'

'Who do you think you are talking to,' Lillian said in her pompous voice. Had it been anyone other than Katherine with the temerity to criticise, they would have been the butt of Lillian's — *I'm the publican's wife* routine — when she spoke as if hers was the highest office in the land. Tonight, she surrendered when Katherine said she'd take her to the toilet and put her to bed.

Over the next few days, Katherine took Eddy to the waterhole where she and Gregory first had sex. Brian stayed back to drink in the bar with others. 'Getting to know the locals', he said with a wink and a knowing grin. They were quiet fellows, and she would miss them when they left, especially Eddy, who was an attentive and kind lover. Being with him was healing, but there was no future in it. In the evening, all three would sit together on the verandah, Katherine content to listen as they reminisced about their university days, talked about their aspirations in medicine and laughed, recalling the antics of erstwhile university flatmates in the magic of the desert nights. They became pensive when they spoke of their families.

Brian and Eddy reminisced about listening to live jazz blues on rainy Saturday afternoons in smoky downstairs bars in Sydney and the buzz of rummaging in city bookshops. These genteel and eloquent city men brought the whole world closer, made it sound exciting. Katherine thrilled to their tales about the novelty and wonder of television, which she'd not yet seen. The kind attention they paid to her and each other shocked Katherine. She couldn't believe she'd become so accustomed to the harsh and often foul ways men spoke to her in the bush, or at least in the pub.

Tuning out, Katherine recalled how devastated she had been when Lillian forced her to relinquish her beloved books as a ten-year-old. Dudley's gambling had meant that the Forsters were on the move, and Lillian convinced her she didn't need them anymore. Katherine cried. She loved her books and pretended the characters were her friends. She missed May Gibbs's little gum nut babies, the horrid banksia men and Enid Blyton's *Famous Five* books that her nanna had given her before she died. Those books led her to become an avid reader as a child, to the extent that wherever they lived, the local library gave her a special dispensation to take out multiple books, far more than other children. As she got older, she would search every corner of every library to find texts that she could barely comprehend but whose ideas came through the complexity, such as Sir Julian Huxley's notion of secular humanism. His brother, Aldous Huxley's *Brave New World*, frightened her because it spoke of social forces beyond human control, as did Fyodor Mikhailovich

Dostoevsky's book, *The Idiot*. That was her favourite book of all time, for she identified with the main character's doubts and fears and the insanity that ensued. The book also spoke of death in intriguing ways, not a topic that many people wanted to think about, but one that fascinated Katherine.

That night, Katherine did not go to her room when the drivers said their goodnights. Instead, she went directly to the back lawn outside the laundry. There, on the cold, damp grass far from prying eyes, the young woman wrapped herself in the beauty of the earth's silence in which even her parents seemed like strangers. The rally drivers came from caring families and were clear about what they wanted from life. She'd never imagined a future for herself, one that might let her explore things she liked. The idea was utterly new. What did she want? For herself? Everyone expected her to find a husband, which, so far, she had spectacularly failed to do yet, for the first time in her life, Katherine felt the stars twinkling with promise, just for her.

21

'Your mum and I talked to Lou a while back, you know when we felt it was best to get you away for a while?' Dudley laughed. 'Lou's alright. You don't want to stay with Elizabeth, my eldest sister. You'll more than likely meet her, but she's the toffy one in the family, or reckons she is because she's the tea lady at the ABC.'

Katherine wasn't interested in Elizabeth, or Lou for that matter. She was still upset that her father refused to acknowledge or even refer to the incident at the claypan. There was not the slightest hope of receiving an apology from either he or Lillian for their betrayal after the William Ringer affair. When Dudley went on to say with pride that Lou's son, Christopher, was in the Army now, Katherine experienced that familiar resentment. Always the boys! Dudley made no secret about having wanted a son. That her father favoured the boys was like a smack in the face every time he fussed over or praised Jimmy, a stranger, not her. The unfairness stuck in her throat like bile. Now Dudley was all praise for Christopher, a boy he'd not seen since he was a baby, just because he was male. OK, Christopher chose the same path as Dudley when he joined the Army. She'd join the Army if they'd let her, but girls were not admitted. They couldn't sign up, certainly not for combat. Dudley acted as though Lillian had let him down by giving him a girl rather than a boy. Could it be that is why Lillian resented her at times? Did she also feel like a failure because she had a daughter, not a son? Katherine was prepared to think the worst but forced herself to stop worrying. She wanted to get away, and that was that.

'Did you hear me, Katherine?'

'Yeah.' Ever since the Ampol drivers left, Katherine had been unsettled. Their departure created a vacuum that nothing could fill. She missed their soft-spoken city voices and vibrant talk of ambition, hope and confident lives. Was it only men who felt like that? Were only men permitted to dream, educated city men, from good families?

Aunty Lou's invitation had come at the right time. Katherine restrained an impulse to fling herself with gratitude into her father's arms, but she didn't want to betray Lillian. Was she becoming as undemonstrative as her mother? Katherine laughed to herself. Her mother's stance on public displays of affection was a joke, especially since Pearl's party. The memory of Lillian with the stationmaster reminded Katherine that she must leave. Her mother was a snob. Yes, she was of the World War II generation. Grew up in British Australia, where everyone spoke the Queen's English (still known as the King's English). Like her forebears, Lillian had spent her life suppressing her needs and desires.

Until now, she ruled over them with an iron will and wanted Katherine to do the same. But, even as she hoped it would salve her pain, the grog undermined Lillian's resolve.

Katherine may wish to be more open than her mother, but her schooling was no more Australian than Lillian's was a generation earlier. School in Katherine's day taught students about England, its Kings, Queens and their British explorers in Australia. White English men became Australia's heroes who died trying to cross the alien Australian landscape. England had trouble making Australia without the help of the Aborigines. Yet, explorers were portrayed brightly in history books that failed to mention women or the Aborigines who helped open the frontiers. Not to speak of the cameleers, finally replaced by the Ghan. One-sided history was not good enough in Katherine's mind.

Photos of colonial women and Aborigines became anonymous adornments to male pioneers. Aboriginal women wore long dresses, and mob caps like downstairs servants in cold English mansions and men were chained together. No wonder Katherine felt shy walking past those old women under the mulga tree when she first arrived in Wonnalinga. Her public-school education failed the very people whose land the British took unto themselves. She now felt ashamed of the commendations she'd received at school for her sketches of white explorers' bearded faces. Nobody questioned the fact that women's domestic work and black faces barely existed in the curriculum.

'You'll be right,' Dudley said, 'you'll find a job in a pub quick enough. They're always looking for good barmaids in Sydney.' Dudley read his daughter's diffidence as fear of the unknown, but his eagerness convinced her she was right; Dudley could not wait for her to go. She lost all urge to hug him.

'Does Mum know?'

'Yes, she's thrilled for you. One of the local boys will give us a hand with the Chaser while you're away.'

Again, the stab of hurt. Katherine wanted to get away, but she had hoped her parents might miss her, not act as though they could hardly wait to get rid of her.

The arrangement was that, in Sydney, Katherine was to make her way to the Clock Tower and the taxi rank at the front of the Central Railway Station where Aunt Lou would meet her. It was the first time Katherine had travelled alone and she had never been to Sydney, so it all felt like an adventure. But it was a long trip, starting out from home, where she caught the Ghan back to Adelaide, then the Overland from Adelaide to Melbourne. From there, she took the Spirit of Progress to Albury in New South Wales before changing to the new Southern Aurora for the last leg. The change was necessary because of rail gauge differences that reminded anyone who travelled by train in Australia that the nation started out as a gaggle of colonies. As they taught at school, the federation was not until 1901.

Nothing, not even Spencer Street Station in her hometown of Melbourne, prepared her for Sydney Central. She was in awe as she walked through the giant-domed concourse that greeted passengers from many platforms. She could almost smell the soot and grime as she looked up to the roof. Although it was capacious, Katherine felt as though she was walking through a tunnel illuminated by neon which made her hasten towards the distant daylight, straight past the array of shops and stalls. She noticed Bex and Vincent's APC headache powder signs and, despite her love of books, kept up her pace past a Gordon and Gotch newsstand. Just as she hit the fresh air, there was a tap on her shoulder. Katherine spun round to see a face as familiar to her as Dudley's. Aunty Lou. They stood face to face, admiring each other. Lou was taller than Katherine (and Dudley, for that matter), which forced Katherine to look up, making her aunt appear formidable.

But the unmistakable family resemblance made it seem as though she had known her aunt all her life. The only difference between Lou and Dudley was Lou's dank, streaky grey hair looked as though it had not been washed for several days, something that Dudley would never allow. It didn't smell musty which pleased Katherine, who was every bit as fastidious about hair as her father. Aunty Lou smelled more like her mother, or pubs in general with a beer and tobacco mingle emanating from her crinkled clothes. For Katherine, the smell was comforting, homely. But nobody had taught Lou not to be demonstrative. Katherine's aunt clasped her niece to buxom breasts and planted a wet, firm kiss on her cheek.

'Daaarling.' Lou drawled in a gravelly smoker's voice, deep with raw honesty. 'You look just like your dad, with a little bit of your mum thrown in. I hope you never get as miserable as she's become in recent years. She was a good sort in her day, you know.'

Lou's Sydney accent was the same as Dudley's, but she had a

permanent chuckle in her voice that seemed to well up from the pit of her stomach. Katherine had grown up believing the Forster girls had no education. Lillian liked to compare them unfavourably with her own forebears, who counted a lawyer and a wealthy businessman among their ranks. Lillian's family once owned half of East Melbourne until a shyster lawyer, as Katherine's nana called him, managed to tie up an entailed will that almost cut Lillian's mother out. The lawyer then retired to Emerald, where he lived, rich but quite mad, writing long political letters to the press on toilet paper until he died. The only thing that Lillian's mother and her three daughters inherited was an East-Melbourne sense of respectability that had them gossiping about Dudley's sisters. They hinted that the Forster girls were prostitutes.

Katherine picked her bag up and looked for a vacant taxi.

'Not that way, Luv,' said Lou, 'we're off to the tram. Then, at Wyndham, we'll change to a train and, from Epping Station, we catch another bus, then we walk. Uphill. I hope your case is not too heavy as I'm a bit old to help. You can have a little snooze on the train if you like.'

Tired from days of travel, Katherine felt her optimism droop with her flagging energy, but she followed her aunt across the road as instructed. At least she didn't have to worry about how to find North Ryde by herself.

Katherine's early months in Sydney were happy. At first, she felt so close to her aunt she began to believe she loved her more than Lillian. She had hoped to look up Eddy and his Ampol mates but had received a letter days before she left for Sydney, saying he had a fiancée. He hoped that Katherine would wish him well. The disappointment was fleeting because living with Lou, who called her darling and brought cups of tea to wake her up for work in the morning, softened the blow. And she had a new city to explore. Still, it showed, class will out. Katherine tried not to compare herself with what she imagined would be a private-school educated girl who would be the right stuff to marry a doctor. Katherine felt for a moment as though she'd been nothing more to Eddy than the publican's daughter, an outback curio.

Katherine soon found employment with Canley Providores near Sydney's Paddy's Market. At school, she passed Dacomb shorthand and touch typing with a 100% mark. The certificate came in handy. Falling a little in love with her teacher had made her try hard in his class, unlike the sewing teacher. That old cow made her feel as though she should crawl under a door and flee.

Katherine's new boss was a middle-aged man who, like her shorthand teacher, was kind but walked around the office hitching up his trousers and giving his crotch a little fondle from time to time. Katherine reckoned she'd seen the lot with men, but this was new. It was hard to hide the giggles that gurgled inside her, but he was a gentleman, so she soon settled in. Her boss arranged for her to be trained on the switchboard, telling his office manager that Katherine was a bright little thing and should be given a go.

She loved working the switchboard and talking to customers. Her pub training, working with people, kicked in, and she was popular with customers. Being in charge of cords on the switchboard and wearing headphones gave her a sense of pride. She took messages and orders, transferring calls without ever mixing up the cords. Among her regulars was a soldier from the Ingleburn Army Camp. His warm, mellow voice excited Katherine when he rang every week to place his order. He flirted, and she liked that, marvelling at the way strangers could form an attachment from the sound of their voices. Katherine agreed to meet him one day with unresolved hopes of marriage until he let slip that his wife was pregnant.

Lou's son Christopher visited his mother from time to time, always wearing his khaki uniform. The young man's face was oval, not square like his dad's, and he had red hair that was not on either side of his family. He was a strange-looking fellow. Katherine couldn't take to him; he was nothing like a Forster (well, he was a Crocker, really). Lou claimed that Christopher took after his father, but Katherine was not convinced. Lillian's family's unkind words about Dudley's sisters being prostitutes came back to Katherine, but she never asked her aunt about such things because she loved her, and Lou adored her son whoever the father might be.

Knowing that Christopher could any day be deployed, taken away just like that, as Lou said, she was generous to a fault with her son. She dipped into private cash reserves squirrelled from a meagre housekeeping allowance. Her husband, Jock Crocker, was jealous of his own son, so different to Dudley and younger men. Although he held it in until the boy left the house and was well out of hearing, he fired up even more for the waiting.

Every day, he'd explode, screaming cruel and unkind things at Lou about the way she treated her son, kept house, and drank. He always referred to Christopher as her son, not our son. Lou cringed from the man and sometimes whimpered before him. What Jock said was true. Even the seating arrangements at the table favoured Christopher, displacing Jock from the head of the table where he liked to sit, from where he could demand dinner, dessert, a cup of tea and anything else he wanted.

Jock had black moods and hit Lou often. Katherine saw it herself one day when Lou came home out of the blue to announce that she had signed up to work at Lifesavers, a lolly factory that produced Peppermint and Spearmint Lifesavers and Katherine's favourites, Fruit Tingles. 'Lifesavers,' Lou would say with a smutty giggle of the sort that kept the girls at the factory going, 'the lolly with the hole'. Jock refused permission for her to work. Her defiance sent him into a crushing rage. Katherine looked on helpless as he took to Lou with his fists, pummelling her on the back of the head before squeezing her neck till she fainted. Lou was still groggy when Jock pulled her back onto her feet, yanking at her arms before landing several hard punches on her chest and stomach. Lou crumpled to the floor in tears, rocking back and forth with her arms around her knees. Jock strode from the house, slamming the door behind him. To reassure Katherine, who stood trembling in the kitchen from where she saw it all, Lou said Jock would not be home for hours.

'Hide in your room, Luv and don't come out until I say. When Jock gets home, he'll be insanely drunk.

Lou never saw Jock again.

22

It wasn't the violence in Lou's household that made Katherine decide to find new lodgings. It was Lou. Although brighter and happier without him, Lou continued to drink herself to oblivion nightly, like Lillian.

Katherine loved Lou for telling stories about her parents when they were young. Dudley's sisters used to worry about their baby brother. They saw the fact that he'd married above himself as an underlying cause of his gambling. Dudley was always trying to impress Lillian, prove himself to her. Katherine knew that phrase from her mother. Lou made out they didn't blame Lillian, who was younger than Dudley and naive about men. But Dudley's constant need to please his wife could even have been to compensate for his failure to satisfy Lillian in bed. Lou gave Katherine a knowing look.

Was Lou inferring that Dudley preferred men? Lillian's family gossiped about that, but Katherine had never seen any evidence. Could that explain why he loved Jimmy so much? If it was true, did it explain Lillian's drinking? Katherine put the thoughts aside.

When it all boiled down, Katherine left because she wanted independence. She moved into a tiny windowless room on Bondi Beach, right next to the ocean pool. The furniture was sparse but adequate; a small dresser, a dark-stained double wardrobe with a slim mirror on the inside door and a wonky wooden chair where wear-again clothes could be draped. She liked to sit, propped up on her first-ever double-bed to read. She was only a short bus ride away from work in Sydney's China Town. Better than the daily trek from Lou's place — half a mile downhill to the bus stop (uphill at night) then from bus to train at Epping Station to the city and tram from Wynyard along George Street and a final downhill high-heeled hike to Canley Providores.

Most of her wages went on public transport, lodgings, food and smokes, so Katherine often skipped breakfast and lunch. Katherine fainted from hunger in a fish and chip shop one pay night while waiting for a hamburger. Someone called the police. When she came to, the two young constables attending insisted they drive her home. Too tired to argue, she complied, but they followed her to her room. One fellow sat on the little chair. The other chose the end of her bed, his hanging legs about four inches short of the floor. He wriggled his bum into the middle of the bed and lay back on her pillow, arms behind his head. Alert to the reek of arousal, Katherine said yes when they asked if she had a friend as pretty her, so they could all get together one night. They left after that.

Katherine found a second job at The Broadway on George

Street, close to Haymarket, the next day. Within a week, she had enough money to move from Bondi to a little cold-water flat in Rushcutters Bay. It was an upgrade with its green enamel, coin-operated gas stove — two burners, but no double bed. Katherine bought a set of bed linen, a towel and tea towel, a few cooking utensils and a one-bar radiant heater and began to enjoy herself in Sydney.

On the way home from work each night, she alighted from her bus at a different spot in Kings Cross. Her first love was the El Alamein Fountain, a WWII memorial commissioned in 1961; the architect, Brian Woodward, himself a veteran. His inspiration was the dandelion. He'd engineered the fountain to refract various colours during the day, and it was floodlit by night. To Katherine, it was lovelier than the ubiquitous brass depictions of suffering young men in slouch hats. The dandelion reminded her of her childhood, blowing dried flowers down concrete lanes in Melbourne with a wish or watching them spin into a million florets in the wind. Sitting on the steps of the fountain at night, she felt protected.

The boss let her take a private call at work one day. Lou told her through tears that Christopher had been killed in Vietnam. Katherine asked for time off to go to her aunt. By the time she reached Lou's place, it was filled with well-wishers. She didn't stay long. Although not grieving, Katherine wanted time to reflect on the enormity of her cousin's death. She visited the fountain where she remembered Dudley's stories about New Guinea in WWII. His father died at the end of WWI from stomach cancer caused, the Forsters declared, by 'the gases.'

Now, a new generation was paying the price for someone else's war.

In the coming weeks, Lou lost her mind. Katherine, who kept an eye on her aunt, was sure of that as she saw Lou sink deeper into alcoholic despair, drinking day and night till rows of empty Toohey's bottles stood three-deep around her chair like sentinels. The ashtray next on her aunt's little coffee table overflowed with butts. Lou stared into space. The booze may well have numbed her against an abusive husband, but its power diminished in the face of this catastrophic loss.

Neither Lou nor the army had been able to find Christopher's father to tell him that his only son was dead at 21. Christopher had always wanted to join the army, but he almost missed his chance with the Royal Military College, Duntroon, when he jumped in a car one crazy night to drive without aim as though he wanted to be caught. Looking back, as you do in grief, Lou told Katherine she should have seen this as a sign, a warning that her son did not want to go to war, that it was not right for him to go to Vietnam, that the war itself was wrong. Now, she raged at the court that was lenient with Christopher, for only seeing a lad from a poor background who wanted to step up by winning entry to the College, a lad aching to serve, to become an officer and leader of men. It seemed irrelevant and possibly trivial in the face of death, but Katherine couldn't help but question whether such leniency would have been shown to a girl under any circumstance.

As time went on, Katherine saw less and less of Lou and spent more time exploring Sydney. Her latest walk took her past the new Les Girls nightclub and cabaret. It brought on the familiar frisson of fear and excitement she felt when walking past the Aboriginal women back in Wonnalinga. The unknown was dangerous, somehow. A man called Abe Saffron owned Les Girls and Dudley, raised in the slums of Sydney, always spoke of him with a mixture of disgust and admiration. He called Saffron one of the biggest crooks in Australia. The giant posters outside the venue boasted men dressed as women — in drag as they called it — wearing giant feathers, pearls and high heels on high-kicking, fishnet-stockinged legs. It all added to the charm of Sydney, like walking home along Darlinghurst Road among the diverse parade of bohemians, artists, soldiers, foreigners — Italians and Greeks — beggars and prostitutes. For Katherine, schooled in ignorance of anything but a white Australia and its British heritage, it was thrilling to discover that so many other worlds and different ways of being existed.

For extra money, Katherine worked three nights a week and on Saturdays at The Broadway Hotel on George Street, where she learned of Beatrice Miles, now retired to the Little Sisters of the Poor Home for the Aged in Randwick (a name Katherine learned through Dudley's gambling because of the racecourse there). B Miles came from a middle-class family and had a university education that she soundly criticised for its lack of Australian content. Katherine identified with her stance because she was aware of the same absence from her own schooling.

Everyone at the Broadway remembered B Miles with a sad smile. She'd lived a bohemian lifestyle, but her love affair with an unsuitable man so enraged her father, he had her committed in her early twenties to the Gladesville Hospital for the Insane. That saddened Katherine. On her release, B became the eccentric everyone remembers. She used to jump into the front seat of a taxi when it pulled up at a stoplight and would refuse to get out until she reached her destination. She did not pay. She recited Shakespeare anywhere for sixpence. B dressed in shabby clothes and wore gloves with fingertips cut off, yet Katherine admired her for being forthright. Katherine found herself bewitched by this unlikely heroine, a woman who would have hated pity, a woman out of place for standing up for what she cared about.

Talking with customers about B Miles made work at The Broadway easier than it otherwise was. Regular working men in the front bar were kind to Katherine, and the boss appreciated her experience. But Katherine didn't like him because he expected his barmaids to wring runner dregs into a bucket at the end of their shift. Not all staff were as careful about wastage as Katherine. But deducting from their pay for every fluid ounce he squeezed from towelling runners was unfair because they weren't even changed between shifts half the time. Dudley would drop dead if he knew this publican poured spirit and wine dregs (from glasses without mixers) back into bottles to be re-sold. That was disgusting, but it was no good reporting it. Health inspectors would probably remain schtum for a backhander. The man served slops. He leered at the girls and laughed with male customers he called mate.

On one of her regular visits to the Cross, Katherine saw Gregory Sharmer crossing Darlinghurst Road near the fountain.

The next day, and for about a week afterwards, she found herself at the fountain, hoping he might show up again, despite her avowal to Paddy that she would never see the man again. Katherine seriously doubted her reasons for this, but she was curious to see him again after reading his diary.

She soon forgot about Gregory Sharmer when the naval seaman she'd often noticed watching her found the courage to sit next to her. They started meeting on weekends to walk around Fitzroy Gardens hand in hand. He introduced himself as Rob Kelly. 'Everyone calls me Ned,' he said with a grin, 'as in Ned Kelly, the bushranger.' Rob was a quiet fellow, a bit naive, but Katherine liked him. He treated her like a lady, which was a nice change.

23

On quiet weekends, Katherine haunted the Garden of Wonders, a second-hand bookshop in Kings Cross. Her childhood love of books, their smell, and their promise of learning still made her feel like she was among friends when she browsed. It was a funny little shop with book-lined shelves from floor to ceiling. Surrounding benches overflowed with paperbacks, hardbacks, first editions, antiquarian texts, collectors' items, and stories from around the world. A foreign language section catered to students and Sydney's growing migrant population. Most books were arranged by topic then alphabetically by author, but some chaotic sections shelved tall, thin books like atlases alongside short, fat poetry collections, defying any logic of order. For Katherine, every shelf overflowed with promise.

Intrigued by young city people who had begun to overthrow the rigidities of their parents' generation, Katherine chose a soft covered book printed like a comic, portraying the new hippy movement abroad. It helped her appreciate the lyrics of her favourite singer, Bob Dylan; the times they are 'a changing'. More particularly, it explored women's growing demand for independence.

One day, long after she had stopped worrying about running into Gregory Sharmer, the American appeared again. He showed no surprise at seeing Katherine. His sudden appearance gave Katherine the creeps. To think that he might have been watching her, stalking, waiting for his moment to pounce, just as he had in Wonnalinga.

'I thought you'd have gone back to America by now.' Katherine pretended to search for something in her handbag to prevent the mix of disgust and lust from showing on her face. Knowing about his carnal knowledge of the little Aboriginal girl repelled at this moment, when he may well be aroused. Recovering her equilibrium, Katherine looked up at Sharmer with an inner smirk. It would never have crossed his mind that she had read his diary.

'It won't be long now. I've booked my fare. Shall we have a drink to catch up on old times?'

'Not now. The pubs close soon.' Katherine could see that he'd asked her against better judgement. That made her curious, but not enough to stay. She wanted to get home to her sailor. Then the words came out, 'How about you come to my place on Saturday, around 7 pm. I've got a couple of friends coming.' Fear gripped Katherine, but it was too late to retract. Why in god's name did she do that? She gave Sharmer her address, and they parted.

She didn't tell Sharmer that Constable Johnstone would

be at the party. It had shocked Katherine to hear from Barry Johnstone, who claimed that Dudley gave him her phone number. He was only in Sydney for a few days to return a thirteen-year-old runaway to his parents. The silly kid found himself penniless and starving instead of becoming the stockman of his dreams. Not yet having the presence of mind to knock Johnstone back when he asked to meet her, Katherine invented a party, thinking she'd be safer to see him in the company of others. She invited all the girls in her building who so far had been oddly standoffish. None of them showered in the morning before work like she did which was weird, and she hardly saw them during the day.

Katherine couldn't understand why she'd invited either man to a party she didn't want and couldn't afford. Deep down, a perverse curiosity told her she wanted to see how the two men would behave in each other's company. The last time they saw each other was when Johnstone was mercilessly kicking an Aboriginal man with his Sergeant while Sharmer looked on, hands in pockets till he vanished on a plane. Well, that's how she thought of the incident now. She'd never heard what it was all about.

On the morning of the party, Katherine woke with a stinging nose, like a thousand ants were crawling in it, and a burning throat. If she had any idea how to reach everybody, she'd have cancelled. She dragged herself out of bed to clean the flat and, by mid-afternoon, had a blinding headache and was shivering with fever.

Her place was not much bigger than a single hotel room. It had a single bed with a blackened wrought iron bedhead that backed onto a pink and green floral curtain. The curtain hid the stove in a strange little corner. God knows where anybody would sit. Still, Katherine set a vase of flowers on the chest of drawers in front of the solitary, boarded-up window as a finishing touch. She tried, unsuccessfully, to get some rest.

As the time for visitors drew close, Katherine examined her face in the mirror for the umpteenth time, checking for weeping mascara or lipstick dribble at the corners of her mouth. When her mum was drunk, lipstick bled into her wrinkles, and she dreaded the possibility that her face might one day betray her as she ages like Lillian's did.

Ronny from upstairs arrived first with a bottle of Smirnoff vodka that she put next to Katherine's Johnny Walker on a small table, beneath which Katherine had shoved a carton of Toohey's Special Bitter and a few bottles of lemonade. She didn't have a fridge, but, being mid-winter, the drinks would stay cold.

The first knock, more of a bang really, proved to be Barry Johnstone. He turned up, empty-handed. Close on his heels, before the door had closed, Gregory Sharmer appeared carrying a half-empty bottle of Crème de Menthe. Rob was the last to arrive, carrying another carton of Toohey's under his arm. Katherine was horrified to see the way Ronny's eyes lit up when Rob introduced himself. Once they got talking, the girl immediately started using Rob's nickname, Ned, in a coy voice before plonking herself in the middle of Katherine's bed to give the sailor her full attention.

Katherine surveyed the men in the room. She only man she hadn't slept with was the constable, who, even now, did not attempt to conceal his lust. That's why he rang her, thinking she was alone, and he'd be in like Flynn, as they say. In pubs, Katherine had seen all the deceitful motives and moves of men like Johnstone who liked to fuck girls they thought cheap and marry fawning domestic types. As a publican's daughter and barmaid, she knew Johnstone only ever saw her as someone to screw on the side. Cruelty shone in Johnstone's cold, blue eyes as he looked inward, paying attention right now, to his arousal. While Katherine again cursed her father for giving him her phone number, she flushed with pleasure, knowing she gave the cop no chance. Not then, not now.

Gregory had been different. At first, his gentlemanly ways had seduced her, almost into believing he might care. Now, she felt smugly superior to him, with his posh airs. He was a certifiable arsehole. That was the truth of the matter. She felt nothing but healing scorn as she observed the American getting drunk with false exuberance, still trying to mimic his idea of the Aussie bloke. Any last remnant of desire for Gregory left her body at that moment; he was no better than Barry Johnstone. He had never known her, had never been interested in what she wanted in life. He was duplicitous. She had read his diary. It was as though he had just rubbed himself on her to get rid of a dangerous lust that nearly brought him and his precious career undone.

Through her fever, Katherine saw things as though the sun had come out to illuminate what had previously been an airless, windowless room in her mind. She stared, but not in disbelief, for she'd believe anything right now as Rob smooched her young neighbour, his unabashed hand crawling up Ronny's skirt on her bed. Almost hysterical in feverish clarity, Katherine began laughing hysterically. She turned the music up loud to blast all the shit from her consciousness, then passed out on the floor.

'Katherine, Katherine, answer the bloody door!' Gregory was slapping her cheeks. 'Wake up; you've got visitors.'

The hammering on the door persisted. Katherine roused herself enough to open it, wondering why the hell one of the others couldn't have done that.

'Turn the fucking music down.' A demand from two tall, strong women from upstairs who Katherine had never seen before. They threatened to call the landlord if she didn't do as they said right now.

'You can tell the bloody landlord for all I care; he's a slimeball.' Her feverish drunken slur reminded Katherine of her mother. 'That man pisses around in my room while I'm at work, rummaging through my drawers, the old perv.'

'Tell him that yourself.' The women turned as the landlord appeared. Anticipating resistance, they'd called him to force Katherine to turn the volume down.

The landlord turned on Katherine before she had a chance to speak. 'Other people live here who need some quiet, you selfish little slut,' he said.

'Fuck of you, you sleazy old bastard!' She turned to the women from upstairs, 'And you, you two, you are nothing but prosti- tutes.' Ronny, new to the game herself, had told Katherine that all the women in the house were prostitutes. The landlord was their pimp.

'We might be prostitutes, Luv, but you're nothing but a charity fuck.' One woman leaned in, threatening to punch Katherine.

'Go on then, go on. Hit me, you cowards.'

'Not here, not inside, come outside, you little cunt.'

On the street outside, Katherine shaped up to the two women. Ronny stayed behind in Katherine's flat, not wanting the other prostitutes to think she took sides. The three men at Katherine's party formed a semi-circle around her, egging her to keep taunting the women. In her fury, an image of Lillian floundering around the Hills Hoist on Myall Station came to mind, increasing Katherine's bravado.

'Go on. Hit me if you're game.'

Minutes later, Katherine woke up by herself on wet bitumen, vomiting and unable to stand.

Constable Barry Johnstone, Gregory Sharmer and Rob, the little matelot who wanted to be a bushranger but fucked her only friend in the house, had vanished. She tried to sit up, her face smarting from a king hit. One well-aimed punch to the head had knocked Katherine unconscious. It could have killed her. She struggled to the park opposite her block of flats and collapsed on a bench. For over an hour, she sat alone, shivering in the misty rain until her hair and clothes were soaked. Frozen through to her soul, Katherine willed herself to get up and go back inside.

As soon as she lay on her bed, Katherine passed out again from the grog, the flu, the punch. She woke the following day to the stench of alcohol and cigarettes, the once comforting smell of home now poisonous with bad intentions, negative emotions and the absence of care. A member of the Royal Australian

Navy, a police constable and an academic — the establishment, you might say — had left her unconscious in the street. Nobody called an ambulance. Nobody bothered to help her back to her flat. They were all more concerned with their reputations than what would happen to a publican's daughter.

There was a knock at the door. This time, the landlord stood facing Katherine with a smirk. He ordered her to vacate his premises immediately. 'This is a reputable house,' he said, 'we don't need trouble-making from ignorant shits like you.'

Katherine rang her old rooming house at Bondi, thanking heaven that they had a spare room. With her meagre belongings packed into her now-battered suitcase, she called a taxi. The driver kindly helped her get her and her fan, heater and record player out of Rushcutters Bay before lunch. She didn't bother cleaning the room and left her few cooking things behind but no forwarding address.

She slept all day and into the night on her Bondi double bed in the room she'd recently vacated. On Monday, it was back to work. The right side of her face was swollen from forehead to jaw and beginning to blacken. When anyone asked what had happened, she laughed and told them a prostitute had king-hit her. Everyone laughed. Then she said, 'Nah, I actually opened a door while carrying too many parcels, and it flew back and hit me in the cheek with the sharp wooden edge.' They believed that.

A week later, a letter arrived from Pearl saying Lillian was doing OK, considering.

Pearl and Barney were waiting for Katherine at the Wonnalinga airport next to their Cortina, now more a trusty rust-bucket than the shiny new red car that had greeted the Forster family when they first arrived. The desert is harsh on Duco. Katherine waved, her heart lifting as she walked towards them. She relished the warm, dry embrace of the bush. For the first time, with newfound clarity, she understood why Pearl couldn't drive. The town had this couple all wrong. It wasn't that Pearl henpecked 'poor old Barney' as they said, but he, like other amiable male souls, enjoyed the power to constrain his wife by pretending to look after her. Being her chauffeur instead of teaching her to drive kept Pearl dependent. No good saying anything to Pearl, of course, she would laugh it off and say she'd never wanted to learn, that it was men's business or some such. Pearl would've had Barney's meals on the table, as and when he liked them without fail, breakfast, lunch and dinner, every day since the day they married. How many years would that be? It made Pearl feel needed, that fuzzy, slightly confused emotion felt by women who never take a day off from sacrificing their needs for others. What would happen to Barney if Pearl became ill?

Pearl opened her arms to Katherine. Although a little taken aback by the older woman's enthusiasm, Katherine responded. She needed that warm embrace.

24

'Where's Mum?' Katherine had expected her mother to be in the kitchen. As soon as she got home from Sydney, she'd resumed breakfast cooking and the laundry chores. Grace still did the lunches with her, but Lillian had taken the dinners back as a cost-saving measure. Katherine hoped this meant her mother was returning to normal. Once, she would have suspected it was so that Lillian could be close to the bar. Now, her mum drank less often.

'She'd be over at Pearl and Barney's place,' Dudley replied. 'She's been going there quite a bit since you left. She missed you until Pearl started dropping by, and soon you'd find the two of them talking all afternoon in the dining room. Your mum goes there a lot.' Dudley repeated in a plaintive tone.

Like Lillian, Katherine had come to like Pearl despite her erstwhile pushy ways. Katherine found that nothing was as simple as it may appear on the surface when trying to understand people. It was not that they changed. They were often not what they pretended to be. One's initial perception of them could prove wrong. Mary Beaming, for example, used to visit Lillian a lot when they first arrived, almost every time she came to town. Lillian and Katherine had assumed a blossoming friendship but, since the New Year's Eve party at the station, Mary only visited the pub to find Lillian when there was not another soul in town with whom she could binge. Lillian was her last resort. As a friend, Pearl was totally different. The more trouble Lillian got herself into, the kinder Pearl became. Katherine remembered how gracious Pearl had been when she apologised for her behaviour at the stationmaster's party. 'That's all right, love,' was all she said.

Katherine let Dudley know that she was going to bob over to Pearl's for a bit. The house was empty, but she'd prepared soup and cold cuts on standby for casuals. Being on the phone, Dudley turned away from Katherine with an irritable shoosh, bringing the mouthpiece to his lips as though to kiss it behind cupped hands. He was placing a bet with his SP bookie.

'Knock, knock,' Katherine shouted, straining to see through flywire down the long corridor of Pearl and Barney's house. Pearl left both the front and back doors open to the rising and dying sun. In summer, when temperatures often went over 100° Fahrenheit, doors all over Wonnalinga stayed wide open to catch the slightest breeze. Nobody locked their doors. Pearl's polished linoleum shone in the setting sun like a sheet of dark glass, a reminder for Katherine to wax the pub corridor soon. It looked as though nobody had waxed it since she left for Sydney.

'Come in, we're in the kitchen,' Pearl's voice was strangely high-pitched, and she spoke fast.

Katherine had expected Lillian to be drunk, but she was sipping a cup of tea. Pearl offered Katherine a fresh scone. She loved to bake, and her scones were prize-winningly famous from Port Augusta to Alice Springs and beyond.

'Jam and cream are on the table. Put the cream back in the fridge after, so it doesn't go off. Even in this weather, it can go fast when it's whipped. The jam's good. I made it myself.'

Instead of the expected female bar-banter, Lillian and Pearl sat in silence, watching Katherine devour a couple of scones. When the scones crumbled, she got flustered, but it didn't stop her delighting in the sweet, vanilla-flavoured cream. The air around the table reverberated with unspoken words and half-told secrets. Katherine felt she should apologise for intruding. It was clearly not a good time to burden Pearl.

'Mum, I'll head off now. I only popped over to tell you not to worry about coming home for dinner because there aren't any customers.'

'Wait, I'll come with you now, love,' Lillian emptied her cup with a glance at Pearl.

Lillian and Katherine said goodbye and headed across the main road to the pub. Lillian looked up at the hotel sign reading 'The First and Last Hotel, Licensees Dudley and Lillian Forster' then turned to Katherine. 'We haven't done too badly here, have we?'

'No, Mum, we haven't.' Lillian's gentle demeanour was uplifting, but it left Katherine feeling a little apprehensive. Would it continue? Although Lillian drank less, Dudley had warned Katherine when she got home that her mother's binges, when they did come, were more excessive than ever and becoming dangerous. A few weeks ago, Lillian fell asleep in bed with a lit cigarette and came close to burning the hotel down. Dudley didn't discover it until he got up for the lavatory in the middle of the night. By then, the mattress had smouldered for hours, filling the corridor with noxious smoke from beneath Lillian's door.

He'd dragged her to a spare room and put her to bed, all by himself, he said. The mattress was too hot to handle straight away. All he could do was douse the smouldering thing with buckets of water. At dawn, he woke one of the young stockmen, a new boy in the area who wouldn't be a tattletale, to help him load it onto the Jeep. Together, they carted it to the dump on the other side of the railway line outside town, where the lad reported later that it smouldered for days.

After dinner, Dudley took himself off to his yippees to give 'his girls' a chance to catch up. Lillian and Katherine both knew he really wanted time to study his race bible.

Lillian invited Katherine to sit with her on the lawn out the back for a while. 'Bring a blanket,' she said, 'to keep warm.' Lillian spread a rubber-backed rug on the grass to keep the damp out and ants off their legs. Once they had settled, Lillian lit a cigarette, inhaled long and deep and began to speak, her voice low and deliberate. She started by telling Katherine she would always be able to count on Pearl Napper if ever she was in trouble.

'Pearl has had a tough life. Did you know that she had a daughter called Rose?'

Katherine shook her head.

'Nor did I, but she told me about her today. Rose was a beautiful girl who, as she blossomed into womanhood, got stuck into the grog. It was her undoing. Men who didn't want to go with Aboriginal women went to her for sex. She was gullible. While gossip had it that she had charged the men like a prostitute, Pearl insisted she didn't. Her daughter was too drunk to know what she was doing half the time. Of course, women, especially station women, gave Rose a wide berth but what upset the girl most was that the men she slept with ignored her in public when they were sober.

'All Rose ever wanted, Pearl told me, was to be loved. Like all girls, Rose yearned for a husband and family, but the way the bush people treated her became too much. She hung herself on the back verandah of Pearl and Barney's house five years ago. Today is the anniversary. Pearl had just finished telling me the whole sorry tale when you turned up. We'd not long moved from the verandah back to the lounge for that cuppa. Have you ever seen Pearl's loungeroom?'

At the mention of the verandah, all Katherine could see for a moment was her mother's disgrace there. How could Pearl live on the site where her daughter took her own life?

'Take time one day to see what's on Pearl's mantelpiece. There's an artificial floral display around Rose's portrait, and the window ledge is lined with dolls and other childhood memorabilia. The wall is smothered in framed family photos of innocent days. Pearl told me that Rose was a clever child and a happy adolescent, but this country, this hard, hot outback place got to her, and that's why I am telling you, my dear girl.' Lillian turned to Katherine and held her face in her hands, close to her own. 'I don't want this country to get you like that. Please take care, my darling Katherine.'

Katherine was in tears by the time Lillian stopped speaking. It was odd to hear from her mother that Pearl's house was a virtual shrine to her lost daughter. How forgiving of Pearl to be kind to Lillian and her. Lillian had not been the only one to abuse Pearl's hospitality at the stationmaster's party. Katherine didn't ask whether Pearl ever told Lillian what happened with Moretti but guessed not because her mother still seemed ignorant of the whole thing. How the story had not been used to destroy the Forster family was a mystery. It didn't occur to Katherine that people might have remained silent to protect her. It remained a puzzle, too, that she was never arrested for beating Moretti. Then again, it could be that the police had silenced everyone to defend themselves. They were both pissed as farts.

Katherine wanted to hug her mother but refrained because of Lillian's resistance to any affectionate display. Even though her mother was relaxed and open, it was not worth the risk of a rebuff.

'There are things here,' Lillian kept her voice low, 'dark forces that people like us from the city cannot understand. We don't know the rules. I think it's time for you to think about leaving home for good, my girl. You're old enough to make your way in the world. You don't have to run off straight away but think about what you'd like to do. I'd like to see you get the hell out of here before... Well, I've said enough. Come on, time for a beer, let's have one together tonight hey?'

25

'Mum's not up yet.' Katherine greeted Pearl.

'That's good cos I wanted to catch you on your own to invite you to bring Aunt Evelyn and Grace to my place.'

'Well, thank you but, why? What's the matter?

'You can bring them to my place any time, whether or not I'm home. Barney won't care. Just make yourself at home. Tongues won't wag about what can't be seen under that mulga tree. At my place, you can relax and talk as much and as loud as you like. Also, Aunt Evelyn may want to share things that she'd be uncomfortable saying in front of others. You never know.'

It came as a surprise that Pearl knew a lot about Aboriginal people, not because of her innate curiosity, which caused her to gossip at times, but from her daughter's friendship with Paddy's family before she died.

Pearl sat herself down at the kitchen table, facing Katherine. 'See if you can get your head around this. Aunt Evelyn and

Paddy are brother and sister. Both are elders in the area. But, because they had different fathers, they were separated as little ones. Evelyn grew up and lives in the Aboriginal town camp in the lane behind the pub. Her father was white, so she went to school. Paddy's parents were both Aboriginal, so Paddy's much darker than Evelyn. He was born and raised out bush and stays in the camp outside town on the flat with other, more traditional, Aborigines. He might be illiterate, but never underestimate him. He is such a wise person and widely respected for his traditional status. You won't know because he always wears a shirt, but his body bears the marks of an elder.' Pearl looked into Katherine's eyes. 'Have you heard about the White Australia Policy?'

'No.' Pearl had her full attention.

'Well, the idea behind it is to keep black and Asian people out of Australia, you know, to keep it white, but it also led to ways of categorising Aboriginal people. Aborigines in the old days were not even classified as human, not really. But, even when they were, authorities described them as a dying race. The idea that you could breed out blackness was popular and probably hasn't fully died out. The government still sorts Aboriginal people one from the other by skin-colour, like they're a species apart: full-blood, half-caste, and quadroon. It's all bloody nonsense. We're not a different species if we can breed with each other, are we? And we can. The government still thinks that white blood will purify the Aborigine — it beggars belief. You'll sometimes hear locals call Aborigines boongs, a word they say derives from the sound of a bull-bar hitting an Aboriginal person when station people used to chase them around in four-wheel drives.

Think about that.'

'That reminds me of the first time I met William Ringer, around the time when you were showing him off as a catch for me!'

'Oh, I am sorry about that. We didn't know you then.'

'It doesn't matter now. That man strode into the kitchen trying to impress Mum and me one day, pissed as a fart. He said with pride that he'd left 'his gin' tied up to an old gidgee tree. I'd never heard that word before, but I guessed straight away it was demeaning from the way he spat it from his mouth. Paddy told me the gidgee is the stinky wattle tree. Anyway, I couldn't believe someone would think they had a right to claim another person as his. His property. Like a slave, I thought. I do not like that man.' Katherine did not confide in Pearl about the claypan incident.

'Well, the truth is, I don't like the man either. He's fathered half the current generation of mixed kiddies in the school here and on his station, just like his father before him. You can ask Grace about that. Ever since the British came to these shores, Aboriginal people have been moved off their land and shoved into settlements and missions. No settler or pastoralist would have been able to get started without their traditional knowledge of the country. Yes, some people's lives took them away from their traditional places of learning, but many, like Paddy, still carry their stories deep within their hearts. They are their stories and, that's got nothing to do with the shade of their skin. The government doesn't seem to get that. Nor did your Mister America, if I may add.' Pearl smiled a curious smile that perturbed Katherine, who hoped Sharmer's diary was hidden well enough.

Despite the sunshine, darkness descended on the moment, making Katherine want to light a cigarette, but she refrained. Chatting at the kitchen table with Pearl was pleasant, and she didn't want to offend. The woman was kind to her mother, and Lillian needed that. Station people and snobs in town saw Lillian as no more than a city woman out of place even though she had grown to love the outback as much as Katherine. Pearl got short shrift from that lot too. And she'd lost her only daughter. Katherine regretted being so dismissive of Pearl with her big spectacles. It didn't surprise her that Lillian and Pearl had become friends. Both women held their whist — as Katherine's nana might have said — and spoke up only in safe company. A bit like the Aboriginal women Katherine had come to know.

One bright day in spring at Pearl's place, Evelyn started talking unprompted about her family. Pearl, who had been sitting with Evelyn, Grace, and Katherine, excused herself.

Evelyn began. 'Me and Paddy are sister and brother. Grace is Paddy's girl, and he is Mother's Brother to my two boys, Sam, my firstborn, and Reggie who was born to my sister. I am a mother to him too. My sister died from chickenpox soon after Reggie was born. Reggie's father was an Afghan man, a cameleer. Old Man Kahn tried to keep the boy, but he took up with a white woman who refused to take on board what she called his Aboriginal brat. That's why Reggie stayed with me, and I raised him with Sam. He's my son in the Aboriginal way, but the authorities still call him Afghan, not an Aborigine like Sam, because of his father. Doesn't matter to them about the mother.'

Evelyn laughed. 'You don't know how many ways that government mucks things up,' she said. 'Take Sam and his dog tag'.

Grace turned to Katherine to interpret. 'The proper name for a dog tag is Certificate of Exemption. It's a piece of paper that promises lots of benefits, as long as holders don't speak their own language. How silly is that? It declares that holders are judged by government officials to be of good character with an acceptable standard of intelligence and development, but it really extinguishes Aboriginal identity. It forces them to break with their family.'

'Names mean nothing,' Evelyn interrupted testily, 'but that tag means the government sees Sam as a white man and no longer an Aborigine. The worst thing is he can't be with an Aboriginal woman unless she is his wife. Now, how is a man going to get a wife if he can't be with her?'

Katherine giggled, as much to hide how she'd felt when Evelyn mentioned Reggie Kahn's name than the older woman's joke. Her mind travelled back to his penetrating black eyes and the way he'd looked at her when they first met at the claypan. She was jerked back into the present. Evelyn's voice commanded silence.

'Now, this is my story. Paddy did not go to school because, in our day, the government said it was a waste to try to educate full-blood Aboriginal children. I got my schooling because my father was a white one. Then, a generation later, we were forced to send our children to school under the threat of having them taken away. There were too many kids taken away. Today, it's a little bit better because black, white and Afghan kids all play together at school as little ones, in Wonnalinga anyway. But it's still tough for people working on stations to follow the rules because they're always droving or on the move for work. Their kids can be taken away for not going to school. Everybody says our people go walkabout, as though moving around is a mental defect which is cruel. We have to follow the work that's on offer for money, such as it is. That's the problem. And people like to work on stations so that they can look after their country. Many carry their stories deep inside. They know their ceremonies and need to stay close to special places, to look after them. If we don't do that, then we lose everything.'

Evelyn paused. Outside, a red and purple sunset bled across the sky. The last streaks of sunlight were streaming through the window, turning Pearl's mustard lounge gold. The lounge room no longer looked quite like the opium den Katherine had imagined when she beat the stationmaster. Now, she could see it as Pearl's valiant attempt to impose elegance on a harsh environment. Katherine felt great warmth towards Pearl, who had shown infinite compassion not only to her but also to Lillian despite watching her daughter spiral out of control in the humpies down the lane. Her precious child, an alcoholic, sleeping with uncouth white men for booze. Indiscriminate men who turned up to take her or any other woman in Aboriginal shelters built out of old kerosene tins beaten flat with galvanised iron castoffs or grass thatch for roofs. The only privacy afforded was behind old hessian wheat bags strung here and there. And here was Pearl, her heart as open as the desert, making space for Katherine to learn from Evelyn. Evelyn started speaking again.

'You'll see in the AIM hospital here, Alice Springs too, black and white people are in the same wards now. But look again. Even the best half-caste women in town, like those married to white men — which sort of makes them a bit higher up, I suppose — are still not allowed to join the Country Women's Association even though everybody greets them in the street. People don't talk about that. No way. There are no rules written down, but you do not see black faces at CWA stalls, do you? And nobody thinks it's strange that there's never been an Aboriginal face inside the hall at the race week ball. There's no law against it. That line between black and white is a bit crooked here and there, but everybody knows where it should be when they come up against it. That's why those boys got beaten up like they did. They stepped on the wrong side, according to the white mob, the bosses. They are still too scared to come back, my boys. Both far away now.'

Evelyn kept talking. Her mention of the claypan incident took Katherine by surprise, and she needed a moment to catch up.

Evelyn's voice softened, and she took Katherine's hand, rapidly changing the subject again. 'You worry about your mum. I can see that. You need to look after her. She could lose her mind. I've seen that before. Nobody told you what happened to her, hey?' As Evelyn spoke, Pearl's words came to mind, *your mother's looking OK, considering.*

'It was that redheaded railwayman. That fettler's from one of the side stations — a bad man that one.' While it had made sense that Lillian had sequestered herself in shame because of gossip about her dancing on the pub roof and swinging on the Hills Hoist at Myall Creek Station. Only now did it make sense to Katherine what her mother was hiding when she spoke about dark forces. It was rape, not gossip, that made Lillian more circumspect in her drinking.

Evelyn continued, ironically sounding a lot like Lillian. 'This country is hard for women; black, white, doesn't matter. It eats their spirit. Many white men, who come here, have a bad past. Criminals maybe? Wife beaters? No education. Rough. There's no culture in them or for them — they're misfits there, they're misfits here — but they believe like all Europeans that white is better than black, and men are better than women. The only safe woman around here is one with a powerful husband or father. Other men respect that. They don't respect women. Before, our people were not supposed to drink, but nothing stopped those rough ones when they wanted sex. They'd bring grog to the camp — town camp mainly — and make everyone drunk, so they could take the girls, sometimes only twelve years old and little, little children saw all that going on behind the hessian bags, drinking, parties, everything. Pearl knows, Barney knows. They lost their girl too. That's all I have to say.'

Katherine sat in stunned silence.

'Aunty, you forgot to say about Paws.' Grace piped up.

'Ah! Yes.' Evelyn waited to catch Katherine's eye.

'You know, we see everything that happens in this town, hear about things from everywhere. No secrets in the bush.' She chuckled. 'But you know that thing happened to your mother before she burnt her hand, what that man did. That's when her mind started to wander, which gave her the accident that sent her away. Paddy felt so sad about your mother's troubles that he searched everywhere for that little dog she asked him to get a long time before. Maybe that old fella did a good thing. Maybe the puppy will help. We'll have to wait and see.'

Katherine chuckled. 'Paws is such a dear little man,' she said. 'Last week, instead of squatting like a girl dog to pee, he stood on tippy-toe on his right leg then lifted his left so high he nearly toppled over. He's certainly growing into the big paws that gave him his name.'

26

Working with Grace in the house halved the workload and was fun for Katherine. They shared tasks or took turns to make beds, polish wardrobes, shine mirrors, vacuum and mop floors. They cleaned bathrooms and toilets daily, alternating who did the ladies and gents. Men peed on the toilet rim, leaving sticky yellow splashes that attracted pubic hairs like a flytrap. Men also left streaks of faeces that glued themselves to toilet rims. It didn't occur to them to use the brush beside the bowl to clean up after themselves. The girls didn't let the stink stop them from laughing as they worked. On the rare occasion when Lillian was up and about before lunch, she'd come to a room, pretending to inspect the girls' work but wanting to join in the fun and hilarity for a few moments. These were happy times for Katherine.

The two also vacuumed and mopped the long corridor daily with Pine-O-Clean, and polished the linoleum with wax once a week by hand. On hands and knees, they'd start waxing at opposite ends using old cotton undies, one pair to apply the wax, the other to make it shine. They raced to see who covered the biggest area, taking turns to start at the front entrance, outside the Ladies Lounge, in case one end or the other posed an inherent handicap.

'I won,' Grace announced, standing up to survey her handiwork.

'By an inch maybe. Well, a foot.' Katherine conceded, feigning shock as she laughed. 'What can we do this afternoon that's a bit different? It's such a beautiful day.' Unlike Lillian, Katherine welcomed the summer heat, even when temperatures soared over 100° Fahrenheit. But she preferred spring with its crisp starry nights and the bright sunny days they were having now.

'Well, how 'bout we go to the old Afghan cemetery after lunch,' Grace suggested.

'Is there one? I had no idea.'

'Yeah. There's not much left of the cemetery, but there are things to see out there. If your legs aren't done in from the polishing, it's about a mile to walk across the gibber, so wear sturdy shoes. And bring water, hey?' Katherine and Grace laughed together. Walking sticks and sore knees were for old women.

'You'd better tell your mum or someone where you'll be too, so, if we're not back by five o'clock, someone can drive out to look for us. You have to do that out in the bush in case a snake gets you or something.' Grace laughed at Katherine's sudden consternation. 'I'll tell Aunty Evelyn. Maybe she might come to chase those snakes away.' The girls went their separate ways to prepare.

Katherine changed into trousers and desert boots that covered her ankles, telling Lillian that she was going for a walk with Grace. Lillian didn't ask where they were off to but suggested they take Paws with them for a treat. Katherine decided against a hat. She loved the wind in her hair, now longer than it had ever been, and the spring sunshine blessing her head. Paws raced ahead and back in excitement as Katherine headed to the agreed meeting place behind the station, where she found Grace and Evelyn waiting.

The older woman led the way, sure-footed, barefooted and silent. Grace wore sandshoes without socks, the sort that makes little plopping sounds with each step. Katherine's desert boots scrunched on the stones. They tended to slide off the big gibber, putting her ankles at risk. Crows cawed in the distance.

'You know,' Grace said. 'That old man Kahn, Reggie's father, his family was one of the first Afghans to come to Australia. Then they moved here from Marree, where there was the biggest and best Afghan settlement in this state. Those old men still wore turbans and funny clothes, but they understood their camels. Those creatures carted food and supplies around the outback. Before the train went all the way, they'd go to Alice Springs too. It must've looked like a train in the desert, too, with packed camels linked together in what they call strings.

'A lot of those men married Aboriginal girls. Some married Chinese, and a few took up with white women. They worked hard and minded their business, building settlements outside the main townships. At first, their mosques were simple mud huts. Those old Afghans didn't mix much. They said their prayers, didn't drink and worked hard. The Afghan names you hear now are all in the Alice Springs cemetery. They're the forgotten people even though they did so much, like the early Chinese who married Aboriginal women. You often find where they lived from creek names. I'd like to know how many Chinaman's Creeks you could find across this country.'

Grace looked to Aunt Evelyn for approval to continue. Their eyes locked knowingly. When Evelyn tilted her head back in answer to the unspoken question, Grace changed the subject.

'My true father is William Ringer's older brother who lives in Alice Springs now.'

Katherine was getting used to the way that, first Paddy, then Evelyn and, now Grace approached a topic obliquely, especially before speaking about profound matters. She was not surprised by Grace's disclosure. Gossip flows through the desert air, and the Ringer stamp was there for all to see on her friend's lovely face. Katherine's heart opened with delight that Grace had enough regard for her to share such an intimate story.

Evelyn walked ahead, giving the girls time alone, Paws at her heels.

'It's all mixed up, you know. Reggie's father was an Afghan man, like I said, which means the authorities treat him more like an Afghan than an Aborigine after his mother. My father's white, and I'm counted as a half-caste. I'm not this and not that. It isn't fair. One good thing that comes out of being half-caste,' Grace spoke with a comical swagger, 'is that I got a proper education down south. Old man Ringer and his wife sent me to a little Catholic School in Adelaide, not Mercedes, where they

209

sent their real daughters, mind you. I stayed with a family that took in foster kids, but I learned to read and write English and matriculated.'

'More than me,' Katherine piped up.

Grace laughed. 'The Ringers said I'd let them down because I didn't go on to become a nurse as they wanted, but I was so lonely for my family and couldn't bear the idea of being away from them for another three years, locked up in some hospital with a mob of strangers. Now, they pretend that I'm the child of some stockman who's gone away. They don't acknowledge me at all.'

Evelyn had settled down for a nap under a shady tree by the time the girls reached the cemetery. Paws rushed over to curl up beside her. Dense clumps of saltbush surrounded a place Katherine could never have found by herself. At first glance, she could see nothing unusual until Grace pointed to ten low earth mounds in a row, some with a few stones on top of them, one demarcated by middle-sized rocks of the same colour. Two rusty iron bed heads, one standing, one fallen, stood as signposts. There was no perimeter fence. An engraved headstone with name and date sat at the head of a tiny, lonely grave set apart from the others. It was the resting place of an Afghan-Aboriginal girl who had died in infancy. Grace explained that the elders told Aunty Evelyn that this was a baby from their mob, a long way back.

'It's as though the Afghan people who lived and died here never existed,' Katherine said out loud, unaware that she had verbalised the eerie sensation that had taken hold of her.

'Yes,' Grace said, 'but you've got all those old date palms up near the police station in town. You've seen those? The Afghans planted them way, way back when there were cameleers all over this country. You have a look, one day. They're a living monument, a testament to the hard work they put in. Their camp was out past the police station, but the palms look back in time; they know who was here.

'Look here,' Grace bent down to pick up thick shards of glass and pieces of broken crockery with edges blunted by sand, time and the weather. 'See, here is some stuff they left behind. You can find these artefacts scattered outside town too, here and there. There, there,' she pointed beyond the cemetery, 'can you see that bit of tin coming up, galvanised iron, more like. Erosion brings things back up from the earth. If you dug in that spot, you don't know what you might find. I found fragments of a glazed bowl here when I was little, an eggshell blue ceramic shard. That William Ringer pinched it from me when he was a boy — he was always mean, that one.'

It was drawing close to 3 pm, the warmest part of the day. The air was still. Katherine and Grace sat down on either side of Aunt Evelyn, tiny, short and skinny as she was, shoving her in fun, saying she was so big they had no shade. They burst out laughing. When silence fell over them, flies buzzed in and out of range, not yet in summer swarms. They took turns drinking the water they'd carried, then contemplated lives lost on these plains, scattered to time like bleached bones in the desert. Camels still roamed, wild now, part of a forgotten cultural and social landscape. To date, Katherine had only ever seen one camel. She'd watched in horror during race week when pastoralists tormented one creature in front of the pub on the main street with a cattle prod to make it throw its rider. For fun. They especially liked to tease new chums in that way.

Evelyn broke the reverie. 'You know,' she said, in a quiet voice that forced Katherine to lean closer to hear. 'I had a daughter. Young one come late in life.' Evelyn inhaled, long and slow. 'Like Pearl's girl, she's gone now too, pregnant from that American. Finished.'

Katherine's heart thumped in her chest. Her breath stopped. There had been no mention of pregnancy in Sharmer's diary. Did he know, or was that why he ripped out so many pages?

'Yes, you know him, that man,' Evelyn said. 'You're wearing the same boots as him today. He came into our world with those boots full of all sorts of promises, like he did with you, but he took the most precious thing I had. She had just turned thirteen, pregnant with his child and shamed. When that baby died, she hung herself in one of them empty shacks in town. Just broke in and put a couple of man's ties around her neck, tied herself to a beam in the ceiling, climbed on a chair. Stepped off. The police — that Sergeant Duke is a bad man — did not tell anybody in town, said he didn't want to upset them. Us mob knew, but we can't talk about those things. He got that constable to cut her down and put her little body in the cells. They made out it was the death of a drunk Aborigine in custody. Nobody would care about that. Next day, our people took her away and buried her the proper way out there on the plains. That's it. I don't say her name anymore. White people have taken all my children away now, Sam and Reggie hunted off their own country by that William Ringer — you know about that one, who calls us gins — and my little girl and her baby finished just like that. That's all I can say.'

Evelyn began to keen. The low, hollow sound brought Paws back to her side. He put his head in her lap, leaning into her, looking up with ears pricked. She rested her arm across his pliant body. The girls held Evelyn's pain in their hearts, wanting her suffering to ease. When Evelyn became calm, they rose in unison and walked back to town in silence. Once they reached the big water tower, Grace and Evelyn turned to go the back way past the Police Station to the lane so they'd avoid meeting anyone.

Katherine continued along the main street, hurrying past the shop and the pub's front entrance to the side gate to get to her room at the back without being interrupted. She fell onto her bed sobbing. Finally, she had an answer. Gregory Sharmer must have left the diary entries behind to expunge the contents from his mind the way he discarded the Aboriginal girl he'd sullied and destroyed, like a piece of rubbish. He vanished, leaving behind a mess with not as much as a farewell to the people whose lives he had invaded. How did he have the gall to watch the police beat the girl's father half to death? He must have known, but he ran. Ran away to get his degree. No conscience. No shame.

27

Recently, Katherine had taken to relieving Dudley in the bar, on Wednesday and Friday afternoons, and Saturday. Like most Fridays, today was frantic. Every pastoralist, stockman, miner, fencer, scalper, rouseabout, and government labourer took a rest from their labours to meet the Ghan and Chaser. As she surveyed the motley crowd over the counter, finding a husband seemed less important than female friendship, excluding gossipy station owners' wives now filling the Ladies Lounge. No matter how hard those women may work on the station, they were little more than perfumed mouthpieces for their husbands' views in town. Is that all a wife is? A man's status keeper?

Janice came to mind. By now, Katherine's absent friend would have had her baby and given it up. It was sad to think they may never meet again. Gone were the carefree days shared in Janice's old shack. Wendy now lived there in sin, an appellation for women, not men. Most of the station wives and a few townswomen ostracised her, but the poor girl was lonely when Ian was out fencing or in the pub with Ringer. A fat lot of good it was for her, having a man in the house.

Katherine served Ringer and an offsider, two men, both legless, standing as close as lovers. Ringer didn't care who it was. He had to have a sycophant to bolster his ego. You learn something every day. Katherine watched the pair perform, master and servant. Ringer's new fellow had it down pat. It must be in male genes or something.

'Come on, Katherine, give us a smile. There's a good girl.' Since the claypan incident, William Ringer had tried hard to ingratiate himself with Katherine but always missed the mark. He was still smitten with Helen Drysdale, the impoverished, private school educated governess at Myall Creek, who schooled and played nanny to the Beaming's offspring. William himself was close to illiterate. His family could not afford to send their boys to boarding school or pay a governess. William's grandfather was one of the first to open the country, which elevated the family to the revered status of outback pioneers. His history, not any personal or professional quality, turned him into a good catch for a girl with aspirations. Helen Drysdale as his wife would add respectability, if not wealth. And, she'd be a good breeder, to put it in bush vernacular. Pastoralists had become the face of a new Australian upper class, born of hardship, scrounging to get ahead then forming copycat dynasties like the British before them. All trace of adolescent fornication with Aboriginal girls was erased from their white stories when they married. As Evelyn said, black blood was never acknowledged, though many bushmen continued their secret liaisons.

Katherine could not believe Ringer had called on her to be a good girl. She hated being patronised in that taken-for-granted way, every bit as much as her mother did. She agonised over how long she could bear to listen to the ugly things that men said in the bar. No matter whether he knew her or not or what class of man he might be, a drunk would think nothing of calling out to Katherine, 'What's wrong with you, girl? You got your period or what?' Men in bars expected to be at the centre of things and, if they didn't get the barmaid's attention, were aggrieved. Katherine had a sneaking suspicion all men were like that to a greater or lesser degree. No exceptions. Lillian often said that the male species expected women always to laugh, smile and dance to their tune.

Like her mother, Katherine was becoming sick to death of struggling to be bright, cheerful and interested in refrains like, 'Ya want a bit.' Words were thrown at her as often as she dared to be unsmiling. This, from men who seemed to believe that the only thing a woman needed was a good root to fix their moods and misery. The message never changed; women must be convivial and amiable to men. Indeed, they had no purpose except as they behaved towards and served men. It was not a complex message to pick up. 'She'll be right when she gets a good poke,' always drew a hearty laugh.

With sweat dripping down her face and neck, Katherine washed dirty glasses and tried to keep up with the customers by herself. From the other side of the room, a heavy voice hooted, 'I'll give it to you, darlin',' if you think you can handle it.'

'You'd be lucky,' Katherine shouted back, forcing a smile while she refilled the man's glass. This man was new in town, not bad looking, but where she may once have found him attractive because of his overt interest in her, she knew, now, that she would never again go out with a man who spoke to her like that. She returned to beer pulling, spirit pouring and drink mixing, one after the other by rote, taking correct change from the piles of cash the men left in front of them on the bar runners when they settled in for the day. Commerce was not allowed to hold up the flow of grog.

Exhausted, Katherine popped her head through the servery into the Ladies Lounge to ask Pearl to find Lillian. She needed help. The men behaved better with Lillian in the bar, especially when her mother was sober. To give Lillian her due, she had built a formidable reputation with her sharp tongue. Most men feared it.

'What'll it be, gents?' Lillian said, walking into the bar with a broad grin that told Katherine she'd already had a few snorts. At least she was upright. Katherine hoped Lillian would stay off the grog until Dudley got back. She looked at the clock; only an hour to closing time. The time could not go fast enough.

Dudley walked back into the bar 20 minutes before he had to call time, filling the breach for the six o'clock swill. He was a good barman, quick and efficient. The three Forsters worked well together in the bar. The faster the service, the higher the takings. Dudley was not one to miss a business opportunity.

'Time gentlemen please.' Dudley's voice pitched itself above the din. 'Come on, fellas, empty your last glass and off you go.

Time please.' It was rare for anyone to argue with him these days, as they had done initially. The people of the area had come to appreciate that Dudley was an excellent publican. They'd had grown to respect the fact that he ran a tight ship. The pub was always clean, well-stocked, and a pleasure to enter.

Dudley called, 'Time please, ladies,' closing the servery as he did, knowing the women would leave as soon as they had quaffed their last drink. He then bobbed beneath the counter to usher the bar crowd towards the front door with a friendly push and a big smile. Lillian took herself back into the kitchen, and Katherine started cleaning up. As soon as the bar was empty, Dudley bolted the external doors and headed to the kitchen for the cuppa Lillian would have ready for him. He didn't drink for several reasons; partly because it made him ill, partly because he had nearly lost his life in a pub brawl as a young man, but primarily because of Lillian. For Dudley, one drunk in the family was one too many. And, so, Wonnalinga accepted their teetotal publican whose implacability won them over.

'I sometimes think I'm getting too old for this.' Dudley plonked into a chair with a sigh and reached for the sugar, piling two heaped teaspoons into his cup. He stirred loudly, scraping the spoon on the base of the cup, tappity-tapping it against the rim.

'Christ, Dudley, must you make that bloody noise.' Lillian was irritable. 'I've got a headache after being in the bar for so long.'

'More like the beginning of a hangover by the look of you.' Dudley did not mince his words, knowing full well she had done just short of an hour in the bar. 'It's about time you lay off the grog altogether. You stopped drinking in the daytime a while ago. Don't go back on that.'

Lillian stood up so fast she tripped as she took herself into the bar. She returned, cold can in hand, sat down opposite her husband, lit a cigarette and stared at him. 'It's about time, you say. Well, I reckon it's about time we introduced counter meals in the bar. We've got Grace now, so the two girls can do them together. We can start with lunch and see how that goes, but I think they'd be a good money-spinner. They'd bring back some of the customers currently heading down the sly grog path to the store. They've started to cook a bit of finger food to attract people. I bet you didn't know that. And don't bother asking why we should start counter meals. We need the money to cover your losses, that's what. You can't take the moral high ground with me, Dudley Forster. It is not me who is running us into the ground. I don't spend anything on myself, nor does Katherine, who works bloody hard for next to nothing. You bought this bloody place with my inheritance, and all you do is you piss it into a bloody bookie's bank every chance you get. Do you think I don't know where you are all afternoon, most afternoons? It was easier to hide when you had Jimmy as your runner, but he's not here anymore.'

Lillian sucked at the beer can through thin lips, slurping slightly in her rage. 'My mother always said you were a no-good charmer, and I can see now that old girl knew what she was talking about.'

'Your mother was a shrew, and you are just the bloody same,'

Dudley screamed, storming out of the bar to take to his room as he always did when confronted by something he could not control. Lillian was so much better with words than him.

'Help!' Katherine called out to Lillian in the kitchen. When there was no reply, she lay for a moment in the puddle of mop-froth where she had fallen, feeling forsaken. Overwrought at hearing the hurt and anger in her parents' raised voices, she had slipped on the wet linoleum tiles Dudley had laid with such pride. Neither of her parents ever listened to the other, so absorbed were they in their disillusionments.

A few days later, Katherine stared at the blank page of her new exercise book lying open on the bed. She'd bought it at the store the day after she'd picked herself up off the bar floor but had written nothing, even though she opened it every day. It was one thing to think about writing a diary, like Sharmer, and another to start. She procrastinated, trying to decide whether to use a pen or pencil. She feared committing something to paper where words became permanent.

Until Katherine discovered Gregory Sharmer's diary, the idea of recording her own experiences had never occurred to her. Jimmy's naming game sowed the seed of an idea about writing, but Gregory's shocking candour on the page showed her the importance of stories. Stories captured the essence of things, made life real. The way Evelyn, Grace and Paddy told stories with defined beginnings and endings gave her other ways to think about how to write. Stories matter to them. They have a purpose and need to be recounted at the right moment, in the right way, told by the right person.

In different ways, all of these people taught Katherine that she, too, had stories to tell. She might even start with the latest family kerfuffle calling it 'The Great Counter Meal Controversy.' By listening deeply to her parents when they fought, as she had learned to do from Aunty Evelyn and even Paddy, it had become clear to Katherine that neither the words Dudley and Lillian used nor the issue in dispute mattered. When they fought, they shrieked about their deep confusion and disappointment in each other and themselves. She took consolation from resolving the counter meal incident by volunteering to give them a go with Grace. It meant longer hours, but she'd do anything to help the pub survive her father's mounting debts.

Katherine closed her diary after looking at the blank first page for what seemed like hours.

When Lillian called her to the kitchen, she poked the exercise book under her mattress with resolve. Next time.

'Happy birthday, darling,' Lillian greeted her daughter the moment Katherine entered the kitchen through the back verandah.

'Happy birthday, my beautiful girl,' Dudley echoed, his voice tremulous. 'Here's a little something from Mum and me.'

'I thought you'd forgotten,' Katherine cried in delight, knowing full well her parents never forgot her birthday. She smiled at the memory of her 21st when they gave her a fountain pen in a silk-lined box, as though foreshadowing her recent decision to write.

'How could we forget our daughter's twenty-third birthday?'

Katherine plucked the sticky tape off the small box her mother handed to her. She didn't want to despoil the shiny gold wrapping paper. Inside a red velvet box, lay a pearl pendant on a bed of white silk. Katherine instantly recognised the pearl as the natural baroque black pearl Lillian had inherited in a ring from her mother. Her parents had it reset in silver and gold filigree. Dudley put the 18-carat gold chain around his daughter's neck.

'Thank you, thank you, thank you. It is so beautiful,' Katherine cried, aching to embrace her parents while they stood, as usual, ramrod-straight choking back emotion as best they could.

'OK, sit down now. No cakes this year, it's just us, and I've cooked your favourite meal.' Lillian pulled a platter of golden crumbed veal from the oven where she'd kept it warm and dished it up with mashed potatoes, peas and carrots on warmed plates with a quarter of a lemon to squeeze on the meat. With the bar closed and no houseguests to worry about, for once, the Forsters could celebrate without distraction. Each glance, smile and morsel of food Lillian had prepared, as though for royalty, was relished with love and laughter. Katherine's heart swelled with the parental love infused into her gift. She felt blessed.

28

It had been easy for Katherine to slip back into the Wonnalinga routine after her Sydney trip. The red earth of the broad main street was pleasingly silent and empty compared to Kings Cross. Did she miss having bookshops to browse in, and the rattle of trams? Katherine recalled the pleasure she got, meandering city streets among strangers. One downer in the bush is that life always available to view, not only in the pub where personal matters belonged to everyone. It was a place where nothing could stay secret for long. Still, her only regret was leaving Sydney before summoning the courage to go to see a Les Girls cabaret.

Living in South Australia, if not the outback had its own rewards, like the sweet taste of Victoria Bitter, one of the oldest and most popular beers in the country that originated in Melbourne, like her. In Wonnalinga, Katherine tingled at the embrace of dry air. She revelled in the vast blue-sky amphitheatre and the desert's red and purple emptiness. Yes, there was a bit of Australian pride in Sydney with its shining harbour and coat hanger bridge, but ferry rides simply did not compete with the outback for a sense of belonging.

Katherine did not miss Aunty Lou, but it made her sad to think of that jovial woman disintegrating with grog and grief. Could she trust Lillian's apparent transformation? When her mother binged now, it was deliberate, designed to make Dudley sit up and take notice. Katherine was not ready to entirely let her guard down but, every time she and Lillian got together, she found herself relaxing into her mother's stories, about missing her long-dead mother and growing up in poverty without a father.

'One day,' Lillian said, 'my two sisters and I picked flowers over a fence before heading, uninvited, to a séance we'd heard about. Barbara was twelve, April eleven, and I was nine. Because we sneaked in, our hearts seemed to beat out loud so, when the mystic said in a sonorous voice that evil would befall those who had brought stolen flowers into her sanctuary, we were terrified.'

'The woman had her eyes closed.' Lillian laughed. 'We scarpered as fast and as far as we could on our little legs, away from that darkened room with its purple drapes and sandalwood incense. At home, we collapsed in tears of giggling fear.' Lillian had returned as Katherine's mother, with laughter.

'We used to tease our eldest sister remorselessly. Poor Barbara died after being committed to a lunatic asylum in Kew for jealousy. Her husband was a philanderer.'

'What's that?'

'A philanderer is a man who cheats on his wife. It can be the other way, of course, but it's mostly men who play away. Anyway, none of her kids ever visited their mum, and who could blame them with her locked in a loony bin.' Lillian's eyes welled with a touch of self-pity and remorse. 'April and I used to tease her so badly.'

Lillian wove her stories into a calendar of relationships like, 'when April had her first baby,' and 'after Barbara came out as a debutante,' or 'at so and so's wedding.' There was no chronology. Young Lillian's identity was enmeshed in connections that marriage stripped away.

'Mum, what do you make of poor old Aunty Lou?' Katherine didn't want her mum turning maudlin. 'When I left, she seemed bent on drinking herself to death.'

'Well, I hope she won't go dancing in the streets now like she did when she was young. We lived with her when we first got married. Today, the poor old bugger'd get locked up for being ugly, fat and wrinkly.' They laughed out loud till Lillian put her forefinger to closed lips. 'Shoosh. Don't let Dudley hear us. He and I've been getting on well lately, for the first time in years.'

Like Lillian, Dudley smothered Katherine with attention on her return from Sydney, confiding his secret plan to throw a party for Lillian to celebrate her birthday. He'd wanted to do something for a long time and, although 47 wasn't a special birthday like 45 or 50, he'd grabbed the moment now Katherine was home.

Given Pearl and Lillian's growing friendship, Pearl and Barney were at the top of Dudley's guest list. Other hotel regulars, townies and bush people were included by default. Katherine thought it odd that the stationmaster was not included. It could only mean that Dudley knew about Pearl's party.

Despite his fear of redback spiders, her father had stacked party supplies out of sight in the back shed. He'd fixed the date for the following Saturday when they had no bookings. He thought it would be like a family holiday. Katherine kept her misgivings to herself.

Dudley and Katherine tried their best to keep the party secret, but the pub was too small, indeed, Wonnalinga was too small for party plans to be hidden from Lillian, given the general air of merriment that filled the town. Playing her part, Lillian feigned ignorance. Even on the day, she stayed in her room until well after 11 am, listening in delight to Barney and Dudley setting up kegs and trestle tables on the back lawn. She didn't hear Pearl come with a massive pot of beef stew and a small gas burner to heat it on later, but there was no mistaking the aroma of her friend's fresh-from-the-oven bread wafting throughout the hotel. No wonder Pearl had won prizes for her cooking in the CWA and the Adelaide Show.

By the time Lillian got to the kitchen, every fridge in the pub — kitchen and bar — was filled with coleslaw, beetroot, pickled onions, cheese, lettuce, tomatoes. Katherine made potato salad with bacon, parsley, boiled eggs and green peas slathered with her creamy egg mayonnaise, and there was enough food to feed an army: trays of home-butchered rump steaks, T-bones and Scotch fillets, loin lamb chops and sausages stacked one upon the other and Lillian's favourite, whiting. By dusk, when the party began, the first keg was already half empty.

'You look pretty, Luv,' Dudley whispered to his wife as she

made her entrance, dressed from head to toe in white. Lillian had not lost her gravitas. Katherine was sure she could see her father's heart swell with longing, seeing his wife sober. Lillian looked lovelier than she had in years.

When Bruno Moretti ambled through the gate, uninvited, Katherine choked back a scream. The man showed up at the precise moment that Lillian appeared. A quick-thinking stockman cleared a path and invited Lillian to join the crowd around the keg. His diversion failed. Lillian's face lit up in brittle party mode the minute she saw the stationmaster. Seeing the sudden shift in Lillian's demeanour, Katherine knew absolutely that her mother did remember the incident at Pearl's party.

That night, Katherine thought she'd probably end up abstinent like her father. She hated the grog. Really hated what it did to her mother. She watched Lillian hold herself together long enough to blow out the candles and appreciate the hearty chorus of Happy Birthday from the guests. But that was it. Even though Bruno Moretti kept his distance, Lillian drank till her legs gave way. Paws clung to her, making little whiny-yappy noises that got louder and increasingly shrill as Lillian stumbled, semi-oblivious and truly paralytic in public for the first time in a long time. Katherine put her arm around her mum to help her to bed. The only light relief that night was Paws urinating on Moretti's left leg. Everybody laughed.

Towering above other guests in his high-heeled, elastic-sided boots and surrounded by acolytes, William Ringer circulated all night. The Beamings appeared briefly. Things had never been the same between Mary Beaming and Lillian since the station's

New Year's Eve party. Roger Beaming continued to act hail-fellow-well-met with Dudley in the bar. There, the tacit agreement among men was that it was safe to appear friendly even if it was a public lie. Beaming managed a light flirtation with Lillian earlier, although not daring to call her Lilly Pilly in front of Dudley. He ignored Katherine, who returned the favour since she'd reliably heard on the grapevine that the pastoralist called her a little slut, 'just like her mother', starting the gossip that she and Lillian had 'slept with everyone up and down the railway line'. His flirtatious acknowledgement of Lillian was intended to appease Dudley, not Lillian. Men, Katherine deduced, are like that.

Around five the next morning, Katherine went out the back to start clearing up. A few revellers were still sleeping in swags on the lawn. One or two lay flat out on the grass without cover. The miracle of alcohol allowed people to sleep anywhere and anyhow without shame, although waking up sober and cold could be a nasty surprise. Picking her way through the bodies, Katherine collected paper napkins, tacky with barbecue grease and tomato sauce, and the odd snotty hanky that had fallen from someone's pocket. No loose undies on view today, thank goodness but, there was a dark patch at the moleskin-covered groin of one of the sleepers who had pissed himself in the night. Katherine carried anything and everything that would burn to the incinerator, recoiling at the faint smell of faeces and foul-smelling vomit splats on the lawn. She would hose that away later.

The party was expensive. Nearly three empty kegs plus the one still on tap which was two-thirds gone. They'd gone through a dozen or more bottles of Johnny Walker Scotch and Bundaberg Rum. It had been a big night, but no fights. Moretti had slithered away to the tune of the crude laughter at Paws' antics. Support for Lillian, though wordless, was strong. Nobody left her alone for a minute no matter how drunk she got. They'd made their point but not making a fuss with Moretti meant they could still do amicable business with the stationmaster, as they must.

29

A couple of days later, Katherine again woke early, feeling guilty about leaving her dad without telling him about the planned outing with Evelyn and Grace. He would wake to a dark kitchen and cold stove and the image of Dudley putting the electric kettle on to make his own cup of tea made her feel sad. Once he realised that she was out, he'd sit alone in an empty pub, waiting for Lillian to get up. But Katherine had to go. Evelyn had promised to share things that were for women only, something, she said, that the American would never get to know.

'With the Jeep already packed, Katherine stowed her swag next to a jerry can of spare fuel and the two jerry cans of water they needed for the camp, and to refill the canvas bags hanging on the bull bar where their drinking water would cool as they drove. Katherine had brought along what hadn't been used of Pearl's bread, tins of baked beans and bully beef, and, as instructed by Evelyn, a packet of tea leaves and sugar. Grace and Evelyn were waiting for her in the lane. They loaded their swags, a billy, enamel plates, spoons and mugs and headed out bush.

The trio was well on the road when the sun touched the horizon, before the town came to life. Evelyn navigated, soon taking them off-road. Katherine obeyed Evelyn's directions, crossing fingers that they wouldn't get a flat tyre from a sharp stone. The older woman found her way across the arid flats where the only signs of life were the ubiquitous flies, crows on whitened bones and an occasional wedge-tailed eagle. No roads, no signposts for 150 miles.

'Look,' Evelyn's finger guided Katherine's eyes to a row of low sandhills leading to precipitous sandstone cliffs rising as if from the horizon itself. Nearby, Katherine caught a glimpse of blue-green as a fresh-water spring materialised before her eyes. She turned the motor off. In the silence, Evelyn announced that this was no ordinary place. It was one of many fresh-water springs that Aboriginal people had once shown to early settlers who would otherwise have perished in the outback.

'There's water all over this country,' Evelyn continued, 'if you know where to look. Springs like this come from a giant underground sea that crosses over Queensland, northern New South Wales and lots of this desert country here in South Australia. Too ancient.

'Our mob have always known about this water, these springs. They have stories, men's and women's stories side by side.'

Katherine learned at school that Great Artesian Basin covered about twenty-three per cent of the whole country. Evelyn spoke in detail about the old people who had traditional names for each and every spring on traditional trade and travel routes. 'It's all in the songs of our ancestors. That's how we find our way around this country. We have songs that hold the past in the present. Some people know some songs and dances. Others have different stories to tell. We are all related to the land and to each other. Like that.'

When Evelyn stopped talking, silence enfolded them. Slowly, from the stillness, bush music arose. In the reeds, sudden swooshes were audible as creatures moved among the sediment mounds left by the spring. A breeze susurrated through overhanging date palms. A frond crashed to the ground, startling them.

Evelyn pointed to a sandy spot close to the water's edge where they could sit down, stay dry and have a good view of the water through the reeds. Evelyn pointed to where Katherine should roll out the swags while Grace searched for kindling and logs of various sizes for a fire. Evelyn piled stones around the fire hole she dug, and when the logs were in place, lay a blackened wire-grille across the flames.

'Where'd you get that from?' Katherine hadn't seen the grille in the Jeep.

'I hide it here.' Evelyn chuckled as she also spirited an enamel teapot out of nowhere and added three heaped dessertspoons of tea.

'You got that sugar?' It was a demand, not a question. Katherine produced a jam jar full of white sugar and a couple of teaspoons. The three women then sat, listening to the desert and watching the flames lick the blackened billy. The tea was too hot to drink straight away, but it was the most delicious cuppa

Katherine had ever tasted; hot, smoky, strong and sweet.

On one side of the spring, a few small salt flats pock-marked the gibber plains. Patches of desert peas not yet in flower could be seen on the low, red sandhills and scatters of saltbush led to an escarpment. Birds whistled and flitted, but Evelyn told them to open their ears to the little mammals in the under-growth and among the reeds. She teased Grace and Katherine, who showed signs of sleepiness, saying they'd have to stay awake all night if they wanted to see any of the night creatures. Katherine recognised ducks, cormorants and egrets on the water. Bronzewing pigeons pecked the ground. Evelyn once told her a bronzewing story without detail because it was not her story to tell. She talked about the bird travelling up from the Flinders Ranges in South Australia right through to New South Wales and on to Queensland. It stops along the way where different mobs camp for ceremony before the next mob picks up the story to carry further into their own country. Nowadays, people can travel long distances with their pastoralists for shows, races and other festive gatherings. That's how they kept their stories and relationships alive.

Evelyn said the spring water could heal because it was fresh from deep beneath the earth. 'But, near the surface', she said with a giggle, 'you hafta watch out for the fish.'

Everybody stripped down to their knickers and waded in until it was deep enough to float. The need for talk faded as they surrendered to the sensuality of buoyant water. Katherine's mind flew back to the pub, hoping her mother and father were getting along all right, the two of them on their own. Then, out of nowhere, a deep sense of shame suffused her body. Here she was enjoying the company of two people she held very dear, who she had not thought to invite to Lillian's party. Or Paddy. Dear Paddy, who had gone to such trouble to find Paws for Lillian.

Katherine clambered out of the spring, took herself behind bushes to towel dry and dress. She called Paws, who trotted alongside her. Katherine hid behind a tree a little distance away and, pulling the dog close, buried her head in his fur to muffle her tears. How could she not have included them? On every social occasion, she'd seen Aboriginal people sitting apart, outside the light of the campfire at the claypan, beyond the verandah at Pearl's place on the night of the fight, on the ground separated from everyone else on film nights, not even on segregated chairs. They sat on the ground as though that was where they belonged. She remembered, too, seeing Roger Beaming chucking chipped, stained enamel plates of food at the Aboriginal women and children and the men when she was at the station. He put them on the ground. Outside, whatever the weather. According to Evelyn, pastoralists treated Aboriginal men, indeed everybody, better on muster out bush when they were working.

Physical segregation persisted like a knife through the heart of the country. At the race week ball, Mary Beaming claimed that Aborigines were the best riders. Yet Aboriginal stockmen never got to jockey any of the station owners' horses. Only white ringers did that. Ingrained, taken-for-granted segregation was a trap, and Katherine had fallen into it. One day, when the women under the mulga tree spoke about going out bush with their husbands, they'd grizzled about how hard it was with all the flies. All the flies. Until that moment, Katherine had assumed that Aboriginal women would not find flies any more of a nuisance than did the cattle their men worked. How could she say any of this to Evelyn?

By the time Evelyn and Grace got back, Katherine was lying on top of her swag, pillow over her face.

'You all right.' It was Grace.

'Yeah, trying to keep the flies off.'

'You can talk up if you like. When we're women together like this, we can talk about anything.' Nothing escaped Evelyn's keen eyes. Katherine sat up and wrapped her arms tight around her knees. She said she was sorry, sorry for not inviting them to Lillian's birthday party, sorry for all the things she'd got wrong. Her shame was so deep she could not look at her friends.

Evelyn and Grace both knelt beside Katherine, surrounding her with their warmth and strength. 'Time's not ready for that, not yet,' Evelyn said. 'I'm not offended. Why? Because you didn't mean any harm. What gets me upset, what gets all us Aboriginal women distressed, is when men who take our women and have babies with them refuse to acknowledge them in public. And, when the roughest of men take our youngest girls without asking and abuse them. That's what makes me upset. Grace, too. All of us.'

Again, Katherine was overwhelmed. Paddy had shown compassion towards her when Sam and Reggie were beaten for saddling horses for her and Janice Cook. And now, Evelyn and Grace forgave her ignorance.

'We'd better have a little kip now because tonight's the night.' Evelyn laughed in the way Katherine had heard Aboriginal women do when they talked about sex, coquettish and full of fun.

As the sun fell, it cast an orange glow over the landscape, and Katherine watched Evelyn wet some white powder she had brought on the trip, and she and Grace each painted the other's face. They laughed when it became clear that the splotches they anointed Katherine with didn't stand out much. 'Not much good that pink skin,' Evelyn giggled as she produced clapping sticks. With faces covered in white ochre, they sat together around the fire in the dark, and Evelyn started clapping the sticks. She sang while Grace explained that Evelyn was singing about the Seven Sisters. 'You fellas call them the Pleiades. These songs are for us women only. We are the Seven Sisters, and we dance to bring them to us here. They are our ancestors. We are the sisters too. The story tells how Moon Man follows us about, but women are too clever for him.'

Evelyn summoned the girls to stand up and dance with her, bare-breasted, around the fire, around their campsite, clapping, singing. Katherine tried to mime the sounds and clap her hands to the rhythm of the sticks, amazed at her lack of inhibition, despite knowing that unkind people may laugh if they saw her relatively plump legs wobbling timid alongside the strong, skinny pins of her friends.

On and off for the next few hours, Evelyn sang. Grace would either sing along or repeat the song afterwards, in translation for Katherine. The three of them laughed. Evelyn sang one story after another about how those sisters tricked the lustful Moon

Man. It must have been midnight before they lay down to sleep around glowing embers. Tired and exhausted, Katherine was thrilled to learn from these stories that women could outwit or be more intelligent than men. Evelyn, Grace and the Sisters had given her a precious life lesson.

Katherine woke at 5 am as she often did lately and stoked the fire enough to boil the billy so tea would be ready by the time the other two woke up. They'd eaten the tinned bully beef on Pearl's bread for dinner, so breakfast was baked beans on the remaining bread, toasted over the iron grille. Their business done, they rolled swags, packed the vehicle and headed home.

Again, Evelyn navigated. Again, they travelled in relative silence, tired and happy.

When they pulled into Main Street, they saw two police vehicles parked outside The First & Last. Katherine didn't recognise any of the other cars.

'Don't worry about us,' Evelyn said. 'Just drop us next door. We'll go through the block now. We'll come and help unload the Jeep later when it's all quietened down.' Police cars outside an outback pub was not an unusual sight, but, in this tiny town, it was strange because the sergeant and his constable usually walked everywhere. Katherine's stomach tightened in apprehension. She parked in the backyard and rushed to the kitchen. Dudley was sitting at the table, head in hands, robbed of life's energy by a force more potent than lightning. Sergeant Duke stood beside Dudley, whose eyes were red with pain.

'Your mum's dead, love.'

30

By the time Lillian's body was removed to the police station's refrigerated morgue, Dudley had attempted to pull himself together.

'I waited for her,' he said to his daughter as she walked in. 'She's usually in the kitchen by eleven, but I didn't want to disturb her if she had a bad hangover after the party, so I hung on till after one. When I got to her room, I thought she was asleep.' Dudley slumped as he spoke until the AIM nurse took over with startlingly crisp efficiency.

'Your mother drowned in her own vomit,' she said. 'She must have been so drunk that her gag reflex stopped. This would have caused vomit to travel back into her trachea and lungs. She might even have had a seizure.'

Katherine stared unbelieving at this atrocious woman who could have said, in a kinder way, that Lillian had died of alcoholic poisoning, which was accurate enough. Instead of remembering Lillian as the immaculate, well-groomed, and self-possessed woman she was when sober, Katherine was left with a hideous, hard to shake, graphic image. Katherine's heart swelled for her mum, whose laugh made her feel warm and protected. For the most part, Lillian kept her own counsel about how unhappy she was as a woman. Lillian was not any old alcoholic to be scorned by this AIM nurse. If it had been Mary Beaming who had died in like circumstances, such horrid words would never have been uttered. It wasn't hard to believe that the nurse knew of the Beamings' stories. Bloody snobs, the lot of them. Could she ever expunge the image of her mother spluttering for breath, choking and soiling herself, being putrid in death, as the nurse had described?

'Get out.' Katherine spat at the nurse. 'Get out of here now.' She trembled in disbelief, rejecting Dudley's guilt, for that was all he offered before relaxing into Pearl's outstretched arms. Still, tears did not come for Katherine.

After Lillian's death, Dudley was like a somnambulist. He refused to close the pub, although he did accept Barney's offer to take up the slack in the bar by bringing in a couple of his railway mates for the odd shift. Pearl took over in the kitchen with Grace. Katherine continued doing the laundry even though it had all but lost its magic. The inexorable cloudlessness of the blue skies stopped beckoning her to greater things. Katherine saw nothing through the window but relentless waves of rising heat over purple gibber and heard nothing but the now harrowing, repetitive caw of crows and buzz of flies; the sounds of death itself.

Katherine convinced herself that Bruno Moretti killed her

mother as surely as his egotistical lack of conscience gave him permission to gatecrash her birthday party. Lillian started the evening intending to stay sober, and he spoiled it for her, for everyone. In an instant.

As days followed each other in an endless chain to nowhere, Katherine's hatred for Moretti spurred her on to work. She spring-cleaned her own room, discarding clothes she no longer liked, then burnt anything that would burn. Katherine developed a strange partiality to the incinerator. She opened her father's room to admit fresh air for the first time in years to eliminate the stench of tobacco, then discarded the cloudy glass of water Dudley kept by his bed for false teeth. It stunk of halitosis. Let him get a fresh glass for himself every night from now on. The ashtray was next to be emptied. It looked as though nobody had ever emptied it before. Nothing escaped Katherine's purifying frenzy. She even scrubbed her father's bedroom walls with Pine-O-Clean, then moved onto pub corners and ceilings, ridding them of cobwebs. On hands and knees, she polished the corridor with such vigour it shone as never before. Her knees hurt, but she relished the pain, which brought her back into her body. With hatred spent, Katherine finally found the courage to enter Lillian's room. As she packed up her mother's life, her resentment toward Dudley started to grow.

'Dad, we have to talk about the funeral. What do you want to do?' Katherine was irritable. Everyone pestered her, the nurse's brand of moralism left her rigid with anger, the police asked annoying questions about her mum, and now the funeral home was pressuring her for plans.

'Long as she's cremated as she always wanted, I don't mind, Luv,' Dudley said. 'Whatever you decide is fine by me.'

'Surely you have some idea. I've never done this before, you know?' How dare her father put her in charge? Lillian might have abdicated her duties by getting drunk, but Dudley did it as though it was his God-given right to delegate everything to do with his wife to his daughter. Katherine sometimes asked herself whether Dudley being trivialised as the youngest of a bevy of bossy siblings had made him a weak man. Or was he just lazy?

'Nor have I,' he replied. 'I am practical. You're a girl, like your mother. You've got a good eye for flower arrangements, food, music, all that creative stuff that a man knows nothing about. Anyway, you'd know what Lillian might like better than me, don't you think? And you'll write a better eulogy.'

Katherine wanted to scream, to tell Dudley to get his head out of his bloody racing bible and quit betting. It was the only thing her father did now, the only thing he brought any energy to, and he wasn't even good at it. He kept losing and yet continued to hole up in his bedroom to mark his bets on newspapers. The only change for Dudley was to go either to the police station or Barney's place to use their phones to place bets with SP bookies across Australia every Wednesday, Friday and Saturday. For a man who was such a stickler for the law when it came to running the pub, ethics meant nothing to him as a man in thrall to gambling.

Katherine bent to kiss her mother on the forehead before guests started arriving at the chapel at Adelaide's Centennial Park. The smell of formaldehyde in the casket was new to her, as was the cold, hard, sponge-like clamminess of her mother's embalmed body, but she did not recoil. The undertakers had dressed Lillian in the white slacks, and knitted top Katherine had given them. They placed her mother's favourite pendant watch around her neck as asked, with its orb at the centre of her chest, where it had always been in life, but the body in the coffin was unrecognisable; the face was wrong. Lillian's cheeks and lips had been cosmetically inflated, rouged and painted till she looked like a clown. Bold red lips on death's pallor looked ludicrous. All the embalmer managed to conjure was a profound absence.

Katherine turned to Dudley, standing docile beside her, head bowed. A flash of pity filled her for a moment, replaced by sudden anger that dissipated as quickly when she asked herself what her father might have done differently. The answer was nothing. He was as impotent as she felt in the face of their loss. Katherine could see in her father's demeanour that his fire was extinguished. She almost forgave him, but a nascent urge to leave him took hold. Lillian was right. It was time to make a new life somewhere away from the bush, away from her father. Katherine decided on a whim, but with clarity, that as soon as Dudley was safely back in Wonnalinga, she would pack up and give Adelaide a try. Lillian would always be with her.

Katherine looked up in surprise when the undertaker's assistant beckoned her to read the eulogy. A billowing semi-circle of fresh flowers and wreaths flowed across the floor in front of the lectern. As she stood there, Katherine felt she was encased in hardened glass. She could see out but could not connect with anything or anyone outside her invisible cocoon. The small chapel was packed. Many came to be seen, not to mourn. Jimmy turned up late, but Katherine softened towards him when he paid kind attention to her father, holding his hand for comfort in a way that she no longer could.

Katherine stepped down from the lectern with nostrils flaring at the stench of well-dressed insincerity that rose like a toxic cloud from the leading lights of Wonnalinga, especially from Mary and Roger Beaming, who were in Adelaide on other business. William Ringer was there to show off Helen Drysdale, now a bonafide member of the bush elite, as his new wife. Katherine pitied the girl.

'Don't worry, Mum,' Katherine whispered, barely able to breathe as she watched Lillian's casket being propelled along a slide towards the hidden furnace. 'It's over now.' Katherine's tears came as the modesty curtains closed behind her mother, sliding towards the flames. In her heart, Katherine gave her mother the words that she had always yearned to hear from Lillian, *I love you, I love you, I love you.*

Outside the chapel, guests were already getting stuck into the light refreshments, small, sweet cakes, cream biscuits and mixed finger sandwiches. While people mingled, Katherine stood apart, as though the glass screen was still around her, protecting her, now magnifying the deceit of those present. She could see through the hairdos, clothes and bodies to the very skeletons of faults, hatred and bullshit. The fairytale about the emperor with no clothes came to mind. They would not have good deaths, these people. Mary Beaming didn't even keep her voice low as she gossiped about Lillian with Betty Duke. Katherine overheard her, saying that Lillian had died a drunk because of 'the change'. This from Mary Beaming, a woman who was an out and out alcoholic herself, was laughable, and, as for Betty Duke, word had it that her husband was close to committing her to an asylum for what he called her irrational behaviour and wild talk.

It wasn't menopause that killed women. It was the bush. It was hard on them. Yet Katherine had seen how women played status keeper to many an unworthy husband, not only on properties but also in town. With varying degrees of success, everyone imitated the pastoralists, the very people who had clawed their way over Aboriginal culture and country to become the new Australian gentry. For a woman, menopause was a humiliating sign that she was of no further use. Fertility over. 'Last chance' sexual urges like those that had afflicted Lillian and, for that matter, Mary Beaming and Betty Duke, saw them mocked for nature's cruelty, and Lillian had thought them friends when she was alive. Hearing those two women gossip about her mother now, when Lillian was not there to defend herself, hurt.

Light streamed through stained glass in shards of green, yellow, red and purple, slashing the faces of mourners with an eerie kaleidoscope that brought a smile to Katherine's lips as she headed outside for air. If there was a God, would He mark them thus with refracted light to show her that He recognised their duplicity? It was beyond Katherine's comprehension that people who did not care for her mother had presumed to attend her funeral at all, but then, humility, to them, was a foreign country.

The game would never change, only the players; pretenders all to a land never theirs.

31

'Who'll do the cooking? How will I manage?' Dudley found Katherine on the front verandah of The First & Last.

'You've got Pearl and Grace. They know the ropes.' Katherine stood up, turned and headed for the kitchen, Dudley in tow. 'You're like a bloody child. You don't understand anything. You made mum's life miserable with your gambling, grumbling and getting angry when you couldn't have your way.'

Katherine turned to face her father. 'You'll find someone. You always do. Why don't you get your precious Jimmy back — that's one way to go — or find someone to replace him? Do you realise how hard I've worked lately, relieving in the bar as well as doing the laundry and housework by myself? Now that Mum's gone, I cook too. I do most of Jimmy's yard work, I meet the train and, because you're so slack, I take care of bookings and the ordering as well. All you do is sneak around the place to bet. Mum's inheritance is drifting south into the giant pockets of your SP bloody bookmakers faster than ever. You've been cutting corners in this pub for too long. Half the time, you struggle to pay Grace or Pearl and Barney when they help out. No, Dad, I'm off. I only hung on this long because, after mum died, I needed comfort from Pearl, Grace, Aunt Evelyn and Paddy. I got none from you.'

Dudley's body wilted at the onslaught. His mouth sagged open. Katherine had never spoken to her father like that before, and she hadn't finished.

'I try to manage, but I can't do it anymore, not without Mum. I'm a publican's daughter in a town that ridiculed her, mocks you and despises me. It's all very well for women like Mary Beaming to say that hard work makes a good bush woman. It hasn't worked for me. Nobody cares...' Before they came, Katherine converted tears of self-pity to anger. 'She's such a bitch. Women like her do bugger all. They've got governesses and Aboriginal women as maids, and they let their kids run wild with the Aboriginal kids — you know why? — because the older Aboriginal girls look after them.'

'At least I pay proper wages, compared to their kind. The Aboriginal station people only get a pittance.'

'Dad, you're saying that just to get on my good side. It's true what you say, but they get something in return. Don't look so surprised. Yes, they work for food and board, but that lets them stay on their own country, their own land. I bet you didn't know that. And did you know that the Aboriginal stockmen live rough on homestead perimeters? Well, they bloody well do. Single men's quarters are for whites — and those with a dog tag, like Sam.' Katherine stopped.

It was no good telling Dudley everything she'd learned from Evelyn. He wouldn't care that those Aboriginal women were forced to dress in fussy, long European dresses with pinafores and mob caps like servants in the early days. To Katherine, the Aboriginal people were the true pioneers of the outback, not the station people. She looked at Dudley with a mix of anger and pity. 'Anyway, it's too late now to try to stop me. I've already booked myself into a hotel in Adelaide, and I don't want you to contact me ever again.'

When she first hit Adelaide, Katherine stayed at the Duke of York in Currie Street. Dudley would never guess that she would stay in the very place where Willian Ringer, the Beamings and their acolytes had once told him he should book his family in elsewhere when he went to the city. The Duke was for pastoralists. They denigrated him in front of Lillian and Katherine, but, for Katherine, the Duke was a convenient hideout close to the Central Market and the tram to Glenelg. She didn't give a bugger what pastoralists might think. Her room was small but clean, and she ate out.

After years in the bush with little fresh produce, the market's abundance tantalised. For the first few days, Katherine wandered among sumptuous displays of fresh fruit and vegetables. She asked about those she didn't recognise; eggplant, broccoli, artichoke and more. Down the side lanes of the market, fishmongers and butchers were full of people talking in languages other than English and all around, seductive wafts of coffee beans, hot baked bread and fresh flowers. The market filled Katherine with joy. It reminded her of Melbourne's Victoria Markets, where she went with her nana when she was little. Some stalls were foreign, dedicated to smelly cheeses, smoked and processed meats and an array of pasta shapes. Even bread stalls had broken with tradition with their unrecognisable range.

Greek and Italian restaurants and cafes lined both sides of Gouger Street. Shops sold dark, sweet, black coffee in tiny shot glasses; cheap enough if you were game to sit down with older foreign men hanging around on tables outside, smoking weird-smelling cigarettes.

Katherine slipped into a daily routine of having breakfast at Dimmies, a 24-hour café a few blocks away in Hindley Street. As she walked across the city in the grey hours of early morning, the city pulsated with promise as people spewed from buses and trains onto its pavements. Katherine collected a daily paper from a delicatessen doorstep or newsstand, leaving coins on top of the pile of papers delivered earlier to stoops. That she might be following the pattern of the old men who propped up Dudley's bar until they dropped out of the social contract frightened her. But it was the only way to find a job and somewhere permanent to live. She chuckled to think that her addiction to *The Advertiser* might echo Dudley's relationship with his racing pages. Nah, she was searching for a job and home. That was not feckless.

On weekends, young women too roamed the streets in the liminal hours still drunk on party heels, their hair and makeup askew, high on hormones and alcohol. Their interest in the handsome young Greek and Italian migrants, New Australians who prowled, elegant and attractive in sharp suits and pointy-toed shoes, seemed to oscillate between lust and disdain. Forbidden men wearing cologne, a pre-dawn brigade who boarded in cheap, dingy rooms with single beds and a bedside table, not much better than single men's quarters in the bush. Loneliness and boredom drove these new arrivals into the night to play so they could sleep away unemployed days.

Dimmies Café united old men, young girls and the isolated, like Katherine, with lonely foreigners. The place fostered a fragile camaraderie over a British-Australian breakfast menu of fried, poached or scrambled eggs with bacon, sausages, steak, chops, tomatoes and toast — or, believe it or not, pancakes. For Adelaide, Dimmies was risqué. Katherine loved it and found herself increasingly eager to experience the frisson of excitement it offered. The place had an atmosphere that intensified her writing aspirations. With determination, she started to take notes. She decided to use Dimmies as the backdrop for stories of crime and corruption. For a time, the café was the Adelaide equivalent of her Wonnalinga laundry, a place where imagination could play with ways in which Australia was changing. This was her Australia, not Dudley's or Lillian's. The war they lived through, into which she was born, was over and a new life beckoned.

32

Katherine found a new home at Trevu Flats, No 2 Torrens Square, Glenelg, opposite St Peter's Church of England. She no longer attended church, but the situation was perfect, a short walk to the tram, shops and beach. Built in the 1930s, Trevu Flats was a two-storey, red-brick building in a city where yellow brick buildings were becoming the fashion. It boasted distinctive twin stairwells with cream rails, both left-curving, which was odd. To Katherine, the way the building's name was etched in red on a prominent cream band at the top of the stairways made it look like it was tied in a ribbon. A group of university students leased the entire complex, which functioned as a single dwelling. Katherine had an upstairs room to herself, which she would share with Paws when he joined her. Pearl promised to put him on the next train as soon as she settled.

Katherine pined for the dog and could not wait for him to arrive. A condition of her tenancy was that everybody could play with Paws, a small concession because Paws would want that anyway. Older than her housemates by a few years, Katherine was the only Trevu tenant not going to university. She guessed that, for all their confidence and brash ideas of overthrowing both oppression and the old-fashioned values of their parent's, the students would all turn to Paws for comfort. As they often claimed, the world was changing, but it was clear to Katherine that most of them were babies at heart.

Once Paws was ensconced, Katherine often couldn't find him when she got home. He'd be tucked up in someone's bed whose exam results had been poor or who'd had a fight. Whenever someone was homesick, they would smuggle him into their room for a snuggle. Everybody loved Paws, and he loved everybody. As Katherine stipulated, his collar and lead hung ready in the hall for everyone to take turns walking him.

With its high, ornate ceilings, the place was cold except in the central lounge room, where a fire burned night and day in a cavernous fireplace. Whoever woke first in the morning stoked the embers and added a fresh log or two. An impressive mantelpiece reminded Katherine of the story about Lillian's father, who had killed himself by hitting his head on one when he was drunk, leaving Katherine's grandmother to fend for three little girls alone.

Katherine was not an innocent, but she was ill-prepared for how freely her domestic compatriots circulated in and out of each other's rooms and beds. They called it 'sleeping around'. Not always in male-female pairs, but men with men, women with women and men and women in multiple configurations.

'You mustn't be frightened to experiment sexually,' a girl called Pamela announced over breakfast one morning. 'We are throwing off the shackles that suffocated our parents.' Others, still half-asleep (Pamela was a high-energy morning person a little like Katherine), nodded assent. 'We are all clean here, but you should see the doctor at the clinic in Ramsgate Street to have yourself checked and get the contraceptive pill.'

'Clean?'

'Free of sexually transmitted diseases — STDs — of course. Then you can join in the fun.'

'Oh.' Katherine had only the vaguest knowledge of such matters and was pleased that Pamela spelled out what STD meant. Until now, she believed only prostitutes suffered from things like that and associated the idea of uncleanliness with sex itself, not a disease. A hangover from Christianity maybe, but more likely, the prudish lives of her parents gave rise to such ideas. She didn't mention that she'd only ever seen Dudley and Lillian occupy the same bed once. They'd acted all their lives as though sex didn't exist.

'Pamela, my poor mother was ashamed of her unrequited desire, especially in her middle years. There was a rumour in the family that dad only married her to avoid the stigma of being homosexual. She got drunk. And, when she did, she'd submit shamelessly to horrid men.' Katherine's stomach cramped. Here she was betraying both of her parents to avoid looking ignorant, yet could not stop. 'You'd never hear the word 'sex' on my mother's tongue. For her, not even the naked body existed.'

'Right. Well, you don't want to get a reputation as a prude, too, do you?' Pamela changed the subject. 'Yesterday, Peter told me he fancied the pants off you, so get the pill, girl, he'll get the courage to ask you soon enough. Get condoms too, they'll keep you going until the pill starts to work. Some men carry rubbers, but you need to look after yourself.' Pamela pinched Katherine's cheeks with her fingers, looking deep into her eyes. 'You have to think about this as liberation. Sexual liberation.'

Katherine tensed with recognition. This young girl — indeed, all the Trevu students —resembled pastoralists with their confident air of superiority except when they were pissed or high (a new concept for Katherine). The only difference seemed to be that rooting like rabbits in Trevu Flats was called fucking. Fucking. Katherine understood that everybody might love it, but would the men still expect to marry virgins?

Not wanting to be the odd one out, Katherine surrendered to her housemates' casual ways. Pamela continued to guide her in matters of independence. And Peter, to whom she had succumbed, was a good lover. Not as good as Gregory Sharmer, who had been the first to ask her for sex, but Peter, a geography student in his second year, pleasured her with purpose and expected little in return. She liked to lie back afterwards, gently pleasuring herself again while he prattled on with unjusti-fied authority on almost any topic. He was, in a word, boring, especially when stoned. Worse than that, he was so skinny his bones pressed into her when they had sex.

Katherine had trouble shaking the belief that, in this house, where everybody had their way with everybody else, a commit-ment was unlikely and not even pregnancy would change things.

Jealousies occurred among the women, confirming that she was not alone in wanting marriage and kids — the whole caboodle — but she had to admit, casual fucks were interesting and stoned sex liberating. That was key.

'Why aren't you at university?' Pamela was curious.

'Um. Oh! Well, I didn't matriculate.' Katherine was not interested in studying, preferring to learn by observation and listening. She was becoming a bowerbird with her collection of memories, stories, ideas, images and behaviours. If Jimmy taught her to name events, she'd learned about notetaking from Gregory Sharmer. And, where the Ampol rally boys inspired her to aspire, Paddy, Pearl, Evelyn, and Grace showed her that life was to be found among the living, not in a textbook.

Peter liked the sound of his own voice to the point of tedium at times, but Katherine paid attention. Paddy telling her she was a good listener or, as he put it, 'she had ears', paid off. Listening to Peter highlighted the depths of her ignorance. She hated him briefly when he said her friendship with Grace and her family bordered on idolatry. When told the tribal name of her friends, she felt shame. But he also trivialised Evelyn, saying that what she taught Katherine about springs linking Aboriginal people and stories across the landscape like physical maps was simplistic. Aboriginal stories, he declared, had both spatial and moral compass. They were spiritual allegories in which ancestral travels and travails created the features of the landscape and defined proper relationships between people, connecting them in both time and space. Maybe, but Evelyn wasn't talking about that stuff. She was talking about how her family was treated by whites. Different stories for different occasions.

Peter did have compassion for Aboriginal people but ultimately saw them as a collection of facts, like Sharmer. They saw knowledge as a commodity, something you could count, put in your pocket and impress those who would advance your career. They did not care about Evelyn's suffering, Grace's humiliations and Paddy's anxiety about mines destroying his country and his people's future. Katherine put people before complex diagrams and measurements of clans, tribes and objectified social structures. Academics seemed to catalogue Aboriginal life as science divides the natural world into species and sub-species and statistics — all measurable within the lexicon of a scientific symbol system.

Gregory Sharmer hadn't paused for a moment to measure the pain he'd inflicted on the community that welcomed him. He saw the girl he defiled and Aboriginal society as things to be known about, used. By reifying them, he could ignore the complexity of their emotions and aspirations. Studying them let him remain separate, outside. As for Peter, he was too stoned most of the time to cause anybody any trouble. She giggled at an image that popped into her head of this soft hippy man recording field notes on a clipboard in a pith helmet, leaning against a Jeep wearing khaki shorts. Would he, too, wear desert boots?

Jokes aside, Katherine learned from Peter that 'gibber' was an Aboriginal word meaning stones. 'Geography,' he said, 'tells us that they are 65-million-year-old fragments of a crust of silica, iron oxides or calcium carbonate worn down and polished by sand and dust.' His facts excited him, whereas Katherine fell in love with the pristine, mystical beauty of the stones through her laundry window. Multifaceted and unequal in size, gibber plains spread across vast areas, glinting and shining under hot sun like a living presence, pregnant with told and untold tales. They called her to hear, to listen and to open her mind and heart.

Peter also liked politics and forever bemoaned the 18 years Prime Minister Robert Menzies and his conservative government spent in power. Katherine remembered only his bushy eyebrows and her instinctive revulsion for the man. She hadn't heard the name Harold Holt who, Peter said, introduced a new Migration Act that allowed non-white and Asian migration to Australia for the first time, overturning the founding myth of a white Australia.

Katherine could see the Australia her parents lived through and raised her in was crumbling. Her father and grandfather had defended a European order in Europe, far from Australia's shores. Cousin Christopher died closer to home in Vietnam, where Australia fought an American war. In these ways, Katherine learned to see the world anew.

33

'Janice, Janice.' Katherine ran, waving her arms at a young red-headed woman sitting on a bench eating ice cream on the foreshore. At a distance, it was hard to tell for sure if it was Janice until she returned the wave. Breathless from her run, Katherine opened her arms to hug her friend. At least Aunty Lou taught her how to do that. But she forgot the tomato sauce in her hamburger. Nor did she notice Janice's ice cream. Realising too late to pull back, they decided the stain on their shirts was a ridiculous blood-and-milk oath. Their laughter mingled with tremulous regret for the years that had rolled by since earlier, innocent times.

'How are you?' Katherine was the first to speak.

'Much better for seeing your smiling face,' Janice replied.

Spring sunshine bathed them as they settled down on the lawn. Both girls saw surprise in the other's eyes at small changes: different dress styles, an extra pound or two, longer or shorter hair than they remembered.

'What do you think of the new decimal currency?' Janice broke the silence.

Katherine laughed. 'After all this time, that's the first thing you fancy talking about?'

Janice chuckled.

'Well, since you ask, I'm used to it from working in bars, but, at first, it was a nightmare trying to calculate what to charge customers in your head. Translating imperial to decimal currency is like working with two languages. I know people are now using pen and paper to add things up, but I'm still too proud to. I take after my father.' Katherine laughed. 'You'd never guess. For a man who had no schooling to speak of, Dudley had no problem changing over. Of course, it would have been impossible for him not to in the pub, but more importantly, he had to change, or it would cramp his betting style. Like the racing industry itself, Dudley was quick to adapt. Where there's a will to profit, there's always a way to gamble. It might be a mug's game, but it requires considerable nous to keep up.'

'Why do you call your father Dudley?'

Katherine lowered her head, her mood switching from frivolous to dark as she searched for the best way to talk about the loss of her mother.

'Lillian's dead?' Janice lowered her voice.

'Yes, she is. And I blame Dudley.' Katherine lifted her head and was surprised to see that the clouds were still white. 'I blame him, but I feel responsible too. At the time, I wanted to accuse everybody, Dudley, all the bloody pastoralists, the outback itself. But the truth is, she might still be alive if I hadn't gone bush with Evelyn and Grace that night. Did you meet them?'

'No.'

'Never mind, I can fill you in another time. The point is that I wasn't there to look in on Mum, make sure she'd been to the toilet, tell her to stub her cigarette out and check on her till she was sound asleep. I still can't forgive Dudley for making me his wife's keeper, but I was. Dad moaned about Mum being a drunk and mocked her in public when it suited him, but he was like a hollow man when she died. I was so confused.'

'I am so sorry you had that burden,' Janice said. 'And I am sorry that Lillian has gone.'

'Thanks, Janice. I know Dad loved Mum the only way he could but, in the end, castigating himself was easier for him than taking care of her. He was weak, a big-time gambler who loved to flash rolls of notes when he had a win. I admit the poor bugger did it with charm. The thing is, I couldn't save her, Janice. I couldn't do a thing because I wasn't there. And I couldn't help him either. At the funeral, he wallowed in grief with Jimmy by his side while the station people strutted around making the right noises. Nobody cared about me.' Tears of self-pity overwhelmed Katherine for a moment. 'It was too hard, too bloody difficult. That's why I came to Adelaide. At least I've got Paws with me.'

'Paws?'

'Lillian's dog. Paddy, Old Paddy, do you remember him?'

'No. Sorry.'

'He's an old Aboriginal man, a friend, who gave Lillian a puppy. She called him Paws. She adored the little fella who brought her and Dad back together for a while. It was quite an achievement for a puppy to unite two people who had forgotten how to show that they cared. I even saw Dudley come out of Mum's bedroom a few times in her last weeks. It made me feel sick at first, but now, I'm happy they spent that time sleeping in each other's arms. After Mum died, Dudley pushed Paws away and refused to acknowledge him. Thank goodness Pearl — you remember her, at the railways, married to Barney — was good enough to give the dog somewhere to put his head while I settled here in Adelaide. Now, he's everybody's friend at my place.'

Katherine sought to turn the conversation around. Janice had been asking all the questions as though she did not want to talk about her own life.

Janice sighed, 'I was hoping you wouldn't ask. It was dreadful, Katherine. It's something I'll never get over. Never. There's not a day that goes by that I don't think of her, my little girl, wonder how she's doing. It's like a life sentence.'

'Can you talk about it?'

'After I left Wonnalinga, I went home to Mum and Dad. They were horrified that I was pregnant, which I'd expected. They are both staunch Catholics. Neither of them asked who the father was, thank goodness. Mum seemed to soften after a while, and she came into my bedroom one morning to tell me she had heard of a place run by the church in Sydney where unwed mothers could stay until they gave birth. She said the church found good homes for the babies. I said I wanted to keep mine, but Mum suggested we go together and check it out anyway. Like a fool, I agreed. It wasn't till we got there that I discovered she had already signed me in. I pleaded with her not to desert me, but she announced that I could never return home if I brought that thing with me. That thing. You cannot imagine the disgust in her voice.'

Remembering how she felt when her parents, and Jimmy, turned on her, Katherine empathised. Did the Cooks think their daughter had impregnated herself? Girls and young women had to take all the blame. Men got off Scott bloody free. Here was her friend, doomed to perpetual inner emptiness at the loss of a child she might have raised.

'Janice, I am so sorry. Did you see your baby?'

'I told them I didn't want to see her, but I was curious, driven. When a kind nurse offered to sneak me into the nursery to have a cuddle, I couldn't resist. I'm so grateful that I had that moment. I call her Susan in my heart, but it won't be the name she has now. It wasn't too bad in some ways. St Anthony's is run by the Sisters of St Joseph, but it supported many girls, like me, to give up babies they wanted to keep. You can't come back from that. Something inside you remains broken forever.'

Katherine wrapped her arms around Janice and held her tight. They sobbed together, each in their personal grief. Beyond her anguish and anger at Lillian's death, Katherine felt a deeply primal pain tinged with desolation in her friend's body.

Janice broke the spell. 'The way they treated me means I no longer care about my parents. There is no love, but I forgive them. Their fear of humiliation was visceral. Revulsion is a gut reaction, but visceral reactions are also cultural. We are lucky that things are starting to change.'

'Well, you'll love my housemates then. They are all students and consider themselves progressive. I don't fit in. They chose Paws, not me. They see him as the house dog, but to me, he will always be a part of Lillian, of Paddy and Grace and Evelyn. Oh! There's so much to catch up on. One of my housemates told me that 'Paws' means traces on a soul. I like that. Most of the house-mates are kind and fancy themselves as spiritual beings. They're not. I presume they get their study done on campus because they get good marks, but I have to tell you, at night, they think only of their next joint and fuck.'

'Ouch! When did you learn to say that with such a glib tongue?' Janice laughed. I'd better come and meet everyone to make sure you're safe.'

'Oh! I'm safe enough, but I'd love you to visit soon. Because I've got Paws, I've progressed to the biggest bedroom in the place, upstairs. It's quiet, and I've got a desk and a typewriter — thank goodness I learned to type at school — because I write stories now. That's my big news. Well, I'm off.' Katherine stood to go. 'I'm starting work at the Bay Hotel Motel on the Broadway in Glenelg tomorrow. Do you know it? Saturday's my day off, so come then.' She handed Janice a slip of paper with her address. 'There's a party.'

34

It hadn't taken long for Katherine to get into a routine at the Bay Hotel Motel. It was a lot bigger than The First & Last, but the work was the same. Downstairs customers got motel-style car parks but single men — young, old and the unemployed-though-not-quite-homeless — rented upstairs rooms at a cheap rate that included a weekly clean and fresh linen on Mondays. Per-night rooms were made up every day; bathrooms cleaned, linen changed, and tea, sugar, instant coffee and biscuits replenished. Katherine made a proper bed with tight envelope corners like hospital beds, and she was quick. The manager told her she had rejuvenated the bathrooms; they were so clean. Katherine didn't have the heart to say that his bedspreads — in various shades of chenille — were so faded the motel rooms looked shabby. The absence of bed bugs in the lumpy, stained mattresses was a miracle.

The manager's wife was pretty little thing, as Pearl might have said, although strict in the way Katherine imagined Lillian might have been when she was young and keen. Soon they both trusted her enough to get her to mind the office for them, take bookings and answer the phone, so they could have a night out together once a week. Counting the tills was the next step, and they were delighted that she could be a backup in the bar, too, if needed. Katherine revelled in her independence.

One morning on her day off, loud and persistent banging on the front door of Trevu Flats forced Katherine to close her notepad and go downstairs. She'd been working on a story about grief and the way it changes people, using Jimmy's idea of naming, but was not making much headway. It was much harder to write than to think about things. Katherine discovered that her thoughts were ephemeral, shifting and shapeless, making them extremely difficult to put into words that might make sense to others.

'Hello, Luv.' Dudley walked straight in, never doubting for one moment that he would be welcome. 'How can you afford all this?' He nodded to the size of the house.

'I'm sharing. What are you doing here?' Katherine was surprised to feel pleasure, seeing her father's familiar face.

'Put the kettle on, Luv. There's a good girl. I've sold the pub. Well, I sold it a while back.' Katherine led her father through to the kitchen. 'There.' Dudley sighed. 'Now you know. Should have told you earlier but had a bit of trouble finding you.'

'Where are you staying?'

'Nowhere. I'm broke.'

'And the proceeds of the sale?'

'Gone.'

'All gone?'

'All gone.' Dudley took a deep swig of tea, holding the cup in both hands, head bowed. He didn't ask to stay; he didn't ask for money. He sat, as dejected as he had been at Lillian's funeral. Her death emptied him, but losing the pub stripped him of the last vestige of self-respect. Dudley was unkempt, had lost a lot of weight, and his luxurious dark hair was now white.

Gone was the proud man who hated his hair being ruffled by a breeze but full of jokes to make her giggle. At least he didn't smell.

'Are you hungry? I can rustle up some bacon and eggs if you like.'

'Yes, please.' Dudley's humility snuck him back into her heart.

'I can't put you up here, but I can get you a room where I work,' she said, 'I'll pay the first month's rent if that'll help. After brekkie, I'll walk you over there and get you settled in. It's not far. Where's your luggage?'

Dudley said he would collect his case from the cloakroom at the railway station later. He smiled as he spoke, eyes brimming with unshed tears of self-pity and gratitude. 'I knew I could count on you, Luv.'

Katherine did not want to take care of her father, but she would. For Lillian, who would have hated to see Dudley like this. Together, they gave her the best home they could. Her parents' marriage survived for all the disappointment and misunderstanding because both Lillian and Dudley maintained a steadfast and enduring loyalty towards each other that Katherine believed was love. Where Lillian had kept Dudley's weaknesses in check, her death opened Pandora's box, leaving him rudderless, loveless, lost and now penniless. He could not figure out how to be, how to exist without Lillian. Katherine could not ignore her father.

Once she'd settled Dudley in, Katherine joined him for a cuppa every day after work. He'd light her cigarette, then his own and launch into a monologue about his early life. Katherine learned patience and forgiveness in the listening, whether he was trying to reintegrate or maybe recapture his humanity through stories as she suspected or was trying to bore her to death.

'I started work as bookies' runner, as a little fellow no more than six I think I was. After that, I became an office message boy, which I hated. So, when I was 11, I joined the navy. I was a 'boy second class' on *HMAS Tingara*. It was permanently moored at Rose Bay on Sydney Harbour. Prime Minister Scullen offered us navy boys a free discharge during the Great Depression. Nobody told us why. That's when my brother Jack and I started to learn about life. We were barely out of nappies and unemployed.'

As Dudley's voice droned on, Katherine began to reconcile her father's youthful anger with Dudley-the-husband, who threw tantrums and chairs and rushed out of rooms with an inner rage he never learned to control. She shook herself to focus as Dudley spoke about how he'd moved up the ranks in pubs after starting out as a dish-hand. Later, the Army put him in the Catering Corps in New Guinea. One day, Dudley Forster was promoted to the rank of Major to manage the Marunouchi Hotel for British

Occupation Forces in Tokyo.

'You did well, Dad. Good on you.'

'Those days in Japan were the best days of my life.' Dudley was noticeably brighter. 'You know, if the Yanks had not joined the war, we would have lost.'

'Yeah, you've told me that before.'

'Well, I didn't like their military men winning our Aussie girls with chocolates and nylon stockings, but, in every other way, a man had to admire the Americans. British Imperialism had its day. Mark my words, Australia will one day be closer to the United States of America than England.'

'You're right, Dad. That's America seeping into our way of life. Look at this new hippy thing that my flatmates talk about all the time.'

Until now, Katherine had known Dudley entirely in the negative, through Lillian's criticism. She'd never heard him talk about himself and his stories were different from Lillian's. Where Lillian enmeshed herself in a network of relationships, Dudley connected his life with history in a social chronology. The world that defined him included footy finals and Melbourne Cup winners. Dudley's was a man's world of politics and wars in which first his father then he had served. He took the misdeeds of politicians personally. His memory synchronised with the public domain. How different men were from women.

When Katherine got home, she made notes.

After a month, Katherine plucked up the courage to tell Dudley she would no longer pay his rent at the motel.

'Dad,' she said, 'I've found you a room with the Salvos in

Whitmore Square. Let's go to town together and have some lunch at the market, then I'll walk you over there.'

'You trying to get rid of your old man, Luv?'

'I am sorry, but you must have known it would have to come to an end.' Katherine cringed at the sadness in her father's ageing eyes.

'I've always held the Salvos in high regard. They do good work. When I was a kid, my mother often got my clothes there, even food when times were tough. I'm a Catholic, but, you know, I repaid the Salvation Army by letting them rattle their tambourines and collection tins in my pubs over the years.'

'Yes, I remember.' At least Dudley had not called the Salvos' work 'God's work'. They sat in silence on the city tram. Katherine shouted lunch at George's Fish Café in Gouger Street, not far from Whitmore Square. A chaplain greeted them at the door and escorted Dudley to his room. Katherine followed them, hoping neither man would sense her guilt. The room was so small it barely contained a truckle bed and a bedside table, but it was clean. There was a lamp for Dudley to light the nights against his demons.

'No point in you hanging around.' Dudley ushered Katherine back towards the front door. She gave a backward wave as she turned to go, not wanting him to see her cry. Her dad, whom she had loved so much for so long, looked little, lost and very lonely, framed in the doorway of what was otherwise a sturdy, reassuring, red brick building.

Within a week, Dudley had vacated Whitmore Square without saying a word, a disappearance that ended an era. Katherine's father had survived the Great Depression. With Lillian, he'd lived through the thick and thin of World War II. From him, Katherine had the sense that she was the offspring of people who, without guidance, had navigated lives in good faith during a precarious and powerful surge in history. Katherine understood now that her father was part of an old order, a world sliding into irrelevance. Now it was her turn to find her path, no matter how daunting.

Six weeks later, a letter arrived. Katherine guessed that Dudley might have scrounged enough money from the Salvos to go back to Sydney, perhaps working as a lay helper at the Catholic monastery where he'd been a choir boy. He'd carried little cards from there all his life, black and white or sepia catechism cards with a sacred image on one side and scripture on the other. He always kept them in his bedside table drawer in a tattered old envelope with an elastic band around it. One was an image of the Virgin Mary, and another depicted St Francis of Assisi, the patron saint of animals. For a choirboy and bookies' runner who no doubt sang like an angel before his voice broke, Dudley's striving in the world of men had been about wealth accumulation — for his wife, for his family — and, in the end, he failed where he had aspired the most. Now, in the absence of all that defined his manhood — his wife, his livelihood — it made sense that he would return to God.

Dudley's letter was brief, with no forwarding address.

Dear Katherine,

I'll be all right now, Luv. Don't worry about me.

Love, Dad.

35

Janice thrust *The Advertiser* at Katherine, pointing to a small advertisement. 'Look, there's a Back to Wonnalinga picnic at Botanic Park next Sunday. How about we go?' Janice never knocked when she visited, which irked Katherine. As for the picnic, the last thing she wanted to be reminded of was Wonnalinga, let alone meet the Beamings and William Ringer or, God forbid, the stationmaster. Katherine said no, old hurts had to be left behind. If she'd thought that there was a likelihood that they'd meet Paddy, Aunt Evelyn and Grace, she'd have jumped at the idea. But that scenario was as remote as finding Pearl and Barney in Adelaide.

After days of Janice's nagging, Katherine reneged. It was now clear that the only thing she and Janice had in common was Wonnalinga. Her friend had thrown herself into Trevu Flats' perpetual party life, often staying for days at a time, smoking dope and having sex for the first time (she said) since giving up her baby. Her friend's return to life's pleasures was lovely to see, but it was getting too much for Katherine. The contraceptive pill made it all both dangerous and thrilling but, as Janice embedded herself in the flat's culture, Katherine tired of it. She was mainly pissed off that Janice had taken over in Peter's bed. It was bloody poor form. It didn't matter that she was never in love with the man. It felt too close. No, Katherine said to herself, it was fucking physically and emotionally claustrophobic.

Increasingly, Katherine found the foggy, drug-filled and often inconsistent discussions about purportedly important things annoying. She saw liberal sex as ridiculous, dishonest and even unsavoury in a small group. Although her desire to find a husband had weakened, she knew that the level of privilege among her housemates ensured they would marry their own kind, and Janice was more their kind than she. They were all the middle-class offspring of academics, doctors, property and business owners, lawyers and politicians whose freedoms were funded by the parents whose values they were trying to supersede, nay, overthrow. Katherine predicted that they would marry their own kind and create perfect new-style permissive families in their own image. Despite how her parents treated her, Janice bore their values and the expectation that she deserved the best. Like the rest of them.

Katherine was under no illusion as to where she fitted in this scheme of things. It was not a surprise to discover she was becoming increasingly frugal and abstinent. Not a prude. No. But she needed to withdraw into herself to write. Without the burden of parents, she was burning with stories about loneliness and isolation, being scared or sad to show other young girls they were not alone.

This new sense of purpose drove Katherine to destroy Gregory Sharmer's diary. She built a sturdy paper and twig fire and watched the flames consume the hateful pages of her shame, cackling as each page turned to cinders. Anyone watching would be forgiven for thinking she was a witch.

On picnic day, Katherine pulled up with Janice in her new, second-hand Morris Mini under the row of plane trees shading the perimeter of Botanic Park, a 34-hectare site situated between the Botanical and Zoological Gardens. City founders planted thousands of trees in the park, which grew into a serene haven for those living on the hot Adelaide plains.

When they arrived at 11 am, the thermometer was already at 100°F. A heatwave caused hot air to rise from footpaths in searing waves that burned the skin on your legs. The people of Wonnalinga had gathered in the deep shade beneath a giant, 100-year-old Moreton Bay fig tree at the centre of the park. The Australian Banyan, as it is known, drew the kids in like a magnet with its massive buttress roots where they could play hide and seek.

At first, Katherine didn't recognise anybody. People sat on rugs in various configurations around the tree, chequered cloths laid out laden with food: cold roast chicken, kabana sausage, iceberg lettuce, tomato, cucumber, boiled eggs, fruit and fresh bread and butter. Salt, pepper and sauce too. Men passed soft drinks to the little ones and took a beer in hand, then banded together to swig from bottles with their mates. The empties were piling up.

'Look, Janice.' Katherine pointed to the pastoralists' wives clustered together on striped canvas folding chairs, far enough away to see everything, close enough to be in the shade. 'They remind me of galahs gossiping on a telephone wire, waiting and watching to see who's who and who is with who. I bet they're talking about what people are wearing and guessing whose kids are really whose.'

Scrutinising faces for family traces was a simple paternity test, but labels stuck if someone's kid was deemed to look like someone other than its mother's husband.

'You're too cynical, Katherine.'

'These women reckon they have the right to trivialise those they consider lower in rank than themselves. Mind you, they take their status from their father or husband, not from anything they've done themselves. They gossip behind each other's backs and smile.' Katherine remembered her mother's funeral. 'The men are no better.' She watched how they strutted around in elastic-sided, high-heeled boots and moleskins, giving each other matey winks and nudges under their Akubras, as usual with grog in hand.

Katherine and Janice made a beeline towards the first people they recognised, April and John Brown, who apparently sold the store next to the pub shortly after Katherine left. They looked well and greeted the girls with smiles, making space for them on their rugs with a generous offer of food. As she sat down, Katherine saw a small group of Aboriginal people at the edge of the shade, sitting on the perimeter as they always did, facing in towards the social and gravitational centre of Wonnalinga's hierarchy. Her heart seemed to stop before pounding so hard her ears throbbed when she recognised Samuel Kingston and Reggie Kahn. Feeling weak, Katherine was glad to be sitting down.

Oblivious to her friend's discomfort, Janice announced to anyone within earshot that yesterday was Katherine's birthday. People came over to join Janice, the Browns and their children to sing Happy Birthday. Reggie and Sam joined in, and Katherine cringed, struggling to hold back tears as they sang along with the rest. This was her first birthday without her family, without Lillian. She clasped her pearl pendant and gave a wan smile of thanks.

Reggie and Sam moved closer to wish Katherine all the best. A surge of desire destabilised her. She wanted to atone for causing the pain and distress they'd endured at the claypan. Katherine turned to Janice for support, but she'd disappeared, so she bent down to the two little ones who tugged at her skirt, asking if they could give her a birthday kiss. Sam and Reggie waited. Katherine held them in her heart as dear friends although, if truth be told, she didn't know them at all except through Grace and Aunt Evelyn. Her only personal contact with them had been when they saddled horses for her and Janice. That was all, except for the piercing intensity of Reggie's gaze and her visceral response so long ago.

'Hey, good to see you.' Sam spoke first, arms hanging by his side.

'Yeah, Reggie echoed. 'You're looking good. This city living might suit you, hey?' No handshake there either. Reggie grinned as he spoke, but his eyes were as penetrating as she remembered. She could barely breathe and looked down for a minute. Aboriginal people did not always look people in the eye as white Australians expect, which made Reggie's direct gaze confronting and confusing. Was he trying to offend? No. As a woman, she could read something more profound. Beyond the desire in his eyes was a plea for her to ignore it.

'I'm doing fine. I didn't expect to see you here. Janice's here, too. Somewhere.' When Janice finally joined them, she normalised the encounter by asking Reggie and Sam what they were doing in Adelaide. It had not occurred to Katherine to ask such a simple question. Reggie announced with pride that he was the first Aboriginal student to study law at Adelaide University and that Sam was working in the office on the docks in Port Adelaide.

'Where's Grace now, Sam?'

'We catch up with her from time to time. She's back at the Royal Adelaide Hospital to finish her nursing.'

'Oh. I'd love to see Grace. We had such good times in Wonnalinga. Please ask her for me if she'd like to catch up.'

As Reggie and Sam prepared to leave, Katherine passed her telephone number to Sam, hoping Reggie would recognise that her invitation was not only for Grace.

36

Katherine pushed on the heavy glass entrance door of The Grosvenor Hotel opposite the Adelaide Railway Station on North Terrace. After the blazing heat outside, the foyer was dark and cold. Goosebumps came out all over her body. She forgot to bring a jacket, and her cotton frock was too flimsy to provide any protection in the artificially chilled air. The concierge sneered at her open sandals, but she refused to react. In her imagination, she thumbed her nose at him. Growing up in pubs had equipped her with a variety of skills for slyly getting her own back. She mentally dismissed him as though he were a lowly footman. She had a right to be comfortable, and it was none of his business. It was hot outside and freezing in here. Didn't he understand that?

Katherine's eyes adjusted to the gloom. Dark timber wall panels, heavy brown leather furniture and a thick, red and black floral carpet made her feel at home. The Grosvenor might be a big city hotel. However, it was still just a pub and smelled like one with its soft furnishings and small spaces redolent with aromas from aeons of tobacco and pipe smoke, intermingled with the bitter-sweet essences of booze and perfume. This unique and heady mix was more potent and familiar than any other scent in Katherine's world. Stronger even than school smells like inkwells, leather shoes and bags wet from rain and puddles, which she hated as much as she had hated school itself. Chalk came to mind, not as an odour but a screech, her screech of misery. Pubs smelt like Lillian's room, like Dudley's room. Like home. She smiled as Reggie walked towards her.

'What will you drink, Katherine. I don't know if you remember, but I don't drink alcohol.' Reggie spoke with aplomb as he sat down beside her. She had not expected it but understood that his refusal of alcohol was political. Despite his elegant Afghan nose and high cheekbones, Reggie identified as Aboriginal and had taken a stand against the stereotype of Aborigines as drunks and drifters.

'I'll have a lemon, lime and bitters if that's OK. I stopped drinking too. After Mum died.' She was afraid that, if she held his gaze, her heart would stop, but she had to look up when Reggie put a big note on the tray, telling the waiter to keep the change. His audacity brought a grin to her eyes.

'Big man now, hey?' Katherine spluttered into her drink.

He returned the giggle in a conspiratorial moment that completely disarmed her.

'Yeah, proper big.' They laughed a bit too loudly, then fell into amicable silence to sip their icy drinks. 'You know I've booked a room?'

'Yes,' Katherine met his dark gaze full on. They rose as one. Without a word, Reggie guided Katherine to the elevator with the lightest touch on the small of her back. She jumped at the clank of the wrought iron doors when they opened. In the elevator, they stood close, not touching but connected in arousal. The room was stark, sparsely furnished. Reggie offered Katherine the chair and sat down opposite her on the single bed, its white chenille bedspread, far plusher than those at the Bay Motel. The walls were a vanilla cream, yet the darkness of the foyer persisted as a presence in the room. A glint of daylight fell on the bed through a skinny window overlooking a brick wall and a bay of garbage bins below.

'I want to have sex with you,' Reggie took Katherine's hands in his. The gulf between them grew huge. Despite her desire, Katherine pulled back in doubt. Was she drawn to Reggie because he was black? A handsome Afghani-Aboriginal man? Was she as low as the American in his fascination with Black Velvet? Her desire heightened and frightened her when Reggie wrapped his arms around her. She slipped her sandals off with her toes. He undid the top buttons on the front of her dress before pulling away to strip. His naked beauty thrilled her. 'Your turn,' he instructed as he watched her remove first her dress, then slip and bra. She stepped out of her panties and faced him, arms dangling by her side. They stood still, facing each other, tracing with eyes, then with fingers. Katherine paused. Reggie kept touching her, bringing her almost to orgasm before entering her.

Afterwards, they lay still. Katherine's satiated body tingled with love for the first time in her life.

Katherine didn't invite Janice to catch up with Sam and Reggie because her friend had recoiled when she learned that Katherine was seeing Reggie. It was one thing, Janice announced, for her to have forgiven a white man for going with an Aboriginal woman, but it was quite another matter for a white girl to be with an Aboriginal man. 'Men can't help themselves sometimes, but what you're doing is disgusting. It's miscegenation. What if you get pregnant? It's against nature.'

Katherine reeled. Janice had spoken with the very religious fervour she had received from her parents. Katherine suddenly understood that Janice's affair with Billy Snowden was about saving him from himself. She wanted to take him away from the half-caste child he'd had with his Aboriginal partner. What did she say just now, disgusting? Miscegenation?

Something in Katherine snapped at the ugliness of her insight. She did not react, although it was clear that Janice was as prejudiced as her parents' rejection of her baby to a man who'd slept with an Aboriginal woman.

'We are all human, Janice; all the same race. We are not different species.'

Janice would not and could not accept that.

After Janice's outburst, Katherine dared not invite Reggie to Trevu Flats. For all the high and mighty talk about equality in that house, she couldn't risk him being insulted. The housemates might be unkind like Janice or, more likely, given their intellectual elitism, treat him as an oddity to interrogate with feigned interest. She could not be sure.

Katherine took to meeting Reggie twice a week on Tuesday and Thursday afternoons, in Polites men's boarding house on Hindley Street, where many New Australians lived. Reggie's room was tiny but clean. Katherine snuck out after lovemaking, unable to bathe until she got home. In Hindley Street, being seen with Reggie was less remarkable than it might be elsewhere, so Katherine introduced him to Dimmies, where they had early breakfast together on Saturdays. There was also a new pizza place, where you could get a nine-inch pizza for 80 cents!

The changeover to decimals happened in increments, starting with the currency, but Australia was changing with it. The world had been in flux during Katherine's Wonnalinga years. Martin Luther King's speech about non-segregation shook American complacency, and Aboriginal people began speaking up for their rights. While Katherine's family's time was spent, the earth itself started shaking towards renewal.

Although Reggie promised to arrange a get together with Sam and Grace, weeks turned into months, and it never happened. One day, Sam rang Katherine out of the blue to say that Grace had agreed to come to Dimmies the following Saturday morning. Katherine thrilled in anticipation. She loved Grace as though she were family, like the sister she'd never had. They had played, laughed and cried together. She'd learned so much from her, from Aunt Evelyn, women's things that she would always hold close.

Saturday came. Reggie, Sam and Katherine ordered one coffee after another and waited. Grace did not show. Her absence said a lot. Aunt Evelyn once told Katherine that Aboriginal people talked with their feet. After a couple of hours, Sam politely took his leave. It would be the last time Katherine would ever see him. For him, there was no escaping the obligations of kinship.

Reggie suggested they go to Botanic Park, where they could sit in the shade and talk about things. Hand in hand, they walked up North Terrace past the Railway Station and Parliament House, past South Australia's National War Memorial, the State Library, Art Gallery and Museum and Adelaide's premier university and hospital. Katherine sighed as they moved through the verdant beauty of the Botanical Gardens to the Park.

They sat in the shade of the same giant Moreton Bay fig where they'd reconnected. Katherine clasped her knees and rested her head on them, content. Reggie began to speak.

'Sorry about Grace. You know. This thing we have, what we've been doing, is wrong in her eyes. It's wrong in mine too.'

Katherine's heart thumped. 'What do you mean?'

'Well, you know, Grace is my wife's cousin, which makes her a sort of a mum to my kids.'

'You have children? You're married? You didn't tell me. Nobody told me.' Katherine was transfixed by how the Moreton Bay's buttress roots grasped the earth with the cruelty of a witch's fingers. She stood up and paced, her arms clasped around her chest. Then she froze. Disbelief followed confusion. Reggie had betrayed her, like Jimmy, like Sharmer. Why?

'No, I didn't. I'm sorry for that.'

Reggie's casual tone reverberated in Katherine's ears. Her body ached.

'Yeah, she lives in William Creek.'

'William Creek.' Katherine reflexively parroted Reggie's words.

'Yes. My wife's family's there to help her while I'm away studying. You know why I'm studying. To help my people. Soon, this country is gonna have a referendum to include us in the census. It'll be the first step towards acknowledging us as humans like everybody else. But it takes time. And it takes dedication. For me to be seen with a white girl, for it to be known that I've been with a white girl, could ruin everything. People won't trust me, and I need their trust to be of any use.'

'You're worried about your reputation more than being adulterous? More than being duplicitous with me?'

'Well, that too.'

The rage that once saw Katherine come close to killing the stationmaster who so flagrantly fucked her mother in full view of everyone in Wonnalinga threatened to explode again at Reggie's dismissive remark. She steadied herself but switched out any attempt Reggie might make to justify himself. He could have told her he was married, given her a choice to be with him or not. But he didn't.

'Working towards that referendum for Aboriginal people to get full citizenship rights has to come first.' He paused. 'Surely, you understood that this could not last?'

Reggie's news sliced Katherine in two. She hadn't asked herself what she wanted from him, not really. Had she ever been prepared to marry him? Would she want to help him in his cause or live by Aboriginal cultural norms? The brutal fact was that she could not; she was not equipped for that. She wasn't ready. Maybe Janice was right, and perhaps Australia wasn't either. Reggie's bluntness forced Katherine back on herself. Yes, she had always wanted to marry and have children yet, here she was, being compelled instead to look at her own motivations in this affair. Had she really considered how Reggie would fit into her world? Did she actually have a world now that her family had gone?

As Reggie continued speaking, a cloud lifted from Katherine's mind. In his few truthful words, Reggie had shown her how out of place she was with him. Men may have used her, scorned her, but, in the end, isn't that also what she was doing to Reggie? Her love for Paddy, Aunt Evelyn, Grace and Reggie was not scornful, but it was naïve. It was about her, not them. As Peter tried to tell her, hers was a selfish love just as self-serving as Reggie's was for her. They were two young people who'd tried to bridge a gap that was too wide. Too fucking wide.

Grace's absence, indeed, her silence after all the fun they'd had together, spoke volumes about relations between black and white, about the damage caused by white male sexual attraction to Aboriginal women and now, Katherine breaking faith with her friend's cousin. Grace wasn't to know that Katherine had no idea Reggie was married. Again, she asked herself, was she any different from the American? Surely it was only a matter of degree? After all, he impregnated a child and left her to kill herself in shame. At least poor white men, who went native, stayed with their Aboriginal wives and lovers for years, most forgoing congress with their own kind to do so. Perhaps the powerful attraction between her and Reggie indicated how beautiful things might one day be, but those times were not yet here.

Katherine felt Reggie watching her. There was sadness in his beautiful black eyes.

'You don't know how hard it is, has always been, for my people.'

'My people, your people. We are all people.' Even as she spoke, Katherine could see how trivial she was being.

'Not really. You don't have to have your every movement recorded, documented and followed. You have no idea what it must have been like to live under a Protector who controlled every aspect of our old peoples' lives; protection that bordered on coercion.'

'No.' Katherine acquiesced. 'No, I do not. And I'm sorry.'

'Having white laws touching our every move, white voices saying who we can and can't marry — although it is changing now — it was like that for Aunt Evelyn and Paddy, you know that. You fellas can just *be* in the world, unquestioned, unless you break the law or something. Things must change, and it is up to my generation to ensure that happens. The time is right for this referendum, and I can't wait.'

Katherine's mind ticked over. How foolish the American's research project had been, making up logical kinship diagrams with lines, triangles and circles. Maybe they'll become useful at some stage, but humans cannot be frozen in a pristine past that no longer exists. As Reggie was trying to tell her, things were changing. He had defined the stakes for him, and she must relinquish her romantic love for Aboriginal people, for it demeaned them. Change, as Bob Dylan sang, was the order of the day.

'I'd better go. Time to leave.' Katherine turned abruptly to hide her tears but felt her courage return when Lillian's words came to mind; *You have your whole life ahead of you.* Yes, Mum, I do.

Reggie stood stock-still, his eyes lingering on Katherine till she disappeared from view.

The End

Acknowledgements

My thanks go first of all to the people I reached out to for information and advice when my research failed, people who generously gave of their time and expertise: Bob Watson and Hal Maloney, who offered insights and details about the early Around Australia Ampol Trials in which they drove, anthropologist Tom Gara from Museum SA who helped me understand the relationship of Aboriginal people to dingoes in South Australia, Michael White and Matthew Davies who enabled me to work out how, in the absence of archival records, wireless and radio transmission might have operated in the time frame of this story.

Writer and well-known South Australian poet Jude Aquilina was the first to read and editorially comment on *The Publican's Daughter* in the rough. I thank her for her encouragement to believe in my story and for her Foreword. Jude launched the book.

I acknowledge the talented poet and gardener Shaine Melrose, who read the finished product and wrote a blurb and In Case of Emergency Press editor, Howard Firkin who kindly did the same.

I thank academic novelist and poet Steve Evans and Elizabeth Fitzgerald, who professionally edited the manuscript and guided me in polishing the text. A special thanks to friends and poet-artists Lynnette Arden and Veronica Cookson for their scrupulous critiques and support. Other literary friends who offered valuable, early feedback are Anne-Marie Smith, Martha Landman, and Danny Wallace. Finally, a special thanks to my dear friend and avid reader, Margaret Luginbuhl, for her unwavering faith in me and the story.

My book would not be as it is without all the help I had along the way, but I take full responsibility anyway.

The Publican's Daughter has the requisite Aboriginal approval as a work of fiction and a story of its time. I acknowledge Jared Thomas, then Arts Development Officer, ATSI Arts at Arts SA, who helped me find the right people to consult.

Author Bio

Lindy Warrell is a novelist, poet and blogger with a PhD in anthropology from The University of Adelaide. Her poems appear in chapbooks, online and in journals. A publican's daughter and mother of three, Lindy lived in Post-War Japan as a child, did postgraduate field research in Sri Lanka, and has worked across outback Australia as an anthropologist. She lives in Adelaide's seaside suburb, Glenelg. *The Publican's Daughter* is her first novel.

Stay in touch with Lindy on https://www.wattletales.com.au.

www.ingramcontent.com/pod-product-compliance
Lightning Source LLC
Chambersburg PA
CBHW030605120726
47904CB00006B/1771

9 780645 312904